Dreams of the
Blue Poppy

Dreams of the Blue Poppy

Angela Locke

Best wishes
Angela Locke

ROBERT HALE · LONDON

© Angela Locke 2007
First published in Great Britain 2007

ISBN 978-0-7090-8282-8

Robert Hale Limited
Clerkenwell House
Clerkenwell Green
London EC1R 0HT

The right of Angela Locke to be identified as
author of this work has been asserted by her
in accordance with the Copyright, Designs and
Patents Act 1988

2 4 6 8 10 9 7 5 3

Typeset in 10/13pt Revival Roman
by Derek Doyle & Associates, Shaw Heath
Printed and bound in Great Britain
by Biddles Limited, King's Lynn

And how marvellously blue – that celestial colour – the whole world was! Blue is at the very heart of romance . . . The high-lying ice of glaciers had a blue gleam . . . alpine flowers like gentians, *Meconopsis*, and forget-me-nots were bluer than any flower I had ever seen. . . .

Frank Kingdon-Ward
Pilgrimage for Plants

For my husband Colin with much love and gratitude

ACKNOWLEDGEMENTS

Many thanks are due to all the people who have helped me to bring this book to fruition, especially my husband Colin, for his patience, and for holding the fort so brilliantly during my trips to the Himalayas. I would also like to thank my guide, Som Bajracharya, who enabled me to understand so much about Tibetan Buddhism, who took care of me on my treks in the Himalayas, and who enabled me to meet the great sadhu of Nepal, and Valerie Scriven, friend and guide, for her intimate knowledge of Nepalese culture. Also my sister, Stephanie Fearn, who first introduced me to the Blue Poppy growing in her Victorian kitchen garden on the fellside, and all those who helped me with much botanical research, especially members of the Lakeland Horticultural Society and Dr Leonard Cama. Thank you to my wonderful assistants who helped me to prepare the manuscript – Diane Scott, who was my faithful secretary for many years, Yvette Sewell, Sue Catterson, and Sharon McLaughlin, who helped prepare the final manuscript. Thank you too for a cheerful smile on dark days, to the staff of the tiny Post Office in Hesket Newmarket in Cumbria who kept my spirits up, and to Tommy Hadwin, in whose Cumbrian garden I first saw a magnificent display of *Meconopsis Grandis* from George Sherriff's original GS 100 seed, for his help and advice. Thank you too to Mike Swift, Head Gardener at Torosay Gardens on the Isle of Mull, whose Blue Poppies, originally developed by him at Lingholm Gardens in Cumbria, I have grown in my own garden, for sharing his extensive knowledge so generously. I would also like to thank my agent Charlotte Bruton for all her help and support.

Finally, I would like to add a very special thankyou to all the people of Nepal who showed me such kindness and hospitality, to the Tibetans whose indomitable spirit and laughter was in part the inspiration for this book, and to Ani Tsultrim Langmo for giving up her cell for me at Samye Ling Tibetan Monastery so that I might have the privilege of being present at the three-day visit of the Dalai Lama.

Angela Locke
Cumbria 2007

CHAPTER 1

In her own wing of the house, Maud Fergusson lay rigid, listening with the blind windows of her eyes. The night was very still. Only the distant call of a lost lamb to its mother echoed through the valley. In her mind, she could see it all; new bracken on the fellside springing up, windflowers closed and sleeping by the beck. And Bambeck Hall, every dark room of it, her prison long before she became blind.

But tonight it felt different. Her grandson had been born, not three hours since. She had heard his cry, the cry of a living child after all those hours of labour. Yet she could feel in her bones that something was wrong. Those years she had spent in the East had taught her to trust her instincts. It was too quiet. No one had asked her to come to Alice. There had just been a brief message from a servant, sounding distressed. Something was definitely wrong. She sat up in bed and groped for the bell on the bedside table.

It was dear John, the butler, who came. He was attentive and quiet and, as always, there when she needed him. He had wrapped her in her cloak and helped her up the stairs. On the way he had confided that his own wife, Violet had gone into labour that very afternoon. It was a little early, but he didn't expect anything amiss. She had had her first pains as she was serving up his dinner. He had taken the big iron pot from her and made her lie down on the bed. Nellie Plaskett, his cousin's wife, had come at once, so that he could get back to his duties. She would be well looked after now. The village midwife would come and do the necessary.

Maud was horrified that John was still on duty after all, at this time of night when his own wife was in labour. Maud reflected how little fuss the village women made about such things, taking them as a part of the natural fabric of their lives. In contrast, for the birth of the Bambeck heir, Dr Nelson had been summoned to the Hall that morning, and Alice had not allowed him to leave. He was an irritable man at the best of times and that would not have improved his temper.

Alice lay and watched her mother-in-law with irritation. Why couldn't she be left alone? She had had a bad enough time, for heaven's sake, and all she wanted now was to go to sleep. Now, with Maud probing her fingers at the baby's chest, he would no doubt wake in a minute and start squalling with that curious, weak cry of his. She had wanted to keep Maud away for as long as possible, but she had reckoned without the old woman's determination.

'Alice, there's something wrong! I know it!'

Maud was really becoming impossible. Quite senile.

'He is perfectly all right. Just go back to bed.'

'Alice! I know. It's his breathing. Can't you hear? I know you think I am just a foolish old woman, but please won't you call for the doctor again? Just to be sure! He is only downstairs in the dining-room. . . .'

'Oh, very well!' Alice broke in crossly. 'Ring for the wretched doctor. You can put up with his sulks! You know what he's like. I really haven't the patience. And how could there possibly be anything wrong with the child?'

In the estate cottage some way down the drive from the Hall, Violet Richardson gave a great screech which set the dogs barking in the yard. Then it was out, back to front and upside down, the cord tangled up somehow round the little throat. What a red-haired little fighter! Echoing its mother's eldritch cry, the baby gave a bellow which set the dogs yelping again.

Nellie Plaskett leaned over the baby which was wrapped in the new sheet that had been sent down from the Hall.

'It's a lass, Vi! Would you credit it! You were that sure it would be a lad! Ay, she's got your hair. She'll be that bonny! Have a look now. You've got a fine bairn.'

Vi smiled weakly in the lamplight, the faces of her friends coming and going in the golden haze. Secretly she had longed for a little lass, whatever John might have wanted. A lass of her very own, to dress, and smock for, and cry over. It was a good feeling.

'Mrs Fergusson, up at Hall, she's had a lad, but I hear tell he's that ugly, looks like summat out of coal hole. She had a bad time, so kitchen skivvy told Nanty. And she's none too pleased with his looks. Maybe she'd like this bonny lass better, with her red hair. They say there's summat wrong with the Fergusson bairn. Dr Nelson's in a right rage on account of he's been wrong-footed. He had to have his supper interrupted to go and listen to the bairn's heart. Ay, the bairn's in bad fettle, so Nanty says. Happen he won't live. And the old lady, she's trying to get madam to feed the bairn herself instead of using wet-nurse what's been waiting about all week. Old Mrs Fergusson don't hold with all them fancy practices. She says mother's milk is best for the bairn. What a carry-on, eh?'

Vi nodded, half asleep. Her insides felt queerly turned over, but the bairn was suckling well, its strange squeaking noises soothing her. It would be all right, though things went wrong often enough. She knew that.

Nellie, watching her friend, bit her lip in worry. There had been a lot of bleeding with the birth and the bairn had come too quickly. Violet was not a strong lass. Nellie herself was built like a barn door, as she would laughingly say. But Violet was a different kettle of fish. Too fine-boned and delicate to bear such a strong lusty lass, this little red-haired creature who already clenched her fists at the world and bawled the moment she was born. Perhaps it would be as well to get word to the Hall and to ask John to get the Doctor to call on his way home. They would have to pay, mind. That is, if that miserable old skinflint of a doctor could spare the time for them.

When Violet awoke again, she felt curiously cold. There were figures in the room, she was sure, but they were shadows. Everywhere was strangely dark. She struggled to sit up, but it was as though she were tied down. Some weakness which hampered her movements. Mabel, the village midwife, was standing over her.

'Just lie there, lass. You won't do a bit of good if you sit up now.'

'But the bairn!' Violet began to twist about in sudden distress. There was a sense of aching loss within her, a cold space where the comfort of the child had been. She groped beside her with her hand, but the baby was no longer there.

'Lie still now.' It was Nellie's voice this time, from close beside her. 'I have the bairn in the basket. Don't fret. I'm just pulling sheets from under and I had to move the little lass. I've sent word for John and he'll be bringing the doctor with him. So stop fretting. It'll all be well soon enough.'

Briefly her vision cleared and she saw the room lit by two candles on the shelf, and Nellie beside her, a bundle of cloths in her arms. At that moment there was a queer twisting pain in her belly. She gasped out loud and felt something come away from her. Looking down she saw her legs, white and huge on the bare mattress, and a welling stain of darkness between them. She heard the voices again, Nellie complaining about the sheets being spoiled and the mattress ruined. She tried to say how sorry she was for all the trouble, but it came out as a cry. . . .

John, serving whisky to Dr Nelson up at the Hall, had received a message from Nellie asking the doctor to come urgently to Violet, who was in a bad way. He had so broken with protocol to approach Dr Nelson as he snoozed by the fire, begging the doctor to go to his wife. But Alice had forbidden the doctor to leave the Hall, and when finally he did get away, he was in no mood to squeeze his bulk into some slum cottage to play midwife to a village woman. When John approached him again in the stable yard, he brushed him aside with his whip and rode off into the dark, impatient for his warm bed, urging his hunter into a gallop through the trees.

CHAPTER 2

Going down that long straight road, so dark with its huge trees, Betty felt like one of those children in the Green Book of Fairy Tales. It was exciting. Perhaps she would never find her way out again. Perhaps she would be enchanted. Betty liked the word 'enchanted'. She thought it must be good to experience enchantment. At least things were different after and you weren't stuck in the same spot with everything going on the same for ever.

The carter had delivered Betty to The George in Penrith and a man called Ollie Plaskett had picked her up in a farm cart. He had taken her down the winding fellside roads to Bambeck, dropping her at the end of this grand road with straight trees on either side. Ollie had told her to go round to the back, but in her grandfather's house there was only one door, so she marched up the gravel, the little stones underfoot crunching in the silence. It was a bit intimidating, with the huge house looming above her, seeming to frown disapprovingly. But Betty was not easily cowed. Hadn't she fought the boys at school many a time and beaten them mostly? Hadn't she bloodied Jacky Tallentire's nose only the week before? There was nothing to be afraid of here.

Betty Richardson had hardly ever seen her father in the years after her mother had died in childbirth. She had been taken, as a baby, from Bambeck village to live with her maternal grandparents, in their farm under the fell at Stainton. Just occasionally, once a year maybe, she would come in from school and her father would be there, waiting. Sitting at the scrubbed table in the kitchen, a big awkward man. He was smart enough in his Sunday suit with a high collar and as polite as you could wish, but the atmosphere in the kitchen was always frosty and the silences very long. There were things she wanted to ask him, so many things, but she never dared.

Around her tenth birthday, Grandpa had called her into the parlour and told her that she was to be allowed to go for one day to her home village, to be with her father. It had seemed like a miracle. Perhaps now her questions would be answered, if she could ever get her tongue around them. But would it be a good thing to know everything? The lads at school had taunted her with names. She was almost certain she wasn't a bastard as they said, but she couldn't be sure. . . .

There was no door knocker, just a thing sticking out by the door like a baby's dummy. She had never seen such a contraption before, but she twisted it and pulled it hard until a faint sound came from inside the house. There was a long pause. She began to feel that she had done something dreadful. At last, after she had almost decided to run for it, the door had been opened by a scrawny lass who just stared at her. She was no more than two years older than Betty.

'I've come to see my dad!' she said firmly.

The gormless lass clapped her hand to her mouth and scuttled off, slamming the door, leaving Betty standing on the doorstep. Almost immediately it had opened again, and her father, red-faced and cross, had hauled her inside by the scruff. It had been rather hurtful to be treated so, but then she had been so fascinated by the smell of the house, a polishy smell like her grandpa's parlour where the Bible was, but this was more intense. Hidden, exciting smells. There was a black and white clattery floor in squares, and above that a gloomy staircase twisting up into the roof like an old painting they had at home of Jesus ascending into Heaven with Angels. Grandpa said it was idolatrous, but her grandma liked it. For once grandma had got her own way and it had stayed hanging on the parlour wall. Here, there were lots of miserable folk looking down at her. Someone had painted them like that, she supposed, but they could have made themselves a bit cheerful, knowing they were going on the walls for folk to see.

She had tried to say all these things to her dad, but they were clattering along so fast it was hard to get him to listen. Then they were plunging down a poky little staircase not at all like the Jesus one, into a big, dark kitchen where there was a lady in a white apron like her gran's. They were all laughing at her, except her dad, who looked right cross. She was afraid she was going to get a skelping, but instead the lady in white gave her a bit of gingerbread and an apple and told her dad not to mind, there was no harm done. She saw him begin to smile as though it wasn't used to it.

There were great big pans all over the walls instead of paintings, so big she thought they must be for giants. Shiny too, so you could see your face in them. After the gingerbread, he had taken her into the garden. Her dad had said they were allowed, though he did seem a bit fearful. A woman was sitting under a spreading tree. Her dad had walked down the side path so as not to disturb her, but she had called out to him. When they got close, Betty saw that she had nice hair, only a bit faded, like the old velvet cushion in grandma's parlour. She was very thin. Betty felt sorry for her.

Her dad seemed a bit afraid and very respectful, so she bobbed down when she was introduced, not looking up. She was given a sugary soft sweet which melted straightaway when she put it in her mouth. Then the lady spoke to her.

'I never met your mother, Elizabeth, but I have heard she was a good woman. Your father, I know, still grieves for her. Her death was a tragedy.'

It was in that moment that all the awful doubts left her and there was just a warm feeling left. Betty knew, whatever else, that this was true. She could face up to anybody now. The lady was smiling at her. It was strange, but at that moment Betty thought she would love her for ever. Somehow this lady had given something back to her, something she would always treasure. No one else had thought to do that, not even her dad.

She looked for the first time at the young lad who was sitting next to the lady.

'This is my son, Charles.'

He was a terrible thin creature, with a funny yellow face like a picture of a Chinaman in the Geography World Reader. But the oddest thing was that he was sitting in a sort of basket on wheels. She was fascinated by this that she let go of her dad's hand and leaned over to see whether he had any legs under the rug. The lad saw her staring. He peeked out at her from under his great thatch of hair. It was so black it made his face look even more yellow. Then she was almost sure he winked. It made her want to giggle.

The lady was talking to her again.

'My son is an invalid, Elizabeth. He requires my constant care, but we give thanks to God every day that he is still alive.'

The lady leaned over then and gave the child's limp little hand a squeeze and smiled down at him. Betty was much affected. There was an invalid in their village. He had fallen down the mineshaft and his legs were like rag doll's legs. He had to live in the downstairs of the little cottage and be carried out to the closet by his father like a baby, although he was forty-three and his dad was more than sixty. So she knew about invalids.

'Can he walk like other folk?' she enquired solicitously, leaning over and inspecting him again. 'There's a man in our village what's an invalid and he has to be carried to the netty!'

She caught the lad's brown eyes watching her. There was a glint of laughter. At that moment she felt some instinctive sympathy between them. She realized at the same time that she had said the wrong thing. The lady regarded her disapprovingly, looking down her nose. Betty wished she had kept her big mouth shut, just for once, but that had always been her trouble, upsetting folks with her runaway tongue.

She was a bit cool now, hoity-toity and not so friendly, as though she were putting Betty back in her place.

'Elizabeth, I promised your father I should give you a position here when you are a little older. In the kitchen to start with, when you have finished your schooling.'

Betty nodded, composing her face into a meek expression and trying to look grateful, even though the thought of slaving away in a kitchen with folk bossing her about was not quite what she had had in mind.

'Thank you, ma'am.'

'You know, child. My son was born on the same night as you. Isn't that so, John?'

Betty glanced up at her father and was upset to see that he was close to tears.

'I always blame myself, Elizabeth,' the lady went on. 'The doctor was so occupied with our dear son, whom none of us expected to live. Perhaps your poor mother could have been saved if the doctor could have reached her sooner.'

She had felt her father tighten his grip on her arm.

'I do feel that the least I can do is to offer you a position, for you to take when you are able. If that is what you would really like?' The lady was looking at her searchingly.

There was no escape. 'Yes, ma'am, that's very kind, I would like it.' She hesitated. 'Excepting, I'm not sure whether my grandfather would approve.'

She had definitely said the wrong thing now. The lady stood up, seeming impatient.

'If you will excuse us, the wind is getting a little chilly and we must retire inside. You must sort it out, John. It's a good chance for the girl. If she does well, she may be able to advance.'

The lad smiled at her with that crooked grin, before his mother gave him a sharp look and began to gather his rugs together to move his chair. John pulled at Betty's hand and, making their awkward goodbyes, they moved off down the path.

They walked rather quickly out of the garden, her dad not saying a word. Down another side path and out into a yard where there were horses poking their noses out of the stables. In the end Betty got up her courage.

'Am I to get a hiding, for saying "netty"? Grandpa would've given me what for. I forgot it were rude. I was just interested. I'm that sorry.'

Then he had stopped, just there in the yard on the cobbles, and he had scooped her up in his great big arms and held her against his shoulder. She was more than sure that he was going to wallop her, but he just held her there, till a lad came out with a big bale of hay from the barn and said, 'Hello, John, and how you doin'?' After that he seemed better and started smiling again.

Then they walked down the long drive once more, only this time it was enchanted in a different way, not scary. Her dad was with her. That was enough. He was talking and laughing as if he had known her always, which he had and he hadn't. 'You're just like your dear mother,' he said at last and she could see he was weeping again. Saying that had just made every-thing perfect, even if it had brought him to tears.

They had walked all the way down to the bottom of the big drive and more horses and a foal had looked at her over the fence from between the big trees. She kept hoping that they would meet some folk so she could show off her dad. She had got to thinking if they had met folk how he would say, 'Have you met my little daughter, Elizabeth?' But they didn't meet a single soul on the road, so she never had the chance to hear it.

And there, at the bottom of the big drive, before you got to the village proper, just on the side of the road, was a little house with its roof sunk in, standing by itself, neglected. There were rose bushes growing wild in the garden and a bit of path, although you could hardly see the door for old weeds which had grown and died back and grown again over the years. Altogether it was fairly ruined, she had liked it straightaway. They stood together by the gate, just looking. Her dad picked one of the blossoms from a rose bush which was growing up where the gate should have been. Now he was holding it against his face just as a lady might, and he had started to sob, big tears coming down his face. She didn't know quite what to do, so she had started crying too, just to keep him company.

After a bit, they had walked further down the lane where there was another cottage much like the first, only not so tumbledown. Her dad said she was to stay with the lady in the cottage. Nellie Plaskett she was called, Ollie's wife, and had been her mother's best friend. They would mind her till he got back from his work.

In the doorway, smiling at her, was a big woman with a baby in her arms and two small bairns looking round the corner. The woman had run down the path and started babbling at her, grabbing her with both arms. She had picked her up, all jumbled with the baby, then put her down again, saying, with a laugh, that she were too grand a lass for that. Betty had looked up into the warm face and seen that Nellie was crying too.

'Ay, lass,' Nellie had said, hugging her so tightly she could scarcely breathe, 'I loved you like one of my own. I remember the day your grand-dad came with a grim face and knocked on the door. He had the cart with him and he made me pack up all your little clothes. He took you away to Stainton to live with him. In a God-fearing house, he said! Ollie was that mad when I told him and so was your dad, when he got back from the Hall. He didn't even know you was going. It near on broke my heart, and your poor father's. Near mad with grieving, he was. But in the end he got to thinking about it, and he thought for your sake, it were for the best. Your grandfather is a respectable man with a good living.'

Betty wished with all her heart that she could have stayed there, in that cosy back kitchen, with Nellie hugging her and giving her bits of things to eat. Betty loved to hear Nellie talking about her mother as though she were there, in that very room. She had listened fascinated, wanting to ask so many questions. But it seemed there was scarcely even time to drink a glass of dandelion wine and eat a slice of bread and jam, before Ollie had come in with her dad. They had told her it was time to go, if they were to catch the carter at The George on his way home.

Everyone had hugged her, and she had hugged her father especially hard. Then they had all stood waving out in the road, her dad still in his butler's uniform, dark and sad among them all.

She held that memory for a very long time. A memory of the May afternoon, with a very high, pale sky. The fell reared up in the background and first transparent leaves were coming through on the trees, with a faint dusting of blossom on the hawthorn. The sun was just sinking in the sky behind them all as they stood on the track waving, their own shadows before them in the dust. She had waved back, until the cart had turned the corner and a bank obscured her view. It was only then that, opening her other hand, she had seen the little white rose from the tree outside the cottage where she had been born. Her father must have put it into her palm without her realizing, when he had hugged her goodbye.

She had kept that flower for a long time, pressed in her Bible with the story of Moses in the Rushes which was her favourite. Until one day she had turned the page and it was gone.

It had been foolish to tell her grandparents everything. She knew that now. Somewhere along the line, probably at the part about the Hall, she sensed, even through her excitement of telling them, that the frozen silence was descending.

She had not seen much of her father after that and Bambeck Hall was never mentioned again. A year ago she had been taken out of the school for what her grandfather called her 'bad ways' and, at the same time, a letter had come for her from her dad.

Dearest Betty,
I am not much of a hand at writing so you must excuse me. Mrs Fergusson did help me with this, just to tell me what I must say but it is my own work. I came twice to the farm but your grandfather has taken against me. Mrs Fergusson would like to see you. She thinks you are a fine lass. Your grandpa and grandma have some troubles with the Fergussons, I don't know why. But it is important to come. I am saying this because I am going away for the War. It is my duty and I will go to be with Mr Fergusson, we will be with Lord Lonsdale's lot, a good bunch of soldiers. I think we'll show them Prussian devils. We are joining with a merry bunch from the village. We are all keen.

You are always my little lass. I think of you often. Your mother would have been proud of you.
                                        Your loving father,
                                        John Richardson.

So, she was to go to Bambeck Hall, to be a kitchen skivvy. There had been a terrible row with her grandfather. He had told her he never wanted to see her again, if she went to work at 'that place'. But she had stood up against him for the first time, out of loyalty to her dad. Her father was her nearest kin after all, and he going away to War. There was nothing else to be done.

CHAPTER 3

There had been a lot of commotion in the house that morning. Charles's father had gone away to the German war with the Border Regiment and his mother was busy and distressed. No one had any time for him. He lay in his bath chair, stranded on the lawn. Connie, the maid, had brought him lemonade and biscuits at eleven o'clock.

'The house is in a scrow,' she said, 'Tweenie's crying. Everyone's getting telled off. You're in the best place, lad.'

As if he had any choice!

They had their own lives. With a wave of self-pity, he realized that they would come to him only when they had to. Their lives ebbed and flowed, while he was forever beached above the high tide mark, picking over the stray bits of news they chose to share with him. Only his grandmother, Maud, had time to spare. But now she was frail, bedridden as well as blind, and no longer such a force in the house. His mother avoided Maud as much as possible. Her obsessive stories of her life in the East, when Colonel Fergusson was still alive, drove his mother mad. Charles found the stories entertaining and exotic. He couldn't hear enough of the Snow Mountains which touched the sky; sacred lakes deeper than oceans; exotic plants; trees and tigers; men with plaits and golden robes and monks chanting spells.

Often, he felt that his grandmother was his only friend. He knew he was spoiled. Most of the time he only had to make a fuss and his mother or the servants would do anything for him. Sometimes he would throw a tantrum just to make them scurry about, to remind them that he was there. But then his grandmother would give him one of her looks, and he would be ashamed.

His mother fussed over him endlessly, her suffocating care something he knew he should fight against, but somehow didn't have the strength.

Grandma was different. She didn't even seem to notice that he was in a
bath chair, pushed and carried about like a lump of meat. She treated him
like a real person. A useful person who might one day do things. Not like
the invalid he truly was, only allowed to walk a few steps at a time from
bed to bath, to sit on a special chair at the dining table, strapped in like a
lunatic because of his weak back.

A few days before, his father had given him a new book as a parting
present, by the plant hunter, Mr Kingdon-Ward. It was a sort of peace
offering. Charles knew deep down his father didn't approve of his grandmother's filling his head with stories. But here was the book, newly
published, all about the Land of the Blue Poppy. His grandmother had
told him about the wonderful Blue Poppy of Tibet. She had been given
one once, by a Tibetan Prince, she told him. It sounded too fanciful to be
true. No one else believed her. She had insisted she had grown it in her
garden in Sikkim. His mother would laugh behind her hand whenever
Maud told the story, looking across at his father and raising her eyes.
Maud couldn't see that they laughed at her and thought her senile. But
Charles could see. It made him hopelessly, impotently angry.

Now, reading the book with growing excitement, it seemed that Mr
Kingdon-Ward had actually seen a Blue Poppy, growing in the Himalayan
mountains. So his grandmother was right. She had been right all along!

Father had come to say goodbye that morning, dressed in his full dress
uniform. He smelled of cologne and leather polish, fresh and excited and
full of energy. He couldn't wait to get away. Charles sensed it, and felt
resentfull. His father had patted him on the head indulgently and told
him that he was the master of the house now, and that he must look after
his mother. They both knew this was only said for the sake of form. They
both knew how hopeless it was. Now he would be doubly alone.

The sound of carriage wheels on the drive had summoned his father
away. They had shaken hands, and his father had said he would be back,
after his training period in Carlisle, before the Regiment's embarkation for
France. Then he was gone. Charles had cried a little, but then he had
bucked up and made himself be brave. He had tried to remember that he
must do his best for mother. He had opened his new book again and
begun to read, gradually falling asleep over the page.

He was there, in that place so vividly described by Mr Kingdon-Ward,
the Land of the Blue Poppy. In his dream, he could smell the fires of yak
dung and the sharp scent of the pine trees on the rocky slopes. In the
distance, far, far higher than the fells which he knew behind the house,

he imagined great mountains capped with snow, mountains which truly
touched the sky.

When he awoke, it had grown colder. Rain was spotting through the
autumn leaves above him onto his face, and a thin wind swept down from
the distant fell. If only he could begin! Take the world and shake it. Make
things different. If only, one day, he could climb that distant fell which
seemed to taunt him, its top shrouded in mist beyond the trees. If only
he had the will to begin. Would it matter if his heart gave out, up there,
suddenly? It was better surely than this living death he endured every day.

But he was afraid. Afraid of dying and afraid of being left alone. As if
to emphasize his helpless state, he was now getting very wet, and there
was no one there to move him into the house. The usual smothering care
he had come to depend on had deserted him. He felt tears of self-pity
welling up. He was, indeed, helpless and alone.

'Mama! Mama!' He shouted at the top of his voice. He rang the little
bell they always left beside him. Maybe it was because of the turmoil in
the house that no one came.

He plucked with peevish anger at the cane sides of the bath chair, calling with all his might. They had *never* before left him out in the rain, *never*
neglected him like this. It was intolerable. He shouted angrily, again and
again, glaring at the house, where it stood smugly, its windows surveying
perfect lawns. Surely someone must be watching! He willed Mama, or
Cook, anyone to come out to him. *If he should catch a cold, what then?*
He had had one once, and his mother never tired of telling him it had
nearly killed him. It would serve them right for neglecting him so long.
He rang the bell again, furiously.

There was a sound beside him. He swivelled round as far as he could.
A girl, about his age, was standing beside the chair, and she was laughing
at him! Hand over her mouth, stifling her giggles. From her clothes he
could see she was an ordinary servant girl. Charles prided himself in
always being polite to the servants. Treating them almost as equals. But
this was too much.

'You! What are you sniggering at?'

His voice was hoarse with shouting and less impressive than he would
have wished. He saw she had red hair and was quite pretty in a fierce way.
That made him crosser still. How dare she laugh at him!

'I'm sorry, sir.'

She bobbed and bent her head.

'I wasn't really laughing, like. That would be cruel. It's just, it looks that comical. They've put you down in a damp spot and the wheels of that chair of yours have sunk up to their bellies.'

What a coarse creature she was! He struggled upright in the chair, trying to untangle himself from the cloying folds of the rugs. He peered over the edge. To his horror he saw that she was right. He was sinking! And now it was raining in earnest, the ground was getting softer and softer and he was tipping slowly sideways.

'Well, do something, you silly little fool!' He exploded. 'I don't know who you are, but just do something. Can't you see I need help?'

'You'll have to get out and walk!' She said flatly, staring at him. 'Then I can lift the chair.'

'But you don't understand.' He stared back at her. She had a brilliant, challenging blue gaze. 'I have a bad heart. I mustn't walk. At any time my heart may go, just like that! I simply must *not* exert myself.'

She shook her head, still staring at him, angry in her turn.

'Well, if you don't mind my saying, I would rather my heart popped off, like, than be stuck in a chair all my life, depending on others for ever. If you've got legs, lad, you should use them.'

No one had ever spoken to Charles so brutally in his entire life. The fact that he had been thinking exactly the same thing made it all worse. His illness was only ever discussed in hushed tones. It was a sacred thing. Once in a while, that fool Nelson came out to see him, stinking of whisky. There would be new medicines and new instructions and then the doctor would go away shaking his head. After his visit a silence, like a time of mourning, would descend upon the house. For a few days his mother would look as though she was about to burst into tears, which made the whole business even more unbearable. He would begin to imagine all kinds of things, sometimes waking in the night, in the black dark, thinking he could no longer breathe. . . .

'I don't know who you are,' he said finally, an icy edge to his voice. 'But in any case, kindly help me extricate myself from this wretched chair and I will say no more about your insolence. Then you may be on your way.'

Once more he found himself on the receiving end of that brilliant blue stare, fixed like a butterfly on a pin. She was certainly very pretty, in a coarse fashion. And when she grinned at him he felt an impulse to grin back. Suddenly he had a feeling he had seen her before, years back, and then she had once made him laugh. . . .

'Please. Help me!'

The bath chair was tilting at a dangerous angle. He was forced to swing out his legs to prevent it falling on its side.

'There!' She pointed an accusing finger. 'I knew you could do it. Now I'll take the blanket off, and you can stand for me!'

He had never stood up outside on his own. Either John, the butler, or his mother always hovered nervously around him. He was thoroughly annoyed when they did this, but it would have been nice if they were here now. But it seemed that now he didn't have any choice. He was blowed if he was going to show himself a coward in front of some brazen servant girl.

As he braced his feet against the ground, the bath chair tipped over completely on its side and he overbalanced, still cocooned in a swathe of rugs. He lay on the ground in a humiliated heap and began to swear. Words he didn't even know he knew, words which he would never have wanted a lady, or even a servant girl, to hear. His glasses had become misted by the rain, and he couldn't see if she was laughing at him. But he was sure she was, the bitch.

Suddenly she was beside him on the ground, unwrapping him from the sodden rugs, lifting him up. There was a smell of lavender around her. He found it unsettling.

'You're a great gowk,' she whispered to him fiercely. 'Do you want to let them boss you about! I wouldn't! Stand on your own pins, lad, and bugger the rest!'

He didn't know whether he was more shocked by hearing a young girl speak in this way – although he supposed that was how servants spoke amongst themselves – or by her unceremoniously hauling him to his feet. He caught sight of her face. At least she wasn't laughing at him. Her face was set in a kind of rage, as though she were fighting a battle of her own. Suddenly, he felt that they were on the same side. That he could trust her. He pushed the thought away, at the same moment fending off her hands.

'Leave me alone, girl. Don't you know who I am?'

Those blue eyes met his for a moment and to his satisfaction, he managed to outstare her. Her eyes dropped. She coloured up.

'Don't you remember, dummlehead? I met you first with your mother crooning over you, as though you were a wee bairn. It were our tenth birthday. . . .'

He squinted up at her, conscious suddenly that he must cut a rather pathetic figure, standing unsteadily in the rain, drenched through and swathed in rugs. He had begun to shiver uncontrollably.

'I have no idea what you mean,' he said at last, through chattering teeth.

'Did folk never tell you? My dad is John, the butler, him as has gone to the war to serve with Mr Fergusson and to polish his boots. Isn't that a fine thing? I've come to work here, now my dad's gone and I've no other folk hereabouts. Only my granddad over at Stainton and we fell out a while back.'

'Why was that?' He found himself fascinated by this strange creature in spite of himself.

She stared back at him with that open look.

'I pushed my friend Mary into the beck and wet her drawers. Then my granddad took me off school. He said I was getting wild. I always was wild. . . .'

She met his eyes frankly. There was an exciting hint of mischief there.

'Not that I weren't a good scholar, mind,' she added hastily, 'and I miss my schooling. It was horrible having to learn with my granddad, though I do love him. He got religion very bad and he used to make out I had to have it too? Specially as I were such a bad lass by his reckoning.'

'And were you . . . are you . . . bad?' He was intrigued.

She shook her head vehemently. 'I reckon I'm as good as any folk if I were given a chance. I'd like to study and make summat of myself and help folk out in the world and maybe make it a better place. Granddad always did set me off wrong. We'd get our tempers up and then we'd both say what we didn't mean. . . .'

She paused and looked down at the ground. Charles was acutely conscious that the rain was dribbling down his neck, but he felt himself held in a spell by this fascinating, irritating girl, whose life had been so different from his own.

'So how did you end up here?' he asked, trying to stop himself from shivering.

'Oh, my dad stepped in and said I was to come here if your ma would have me. There was another big fight between my dad and my granddad but I came here anyways.'

He looked at her, puzzled.

'No one tells me anything! I didn't even know you were coming.'

'Well, I'm telling you now. I'm Betty Richardson.' She grinned at him, tucking back the red hair which had straggled out wetly from under her cap. 'And you had better get yourself inside, lad, before you catch your death. Let me wrap you up. . . .'

He shook his head determinedly.

'No! I want to know more about you! It's true! No one tells me anything. You have no idea. What do you mean, we share the same birthday? I don't care if I catch a cold. I want to know. . . .'

She ignored his questions and began to wrap him tighter in the rugs. He smelt again that unsettling feminine scent of lavender.

'No, lad. Connie sent me out to get you, and I'll get my backside paddled if I don't do as I'm bid. This is only my first morning, and I don't want to get into trouble already. Here! Let me put you up a bit. You're thin enough, lad, but I doubt I can carry you back all the way. . . .'

'Charles! What on earth is going on?'

They both turned round. In that second he thought they must look like conspirators caught stealing apples in the orchard. Another thing he could never do. His mother was striding towards them over the lawn, Connie trotting behind her with a black umbrella. 'What are you thinking of, out here in the wet? And you, girl, why didn't you bring him in as you were told?'

'I was just doing it ma'am. Only. . . .'

Could this be the same girl, so submissive, her hands clasped before her and eyes cast down to the ground. Despite the rain dripping down his neck and the way his back ached, he wanted to laugh.

'If I may say so, Mother, it was all of you who left me to get wet, and this girl . . . I'm sorry, I don't remember your name. . . .'

'Betty, sir.'

'Betty here was helping me. She was having rather a struggle with the chair, as you can see. . . .'

The hated bath chair squatted under the tree, tilted over at a drunken angle, one iron wheel stuck firmly in the muddied ground.

'Well, no matter,' his mother interrupted him, brisk and impatient. 'We shall have to carry you in. I don't know what Connie and Cook were thinking of, leaving you out here. I fear you will take cold, and then what may happen, heaven knows. If John hadn't deserted us and gone off to the war, and your father too. . . .'

She paused for a moment and, looking at her, he could see that she was close to tears.

'If I hadn't looked out of the window and seen you. . . . My poor child. How we neglected you today!'

It was embarrassing, all this mollycoddling! He felt it for the first time. That damned girl. She had stirred him up somehow. How could he have such contradictory thoughts, loving his mother as he did above anyone in the world? He felt a sudden irrational guilt, as though this brattish creature and he had shared some secret.

'Lean on us both now!' his mother commanded, 'Betty can bring the chair. I shall call Dr Nelson immediately. You must go straight to bed! I fear this may be a disaster, just as your father is leaving us alone!'

Despite Connie's ineffectual efforts with the umbrella, the drenching rain now soaked them all. He was in despair. For a few moments there had been something else, but now it was gone. Everything would go on the same for ever. He didn't even turn to look at the red-haired girl. She would be laughing at him again, under that subdued look she had put on for his mother, the little minx. Laughing behind his back, no doubt.

Helped now by the under-butler, Tom, a lad hardly older than himself, he was carried up the stairs. But, as he reached the top, he pushed them all away.

'I prefer to walk by myself, Mother. You really must stop namby-pambying me, you know. Leave me to do it. I am to be the man of the house now that father has gone. You will have to depend on me!'

He turned to give his mother a straight look, while she stared back at him in astonishment. Then, glancing over his shoulder, seeking he didn't quite know what, he saw, with a queer twist of disappointment, that the red-haired girl had gone.

CHAPTER 4

It was not until her grandson, Charles, had been born, on that dramatic April night thirteen years ago, that Maud had felt hope was reborn again in that frail creature. The memory of holding her grandchild on that first night was still with her. He had turned out to be everything that Thomas, her son, had not been. But Charles was trapped for ever in a bath chair, a crippled body, kept prisoner for ever by that fluttering heart.

In her darkness, Maud Fergusson thought about her son. Now he had gone away to the war, she realized how much she had failed him. When he had been born in the dak bungalow in Sikkim, she had felt that this was a beginning. That at last she would have something of her beloved, Thomas's real father, to keep for ever. But as he had grown, it had become obvious that, despite all her efforts, it was not to be. He had grown into a gentle, kindly man, but typical of his class, more at home with his precious horses than with her dreams for him. They had little in common. In the end he had become no more than an English gentleman, skilled in all the blood sports. He was the son that her husband, old Colonel Fergusson, had been proud to boast was a 'chip off the old block'. If only he had known the truth. . . .

But her grandson. Ah, how different he was! She remembered it all as if it were yesterday. She had held him to her fiercely that night, until they had taken him away. She had given him her last remaining strength. She knew she had saved his life. He had belonged to her ever since. If she could have done, she would have fed him herself, so strong was her urge to help him survive. But in the end she had made Alice do it. She had her own milk, after all, although it was not the fashion to tire out women of her class with such a lowly activity. A wet-nurse had already been brought in from the village in preparation. But what could be more powerful for a sick baby than its mother's own milk? She had bullied Alice into it, shamed her almost, and Alice had never quite forgiven her. But she had done it. Maybe, in the end, that had tipped the scales. Miraculously, her tiny grandson had survived.

Her memory began to wander far away from the cold house on its northern fells; the house she had hated since being brought home here. So far away from everything she loved. Once, she too, had held her own child like this, Charles's father, Thomas, with this tender passion. She had fed him too, in the fashion of the hill women and was glad to do it. He had been all she had left, the new-born boy. Their child, not marked with that red-haired look of the hated Fergussons, but dark like her Tibetan prince. At birth he had those strange eye-creases, the cheekbones giving away his parentage. Kadji's wife had seen it, and they had looked at one another.

'It is a blessing Sahib is away in hills, Mrs Fergusson. This look will go away.'

The two had been very close then, mistress and servant. She had been ill with a fever after the birth. Maybe, in her delirium, she had spoken of Kensin Lo and his promise to return. Kadji's wife kept her own counsel. But she had known, from the sheets perhaps, that she had taken a man into her bed. She had known too, in that mysterious way that servants know, that her husband had taken her brutally again on his return from Delhi, and would think the child his. Maud had written it all down in her private diaries and given them to Kadji's wife for safekeeping, in a box, with the precious amulet from Kensin Lo. The box would have crumbled by now, rotted in the monsoon. She was the sole repository of all its secrets. They would die with her, when she too crumbled away.

She had failed with her son. She had tried to keep alive in him the spirit of his true father, Kensin Lo, but she had failed. Ah, but now he had gone away to the war and she missed him, wished she had been kinder. She had talked to him, read him stories of the high Tibetan hills, spoken to him of bells, mysteries and monasteries, and of the high lamas. She had been sure that her son would return to the East, that she only had to sing the right songs, inspire him with dreams and he would go back for himself, find out the truth about his parentage, understand what she had found. But it was not to be.

Who could blame her for finding a lover elsewhere? Her husband had taken advantage of that good Quaker girl, her own servant, Hannah. And his bastard child was red-haired, so they said. Matthew Bowman, the preacher from Stainston, had taken pity on the girl in her disgrace. He had married her to give the child a name. . . . Had they all known, all the servants laughing behind her back? And how often had it happened before? But it was all past now. The letter which Matthew Bowman sent to Maud, returning the money she had tried to give for the child, was the finish of it. Matthew had made it clear he wanted nothing to do with the Hall ever again. Now he too was probably dead. She doubted if anyone living knew the whole truth.

Only the anger was left. She had never forgiven her husband. How could she? Even long after his death, the pain of betrayal was as sharp as ever.

She sighed, coming back to the present. How dark the world was without sight. And when would he come to her, her little grandson? She was almost sure that she had called for him. It was so hard to remember, when the past lived so strongly in her mind. He was like her, dependent on someone to carry him about. They were so alike now; the young and the very old, both of them dependent on people who didn't care. It was a bitter world. They dreamed their dreams together – both of them trapped now, by their physical frailty. Dreams of the East, of the Snow Mountains of Tibet, and the Blue Poppy her prince had given her and which she had planted in the garden of the bungalow.

A shudder passed through her old bones.

Her grandson, whom everyone treated as helpless, had become her confidante. She had inspired him, given him her strength, her dreams. Kensin Lo lived again through him. He wouldn't always be an invalid, confined for ever in that wretched chair, only able to take a few steps from his bed. Although she was old and desiccated, and felt she had nothing left, yet she believed with every fibre of her body that he should be given a chance to live. Didn't she love him? Didn't she want to keep him safe and protected? Any exertion might spell the end. That little heart might just give out. But if he never began, he would never know and his own life would be a living death in this cold house. She knew what that was like. If she could pass on a little of her spirit, it would be worthwhile. It was all for his sake, in the end.

The sound of the bath chair wheels clattering along the stone floor brought her sharply back to the present. He had come, at last! It seemed like days since she had seen him. They both depended on someone lifting Charles up the stone steps and pushing him into the annexe where she lived now, away from the main house. Maud sometimes felt that Alice had arranged her accommodation like that on purpose, just to spite her. She supposed she should be grateful for a residence of her own, the pretty little Queen Anne house set in the grounds of Bambeck Hall. Her son had described it to her in great detail. There were even roses round the door. But she had pointed out, with some asperity, that she couldn't see them anyway and she was, after all, confined to her bed. She was sure that, for all her comforts, it suited them that she wasn't too near her grandson. She had overheard Alice say once that too much contact with Maud would fill his head with silly ideas. He might be encouraged to behave recklessly, she had said. One had to be so careful. What bunkum! They were turning the child into a milksop. She loved him, perhaps more than anyone in the world, but even without the use of her eyes, she could see that he was being smothered. It was the ultimate cruelty to deprive her of her grandson's company, when she needed him so much, and he, perhaps without realizing it, truly needed her.

'Grandma!' The sad little voice was next to her bed. She reached out and found his cold hand.

'How are you today, Grandmamma? It's all right, Tom. I will ring when we need you. . . .'

'Where have you been, Charles? I've been waiting for you. I've had no one to read to me!'

'I've been ill! Didn't you know?'

'No!' She shook her head irritably. 'No, I didn't know. Your mother never tells me anything.'

'I expect she didn't want to worry you, Grandmamma. Anyway, I was very, very ill. I had a fever. I got wet in the garden because the servants forgot about me, and Dr Nelson came three times in one day. . . . In fact I nearly died. Mama was so worried!'

Maud sighed with exasperation.

'Charles, much as I love you, and of course we all worry about you, I do wish you wouldn't talk about your ailments all the time. You do seem to take rather a pleasure in your delicate state of health.'

He was silent. She could feel him sulking beside her. She wished she hadn't spoken. Anything rather than drive him away. But it had to be said and there was no one else to say it. Really, her beloved child was turning into a terrible namby-pamby, and it was all his mother's fault.

'I was stuck under the tree,' he went on at last. 'It was dreadful! You have no idea. Then this girl, this new servant, came out and helped me.'

'Could you not have walked indoors by yourself, just for once, Charles? After all, you haven't lost the use of your legs! But if you don't insist on walking more and stand up to your mother, very soon you will be unable to walk at all.'

She felt him pull his hand away.

'Grandmamma! If you're going to be horrid, I shall go away, and I won't read to you at all. I thought you loved me. . . .'

'My child, I love you more than you can imagine. But it is because I love you so much, that I want you to start growing up and to stop feeling sorry for yourself. Don't you think I worry about you all the time?'

He sighed, and was quiet for a moment.

'Anyway, Grandmamma,' he went on as though she hadn't spoken. 'This girl came out to take me in! She was so rude! I almost asked mother to dismiss her after the way she spoke to me . . .'

'Was it her fault that you were left out in the rain?'

'I have no idea, Grandmamma.' He paused. 'But actually, she was quite nice, in a horrid way. Different. She told me to . . .' he hesitated.

'What?'

'I'm sorry Grandmamma, I am going to shock you now. She told to me to stand on my own pins and . . . bugger the rest. I didn't tell mother, of course. She would have dismissed her immediately.'

Maud gave a snort of laughter.

'Charles! You are a trifle priggish at times! Who is this new servant?'

'She said her name is Betty. She said we shared the same birthday. She's John's daughter. Mother has taken her in as a kindness.'

'Oh yes, so she can scrub the floors, no doubt.'

'Grandmamma!'

'She must be the child who was born in the village that same night . . . the night you . . . almost died. Poor John! He kept asking for the doctor to go and see his sick wife. I remember it well. She was bleeding. But the house was in such an uproar about you, that no one took the slightest notice of him. I remember it all so well! Poor dear John. He is far too gentle for his own good. There he was, serving whisky to that odious doctor and, all the time that poor man's wife was bleeding to death in the village.'

There was a silence. Maud could feel her grandson thinking. She knew him so well. He could be such a fine young man, if he were given half a chance. He felt things deeply and, underneath, he cared for people. But it would all be lost, if he didn't cut his mother's apron strings very soon, and start to stand on his own feet. She wouldn't be here for ever.

'But that's dreadful!' She could hear the unhappiness in his voice. 'I wouldn't have that happen for the world!'

'That is the world, Charles, I fear. You have been very protected from it. Most people are not like us. Most people face cruelty every day. I'm glad to hear you have some sensitivity. Just remember that servants are people with feelings. They have their own lives.'

There was another pause and she heard him sigh. Her heart went out to him. It was so difficult for him after all, but the last thing she should do was to feel sorry for him. He had had too much of that.

'Come now! I've missed you. Give your poor grandmother a kiss.'

She held out her cheek and felt him lean forward onto the bed, and brush her face with his lips. She smelt the fresh soapy smell of him. She had never seen him except in her mind, yet she loved him with such savagery. If anything were to happen to him. . . . Yet it couldn't be long now until she left him alone, to cope somehow by himself, wrapped for ever in cotton wool until he died, a prisoner of his poor heart and his mother's suffocating care.

'This servant . . . this girl. Tell me about her.'

'Well, she has blue eyes and she is very rude. She uses swear words, which no lady would do. But, otherwise, she is not like a servant at all.' He hesitated. 'She was funny. Really, I quite liked her. She made me want to do things. Get up, walk about, I don't know. . . .'

'So this was John's child! Poor, dear John. He was always so kind to me and now he has gone off to that awful war! I would like to meet this girl. Why hasn't she come to see me?'

'You know mother! Everything has to be orderly. And Connie is your maid now. Anyway, she was in disgrace. Connie got her into trouble and said it was Betty's fault that I was left out in the rain. That's what Tom told me. She has to do the grates and the floors for a week instead of the tweenie. Betty is in a frightful temper about it and she's been cheeky to Mrs Callerthwaite.'

Maud found herself smiling.

'Well, Charles. I would like to meet this little firebrand, if you can arrange it without upsetting your mother. Perhaps, if she can read, she might read to me sometimes. It is such a nuisance to rely on Connie, who can hardly read the headlines in the newspaper. And you, after all, have your studies. You can't be here all the time.'

'Yes, Grandmamma.'

'But for now, it is your turn. I believe we were reading Joseph Hooker's "Himalayan Journal" before your illness. The copy I gave you for your birthday. It is rather exciting, don't you think? Can you imagine the first time he saw the crimson rhododendron on the slopes of the great snow mountains? Ah, how I long to see those mountains again! It would be like going home. Please, my child, do begin, and after, if there is time, I will tell you about the great plant hunters I met in Sikkim. They were such happy days.'

CHAPTER 5

Betty attacked the kitchen grate in a rage. Flakes of soot flew around her, landing unheeded on her white apron. She had never been afraid of hard work. But this was so pointless. Scrub this table! Clean this step! Blacklead that grate! Polish this floor, again! Never mind that it was done yesterday and the fire hadn't been lit and the floor only walked on by a lady in satin slippers.

What a waste of energy it all was! When she could have been doing something useful. Even reading. Betty had fallen out with her grandfather once or twice about the value of reading. The trouble was her grandfather's choice of reading was bread and water stuff, the kind of thing you got fed as a punishment. Especially after she was taken away from the village school for fighting the boys and for pushing Mary in the beck. All she was allowed by her grandfather was the Good Book with all the exciting bits taken out, and stories of poor folk who had died young from the Demon Drink. But the first day she had been allowed into the library at Bambeck Hall to blacklead the grate, she had seen a different kind of book, gold-lettered books full of dreams, with fancy names. Ay, you could go somewhere with them kind of books, away from grates and spiteful cooks and sudsy floors and all the boring palaver of cleaning and shining day after day after day, enough to make you nicked in the head.

When she had finished, she would sneak up to the library, just for a few minutes. Surely, no one would miss her and she could spend a little time alone there. She had to think about something important. She had just had a letter from Stainton, from her grandfather's neighbour. Both her grandparents had been taken ill. The letter said that her grandfather had been poorly for a while, but had been too proud to take to his bed. Now her grandma had taken bad too. There was no one to look after them. She would have to go to them. But would Mrs Fergusson give her leave, when she had only just started at the Hall? She hated the job, but it was a position nonetheless, and her dad had got it for her. She didn't want to lose it. It was all very worrying.

Yes, she would go up to the library, where she would have a little time alone to think. Cook had said that the elderly governess was away with her 'young man' (much hilarity in the kitchen) and that Master Charles would not be having any lessons in the library. She would have a few moments of peace and quiet, to work out what she should do. . . .

Charles was working alone in the library. Poor old Miss Hopkins had abandoned him yet again, to do her courting in the village. He was glad to be rid of her; she had become more of a nuisance than she was worth. And it was embarrassing to them both that he was so far ahead of her, though he would never tell his mother, because he knew how much Miss Hopkins depended on her salary.

Encouraged by his grandmother, he was working towards the entrance examinations for Cambridge, not, however, with any hope of actually being able to go up. How could he ever manage to study away from home when he could hardly walk from one place to another? But it gave him an aim in life and even his mother, in a vague sort of way, had said that must be a good thing. Now his father had gone to the War, life could be rather empty, and he often found himself feeling very depressed.

For the tenth time that morning he laid down his book and gazed out of the window. Miss Hopkins might be a poor, grey creature but she had made him concentrate. It was hard to discipline himself when he had no one to make him do it.

He turned at a slight sound behind him. Slowly, the door was opening. A face appeared, caught sight of him and was as quickly withdrawn.

'Come here. At once!'

There was a moment's hesitation and the door began to open again. The face peered round, looking sheepish.

'I said, come here!'

It was the girl from the garden. The one who had laughed at him when he had fallen out of the chair.

'What are you doing here? Have you been sent to find me?'

She was looking at him uncertainly. Yes, he considered, she was pretty, in a rather outrageous way; violent colouring, that red hair and the most brilliant blue eyes he had ever seen. He suddenly knew, as though he could read her mind, that she was thinking of telling a lie. Then, maybe, she thought better of it.

'Truth is,' she said at last, 'Well, I did think there wouldn't be any folk in here. I couldn't hear no voices and. . . .' She paused and looked up at him meekly. 'Cook said, "Miss Hopkins was gallivanting, so you wouldn't be having your lessons".' In a flash, she had conjured up Mrs Callerthwaite and her mincing tones.

He made an effort to look stern, but laughter kept bubbling up in him, unbidden, 'You do know that the library is out of bounds to servants? You really have no right to come sneaking in here!'

Suddenly, he felt horrible saying it. It was a stupid rule. None of the family cared about the library anyway. He was the only one who ever used it.

Her face fell. 'Ay, I know. I'm that sorry.'

He wanted to wipe away his pompous little lecture. It hung heavily in the air. He wanted her to make him laugh again, but she was white-faced and contrite now, not smiling, the mischief gone as though it had never been. It was all his fault.

'Truth is,' she said quietly, looking down at the floor, 'I miss my books. Me grandfather had that many, and I thought at the time I wasn't really interested. You know how it is when you're a little lass. He were such a dry old stick. I miss seeing him now.' She stopped and swallowed. 'And I miss my books too. It's as though summat's speaking in my head. Come on, Betty, it's saying, if you don't do anything with your life, there's no folk going to stretch a hand out to you, and you'll stay a kitchen skivvy all your life! Then what'll your father say when he comes home from the War. . . ?'

He felt a sudden surge of sympathy.

'I say, I am awfully sorry.' he said stiffly. 'It must be jolly hard for you. I take all my privileges for granted. Grandmother is always telling me so. I get bored up here in the library and sometimes I would do anything to get out of studying. But I suppose if someone took all this away . .' he paused, waving his hand around the silent shelves of leather-bound books.

She was looking at him, nodding.

He went on in a rush of confidence, 'Actually, I'm having the most beastly time. You can't imagine! I do need a hand with these wretched books. I'm not allowed to climb up to the top shelves, you see, because of my heart. I'm rather frail, you know! John used to get all the books I needed in the mornings, but John's gone off to the War and left me absolutely stranded. It's so inconsiderate. . . .'

He stopped. Inexplicably, the girl was standing there, eyes downcast, tears rolling down her cheeks. With a sudden cold feeling, he remembered that this was John's daughter. How could he have been so tactless?

In a moment of revelation, he saw for the first time what it was like to be another human being. Other people had troubles, and battles of their own. It was going on all the time, while he had been feeling sorry for himself. Astonishingly, all at once he didn't feel so alone.

'I'm so sorry. I should have thought. I was so wrapped up in my own problems. You get like that when you're ill. Rather preoccupied with yourself and what's wrong with you. A bit selfish.'

She was wiping her eyes with a corner of her rather grubby apron.

'It doesn't matter. It's just that I've had word, a letter from Stainton, my grandfather was taken ill some time since. Grandmother's poorly too. I don't know who's looking after the stock. We fell out, about my working here, in this spot. And we haven't spoken since. . . .'

'Of course you must go to them. I'm sure my mother will understand. And your father would expect you to go, wouldn't he?'

She sighed.

'They're my mother's folk, like, and they don't get on that well with my father. But of course I'll have to go. I came up here to think. I keep thinking my dad'll walk in through kitchen door, and he'd tell me what to do.'

There was a long pause. Charles looked out of the window, trying not to look at her weeping quietly into her apron.

'I say, I'm awfully sorry. I suppose we have something in common after all. I do miss my father a dreadful lot, and I get lonely up here. Miss Hopkins isn't very good company. And your father was very good to me.'

He turned back and found that she was looking straight at him, wiping her eyes again on that grubby apron. He was conscious of a flush of embarrassment. It was the nearest he had ever been to a real, live girl, at least in a personal way like this. He tried to distance himself, but she was so real it was hard to do. He was saying things he never thought he would ever say to anyone.

'I say, why don't you just go and talk to my mother? She's not a dragon, you know. Tell her about all this. She'll understand, I'm sure.'

She managed a smile, her eyes violet and hazy with tears. An odd feeling, not pity, made his insides turn over.

'You're a good-hearted lad, despite all that fussing.'

Was she laughing at him again? He tried to believe she wasn't. It was perhaps just her way, to be so direct, forgetting the barriers between them.

'You've been that kind. I'll not forget. I'll come up and help you. Though I don't know I've enough brain to take in all this clever stuff.' She nodded towards the pile of books on the table. 'Any road, you don't need to be so bound up in that chair thing. You could do more for yourself!'

He was taken aback. Why couldn't she behave like a proper creature? Why did she have to take advantage so?

'I beg your pardon!' He put as much hauteur as he could into his voice.

She shook her head fiercely. 'You don't have to be so tied up. It's only what other folk say. It's up to you to fight! It's the same for me! Folk want to put you into a little box and stick a big label on it. That way they'll never have to think about changing their minds again. Maybe it's comfortable having other folk tell you where you stand in the world. Saves a lot of thinking about it for yourself, eh, lad? It makes it harder if folk means to be kind, as you've still got to fight. You have to fight for your own life, lad, no one else will do that for you in the end!'

He looked at her and felt astonishment at her speech mixed with annoyance. She was looking at him with that look of hers which made him so uncomfortable. Suddenly, it was as though a door was opening in his head. He turned away and again looked out of the window. There they were! Those great hills he dreamed about. A first step.

' 'Tis only one step! Tha doesn't have to dream all the time!'

How did she know so well what went on in his head? He turned back, furious with her. But she was no longer looking at him. It was as though she were speaking to something in herself, her eyes clouded and lost. With an effort, he put aside his annoyance. Maybe they could help each other after all. Instinctively, he trusted her. With a wave of self-pity, he suddenly realized that he was, indeed, terribly lonely. After all, what did he have to look forward to? In a lonely world, she seemed like an ally.

'I say, if you do come back, would you help me? I could do with some company, someone to study with. I get rather lonely sometimes. My grandmother also suggested you might read to her. Then you'd have even more books to read! She's awfully lonely, too. Connie reads her the headlines from the newspapers, but that isn't much. She's stuck away in her house, down in the grounds. She would love someone new to come.'

He hesitated.

'She has suddenly become very frail. Mother says I'm not to worry, but she is so old. Of course, I know that, but to be honest she has really been my only friend.'

She stood in front of him, staring at him, uncertain at his change of tone. She had thought him such a spoilt creature, arrogant and difficult. Now she could see him in another light and her heart went out to him. It couldn't be easy for him all alone in this dark house. It gave her the jitters, if she were honest, especially the back stairs. And he was so dependent on everyone to help him.

'You haven't had much of a life, lad,' she said flatly.

He swallowed down sudden traitorous tears.

'Grandmother is always reminding me that I am impossibly privileged', he said in a tight little voice. 'I've been awfully spoilt, you know, because of my heart. But underneath, I do mean to be a decent sort of chap some day. I'm not really as bad as I look.'

Yet what was he thinking of, talking to a servant girl like this? He was suddenly conscious of a new humility, that something was changing in him. It was like sloughing off an old skin. It was actually such a relief to talk to someone who seemed to know what he was thinking! Uncomfortable, yet rather exhilarating.

'I say,' he went on, when she said nothing, 'How about your taking me down to see grandmother? You could get her on your side about having time off to see your grandparents. And even about working here, reading, in the library. She is very much in favour of education for women, you know. She's a lot more modern than Mama. But then she has travelled a lot. Anyway, she could speak to mother for you. Actually, they don't really get on, but mother does have to listen to her. Grandmother Fergusson is still the head of the house, though mother hates to admit it.'

'Your grandmother sounds a sharp old lass,' Betty nodded. 'Seems as though she's got her head screwed on all right.'

This description of his grandmother was so delightful that he almost burst into giggles, but then remembered that he might hurt Betty's feelings. In tune with his new mood of caring about people, he didn't want to upset her. She was really all right, a good chap even.

She was staring at him again, and he felt himself blush.

'If tha's thinking we can't be friends because I'm a servant here, that's right enough. We can't! We'll just work a bit together up here, if your mother will allow it, and in between my other work, like. Though heaven knows, I get no time to myself. And, maybe, I'll read a bit to the old lass if she likes. But as for being friends, I have my own life too.'

He wished she wouldn't do that. Get inside his head just when he had sorted himself out, catching him at a disadvantage with that sharp gaze.

'I say! Do we have to tell Mama? She is rather stuffy about such things, you know. Couldn't it be a secret? Anyway, I give you permission to be here,' he added grandly.

She looked at him sideways.

'Ay lad! Well, we'll see about that. And another thing. I may have Cumberland speech and a clarty apron, but don't you forget I'm as good as you!'

She smiled at him, diffusing the temper he could feel rising in him at her infernal cheek. What had he started after all?

She turned at the door and gave him a wink.

'Now I'm off to do the dinners but I'll be back after. We'll go to see your gran then. Mind you're ready now! It'll be hard enough to get round old Ma Callerthwaite to let me off them blasted grates. I'll have to wait till she's having her forty winks, like as not. . . .'

The door closed behind her and Charles was left feeling apprehensive. What if his mother were cross with him? She was bound to find out. He had never, ever deceived her. And, worse still, what if Betty took advantage of their friendship and 'got above herself'? It would all be his fault. But then he remembered her grinning across the room at him, a fellow conspirator. His spirits rose. Nothing could be worse than being alone. The whole adventure might even be fun.

CHAPTER 6

Betty was pushing Charles through the gardens to see his grandmother. There was a late autumn smell of burning leaves, and the sharp, acid scent of chrysanthemums. Ollie acknowledged them with a nod.

'Haven't I done a good job, Ollie? Everyone says so.' Charles shouted as they came closer. 'We're going to have the Walk over here, and a Rose Arbour and the new foreign shrubs just here. Grandmamma knows all about those. They come from China. And I have a plan to build some new glasshouses with special heating for tropical plants.'

Ollie dug his fork savagely into the soil of the new bed.

'That's all very well, Mr Charles, but who does all the work for your fancy ideas? Some poor bugger's got to do digging to start with and that new garden boy's as useless as a pile of clart. I'm a sheep farmer by rights, you know. If it weren't for the War taking folks away, I'd still be tending my sheep on fell!'

Betty gave him a sharp look from behind Charles's chair. Charles looked downcast.

'You're quite right, Ollie. I was forgetting. I do get rather carried away.'

'Nay, lad.' The old man's face relaxed a little. 'I don't begrudge it. And I've the new garden boy to help me with digging. Though, as I was saying, he's that useless I could skelp his backside for him. Never mind, you could still do a bit of planting when it's time. I'd be glad of a hand.'

Charles's face lit up.

'Could I really? I would love that. But do you think mother would let me?'

Betty had been standing behind the chair, trying to restrain herself from bursting forth with some unwanted advice but this was too much for her.

'I've told you, lad. The more you get out of that blasted chair and fettles for yourself, the better off you'll be!'

'Ay!' agreed Ollie, laconically. 'She's right enough.'

Charles found himself torn. He felt duty bound to protest: how dare the servants criticize his mother behind her back. The insolence of it! But some instinct was also telling him that these two cared about him, and wished him well. Ollie had been there as long as he could remember, carrying him about when he was sick, bringing him flowers for his sickroom. Sometimes, he would appear at the door, cap in hand, in his 'gurt' boots, with a bunch of roses or freesias grasped in his fist. Their perfume would linger for days, overwhelming the horrible smell of medicines Charles had lived with all his life. Ollie had even shown a grudging enthusiasm for the new rhododendrons and some of the other exotic plants Charles and his grandmother had chosen from the Bees catalogues.

The old man resumed his digging. They stood by him, looking down at the shiny sods coming off the spade with their smell of damp soil, lulled by the quiet autumn afternoon.

'You know, Master Charles,' Ollie said at last, leaning on his spade. 'You have a way with plants. That fancy thing I brought you in a pot last autumn. It were near dead, I reckon, in right bad fettle, but with you looking after it for a few days, it took off like a fox with hounds on its tail. It's in glasshouse now, climbing all over walls and making a bloody nuisance of itself.'

Charles flushed with pleasure.

'Ay, you've got green fingers, lad, right enough. Just get them fingers in the real clart and there'll be no stopping you.'

A mischievous wind had sprung up, galloping down from Bambeck Fell with a hint of snow in its breath. Charles shivered, and Betty, suddenly conscious of her responsibility to her charge, bent down and released the brake on the bath chair.

'We'd better be going.'

'Ay,' the old man nodded. He looked down at Charles.

'My wife, Nellie, brought Betty into the world. We're that fond of her, and it's grand to have her back again, in her own spot. She's a good lass just like her ma, excepting she's a temper on her sometimes like a mad bull. Where she gets that from, I'll never know. Violet, her mother, were the gentlest lass you could ever meet, and that bonny. I'd have wed her myself, though our Nellie would have had a bit to say about that! John were that keen on her. He were broken-hearted when she died. Ay, it were a terrible thing.'

There was an awkward pause, both of them astonished at Ollie's burst of uncharacteristic confidence. Betty thought with sharp sadness of her mother, the mother she had never seen, except, she supposed, in those first hours after her birth. When she thought of her, there was only an empty space in her mind, filled unsatisfactorily by her father's occasional comments. He seemed to find it all too painful to talk about. She sometimes visited Ollie's wife, Nellie, on her rare days off. Nellie had loved her mother dearly and had been able to fill in a few of the gaps. But mostly it was a mystery, and in Betty's dreams, her mother had become an idealised, shining figure. . . .

Betty pushed the chair in through the open door of the Lodge. It was a pretty spot, much nicer and more friendly than the Hall's sombre atmosphere. There were late roses still around the door. Betty stopped pushing the chair and, leaning over, buried her nose in a full-blown flower. Charles glanced up at her face. She looked sad. What could he say after all to make things better? There was nothing. Silently, he reached out and plucked a half-open bud from the stem which was nearest to him.

'Ouch!' He sucked his finger.

She grinned down at him, that grave, distracted look wiped away.

'That's a lesson, lad. All the bonny things in life have thorns. No doubt about it!'

On impulse, Charles turned in his chair and held out the bud to her.

'This is for you, Betty! I can't do anything to say sorry, but I *am* sorry about your mother. I'm sorry about everything. It was rotten for you.'

Instantly he was embarrassed. Whatever had made him do that? She would think him an absolute fool! He kept his gaze fixed on the ground. The next moment, there was a faint scent of lavender and her face was close to his, blurring his vision. He felt the faint touch of her mouth on his cheek.

'You're a kind lad, Charlie boy. I love you for it!'

Then the chair was propelled at double speed along the stone corridor. Charles, furtively touched his cheek, overcome with a strange mixture of emotions. She had definitely kissed him! He didn't know if he was more horrified than pleased. What would his mother say?

The door to Maud Fergusson's room was open. Maud's bed was under the window, looking out over the fell. Though she could not see those great hills for herself, she could at least sense them there, looking down on her and, from that angle she could feel the afternoon sun on her face. She had fallen asleep, but on hearing the chair approach, she opened her blind eyes.

It was several days since Charles had last seen her. He was shocked to see how wasted her face looked. She had become very frail.

'Grandmamma! Are you sure they are looking after you properly?'

She smiled in the direction of his voice. He grasped her hand, where it lay on the coverlet. It was thin and papery, like the old skeleton of a leaf.

'My dear child, don't you worry. I'm just very old. There's nothing anyone can do about that. We all grow old. Now, whom have you brought with you today? He is certainly speedy with the bath chair!'

'No, Grandmamma! It's a girl.' And she has just kissed me, he thought, with a guilty thrill. 'I've brought the new maid, Betty, to see you. You remember, John's daughter. You asked me to bring her.'

'Come around here, child.' Maud gestured to the other side of the bed. 'Let me hold your hand. My, you have warm hands. Come, sit by me.'

'Excuse me ma'am. I'm not allowed to stay for very long. Mrs Callerthwaite wants me in the kitchen and I'm already in trouble.'

The cool, bony fingers began to touch her face.

'Fine bones. And a fine nose! Tell me, Charles, is she pretty? No, of course, you wouldn't notice such a thing. Yes, my girl, I think you must be rather pretty. What is your colouring?'

'I have rather red hair, ma'am. And my eyes are blue.'

'Red hair! Sometimes a sign of an incontinent nature. It was certainly so in my husband's case. I trust you have a calm temper, my dear?'

Charles grinned at Betty across the coverlet, enjoying her discomfort, their quiet moment by the door almost forgotten.

'No, she hasn't, Grandmamma. She gets rather cross, and she is always in trouble.'

Just because she had kissed him, he wasn't going to let her off the hook!

Betty glared across at him. What a little brat he was, after all! She longed to box his ears.

'Now! You must tell me everything about yourself. I am so fond of John, you know, my dear. He used to take care of me so well. It was such a tragedy when your dear mother died, so soon after you were born. But here you are! Tell me, child, has your father taken care of you by himself all these years? I am surprised he didn't speak of you more.'

'I lived with my grandparents, ma'am, after my mother died, and I've hardly seen my Dad. First of all, Nellie Plaskett took me. My Dad won't talk about it at all, it seems as though it hurts him too much. When I were six months old, my grandfather at Stainton, he came with the cart and took me back to his folks and my Gran brought me up.'

'Stainton! I used to know people at Stainton. Who was your grand-father?'

'Oh, we're just ordinary folk, but my granddad had some education like, and he taught me a fair bit. He were a miner up on Bambeck and he made a pile of brass. He has a spot over Stainton way, a farm and some beasts. Since my mother died, he took religion hard and he became a preacher. He fell out with most folk. I do love him, but. . . .'

Betty broke off. Charles, looking across at her, saw that tears were running down her cheeks. Maud, listening to the sadness in the girl's voice, leaned across once more and took her hand.

'Are you in trouble, my dear. You must tell me! Perhaps I can help.'

Betty found a rag in her apron and wiped her eyes.

'No, it's only that we fell out, my grandfather and me. He always took against this place, though I never knew why. He was a hard man. My father wrote to me and said he'd got me a position here, before he went off to the War. I felt duty bound to come, but my granddad were that angry. He said he didn't want me back home ever again, if I came here. . . .'

'That seems quite unreasonable!'

'Ay, well, no doubt he had his reasons. But now I've had a letter from my grandma's friend, Jinny, her that lives close by. They are both in bad fettle, my grandad and my grandma, and no one to help them out. I reckon I should go back and patch it up like, but I don't want to lose my job. . . .' She stopped.

What was she doing, pouring out all this to a total stranger? But the pressure on her hand continued, and looking up at the face with its blank eyes, she saw that Maud was nodding sympathetically. She felt a sudden rush of warmth for the old woman.

'I'm sorry like. I didn't mean to tell you all my troubles.'

Tears were running freely down her face, as they had in the library. Charles, looking across at her, was suddenly ashamed that he had teased her. The rose lay forgotten on the coverlet. He reached across and pushed it towards her with an inky forefinger.

'Sorry!' He whispered. Betty managed to give him a wan smile and blew her nose on the scrap of rag.

'There!' Maud exclaimed. 'I'm so glad you've told someone. It is always better to share a trouble if you can. I hear you have been encouraging my grandson to walk about and be a little more independent. I am so pleased.

You know, I am getting very frail and I can't fight his battles for him any more. You and I must be allies. As for your own troubles, I shall speak to my daughter-in-law and explain the situation. You must go today to see your grandparents. I will send you home with my own carriage. You shall have leave to remain for as long as you need.'

Betty was staring at her, astonished.

'No ma'am, you don't have to do anything for me. I have to fight my own battles. I always have. I'm that grateful, mind you.'

'Nonsense, my dear. You have no idea how hard it is to fight *any* battles in this house. But I do want something in return. I want you to promise that you will make this young man into something for me. I don't have very long to live, and I would like to think that someone else is keeping an eye on him. He does rather descend into self-pity when there isn't anyone around to reprimand him!'

'Grandmamma!' Charles protested.

'No, Charles, I am only telling Betty the truth. We have discussed this many times. She is a strong young woman. Just what you need. Now, Betty, I want you to promise me you'll look after him for me. . . .'

Betty looked across at Charles and, under her breath she said, 'Ay, ma'am, I'll kick his backside for him, for my own sake as well as his. No trouble at all!'

Charles was shocked. He looked across at his grandmother and saw to his astonishment, that her frail shoulders were shaking with laughter. . . .

CHAPTER 7

Betty's hands were trembling, as she sat at the table, trying to fill the lamp with oil. Outside she could feel the great loneliness of the fells. She too was alone, with the dead. She had never been one for fancy thoughts, but now all sorts of awful possibilities occurred to her.

The whole house seemed full of the powerful presence of her grandfather. He had never known that Betty had come back. He'd been unconscious since her arrival late at night. Hannah had died only days before, from the pneumonia which was to take them both, and was already buried. Weakened by influenza, they had struggled on alone. Matthew, too fiercely independent to ask for help, had been feeding the beasts in the unseasonally bitter weather, until he could go on no longer. It was all her fault. She would never forgive herself for going away.

There was a knock at the kitchen door. She jumped up, spilling lamp oil on the table. Who could be calling after dark? Fearfully, she took up the other lamp and moved towards the door.

'Who is it?' she asked in a tremulous voice.

'It's Jinny, lass.'

Relieved, she unbolted the back door. Old Jinny Ridley, from the next farm, bustled inside. She had kept an eye on the sick couple. Matthew had refused to have a doctor and wouldn't take any help. It was a terrible thing, the both of them dying like that within a few days of each other. Now the poor lass looked scared half out of her wits. Impulsively, she stretched out her hand and clasped Betty's own cold ones.

'Come on now, sit yourself down and I'll make you a cup of tea. You can tell me all about it.'

Betty had seldom been so pleased to see anyone in her life. She sat down at the table, while Jinny busied herself in the kitchen. Jinny knew the kitchen well. Within minutes she had found a crock of butter, some bread and an egg and she had made some food for the lass. The poor thing didn't look as if she had fed for a while. While she busied herself, she listened.

'I should have been here, Jinny! I should have been here to help them.' Betty burst out. 'It was my fault, if I hadn't been so headstrong. I could have stayed here. Maybe they would have never taken cold and died like this!'

She was a queer one. When she was cracking on like that, half the time she was talking in their own speech, half the time like a lady. That was Matthew's mark on her. He had always wanted something better for her. But in truth, she had been left neither fish nor fowl. Not much good at the practical things that needed doing, her head full of dreams. And there was always something about her that marked her out. Jinny, who had been Hannah's best friend, was one of the few who knew why. The poor lass would have to be told soon, before the funeral, because it would all come out then anyway. Some busybody would whisper in her ear and it would be far worse to hear it from a stranger.

Together they began to collect the stuff for washing and laying out. Jinny was used to it. She was an old woman and had seen many deaths. The bairn could not stop shaking. She was as white as a sheet, those freckles standing out on her face and her red hair like fire in the lamplight. Poor mixed-up lass.

'You see, Jinny, what else could I do? My Dad wanted me to go to the Hall. He'd been well treated there, you see. But my grandfather was so set against it. Why are folk so difficult?'

Ay, this was the time. There were no other folk left to do it. No wonder the lass was in such a muddle.

She took a deep breath.

'Betty lass, before we do anything for thy grandfather, just sit down and take this food and a cup o' tea. Ay, just sit down and settle thyself. I've summat to tell you. Perhaps you'll feel a bit easier when I've told you. Maybe not.'

'Your grandfather was not your own kin,' Jinny said quietly, as she moved across the kitchen with a big pan of water to boil up on the stove. Betty, sitting at the table, was just about to take a bite of bread and butter. She dropped the bread back on the plate, and stared at Jinny.

'Your grandmother was expecting when Matthew married her. Most folk don't know it, but Hannah was my best friend. She and I always knew each other's business. Folk all thought she were pregnant on account of Matthew. And no one said nay to that. Ay, it's common enough. But the truth were different. And perhaps you should have been told. If you had, perhaps you could have made a few decisions of your own. But your grandfather, God bless his soul!' She glanced upwards, hoping he would forgive her if he were listening. . . . 'he was such a stiff man, couldn't bring himself to talk about anything like that. Even when the bull came to the cow, he kept the shutters closed!'

The child was looking at her, white-faced, uncomprehending. Mentally, Jinny scolded herself. Why had she to make such a hustle and mustle about it all? For a moment she wondered if she should go on, but then, it was half-said already. There was no stopping now.

'Your grandmother used to work up at Bambeck Hall. Just like your father, and that were one of the troubles. When Violet, your mother, started walking out with John, your grandfather would have nothing to do with it. He reckoned all them Fergussons were bad, after what happened to Hannah. It don't matter that old Mr Fergusson, him they used to call the Colonel, was really the horse of a different colour. Ay, there were bad blood in him, right enough. He had got several lasses into trouble, so they say. And Hannah, your grandmother, she was no more than sixteen when he got to her, that wicked creature.'

The food lay uneaten on Betty's plate. So much was falling into place. It was all becoming clear now. No wonder he had been so angry all the time, that poor old man lying upstairs dead and beyond speaking to.

'Come on, lass. We've this job to do. Help me with the water, and the clean rags. It'll be better if we have summat to do. At least if we get it all sorted out, you'll be able to pay your last respects to them both, though I could have chosen a better time to tell you.'

With an effort Betty got up from the table. Her legs felt leaden. With shaking hands, she picked up the lamp.

'Ay, lass. You can take the lamp and the basket, and I'll manage the water, if you can light the way. Never fret lass, I'll stay with you tonight. I won't leave you alone. We can talk as we work. There's nothing to be afeared about now, 'tis only a body; the spirit has gone away. And I've done the same service for your poor old gran, already. It's nothing to fear.'

Betty followed Jinny numbly up the stairs, like a sleepwalker in a dream. Yet her quick mind had run ahead, and she could already begin to fill in the gaps in what Jinny was saying.

They began to sponge down the old man's body. How would he have felt, exposed to the gaze of two women, Betty wondered. She was embarrassed and horrified, but for Jinny it was a last service to a friend, however ill-natured he had been in life. Besides there was no one else. The lass couldn't cope with the task by herself. It just had to be done whatever your feelings, and that was an end of it.

Mercifully the job was finished. Now he was as clean and holy as he would have wished, wherever he was going.

'Come on downstairs, lass. We'll clear up this scrow and have a talk. I can tell you the story as Hannah told it me. You mustn't be too shocked, nor judge some folk too harshly, for all that.'

Downstairs again, she bustled about, trying to fill the silence: The lass was awful quiet, had hardly said a word all the time they had been working. It was a shocking thing, all of it. Why had she been so foolish as to tell such a tale when the lass was shaken enough. But what was a body to do? There would be a funeral the day after tomorrow, and the reading of the will. Betty would have to face it all with folk looking on and gossiping. No, it had to be done.

Gently placing a fresh cup of hot tea in front of the silent girl, she took a deep breath, sat down beside her and continued with her story.

'This was always a good Quaker house. We had Meeting in this very kitchen. I mind when I was a little lass, sitting with Mother on a bench against the door. A good holy house and Matthew was a fine lad from a good family. When we grew up he followed his father's trade, mining above the fell there. There were good seams of copper up by Brandy Ghyll in them days. Folk had taken copper from there since the Elizabethan times, so they say. Then when his father died, he took on t'farm as well, looked after the old lady, and he made a good living besides. He were a warm man in them days, and a good catch for any lass. And he were bonny. All the girls liked him, but there was never any other lass for him but our Hannah. It were the same for her, allus the same. From when she were a lass, all the valley knew she and Matthew were meant to be married.'

'Then she went into service up at the Hall. Oh, dear me! One night, when she were taking the mistress's tea up last thing, as she always did, he got her on the stairs. The old Colonel. That devil. It were over in a minute, and he left her crying her heart out. Did you ever hear such a wicked thing? Of course she didn't dare tell. And when she found she was expecting the bairn, she were dismissed and had to come home in disgrace. Where's the justice in that? And Matthew, he was a fine man, he stood by her even though he was a bit strict, like. It must have shocked him terrible. He was in that much of a rage, he went up to the Hall. He never did hold with bowing down overmuch to them high-ups. The old man was away then, but he saw Mrs Fergusson, Maud they called her. She were a kind soul. By all accounts there was a terrible carry-on. But she were a fair woman and she knew Hannah were a good lass. Matthew had that way with him, folk always knew he was talking straight, even when it were a bit uncomfortable. She must have put to two and two together. It would have been a terrible shock. 'Tis said she never forgave the old Colonel. She sent money for the baby. But Matthew had married her by then, and he sent it all back, every last penny. . . .'

The lass stirred, as though she was coming out of a dream.

'So my mother. . . ?'

'Ay, lass!' Jinny said softly. 'Your mother, Violet, was the child of old Colonel Fergusson. There were no others. Hannah, poor lass, bearing a child so young and her always as thin as a fencepost. It damaged her. There were no other bairns.'

Betty put her head down onto her arms on the wooden table and began to sob.

Jinny, rung to the heart, got up from the table and put her arms around her. She was crying like a poor lost lamb. After all, the lass had never had a mother to give her a hug when she was a wee bairn. Hannah had tried her best to be a mother, but in this sad house, it couldn't have been easy. . . .

'There! There! Don't get thyself in a state, lass. It is a terrible time to be telling all this. I wish you could be spared. But day after tomorrow you have to face all the folk in the valley. Who knows what will get said when some of them start blathering. Folk have long memories. 'Tis a miracle you never caught it all before this. . . .'

'At school they used to call me names. . . .'

'Ay, lass, I know. Folk can be that spiteful. When your mother, Violet, was walking out with John, and she fell with you, there was another carry-on. Folk from the Hall, guddling about in other folk's lives. That's how Matthew saw it. "History repeating itself", he said. But it were different. John and your mother could not have loved each other more. They were married before you were born. But of course when your mother died, it were the end. Poor Matthew would never forgive John. He had become that stiff and bitter in his old age.' She sighed. 'So that's the end of it, and too many tears shed. It's all over and done with now.'

The whole of the next day, Betty walked about in a state of numbness, willing herself into hard work, deliberately keeping her mind empty. Thinking, with all its implications, was just too painful. Evening came and Jinny visited again. She had all sorts of practical help for the preparations for the funeral on the morrow, and a warning that folk would be calling. She did the evening milking, gaining some comfort from the warm flanks of the beasts, the rhythmic spurt of milk into the bucket. Real things. Real beasts. You knew where you were, after all.

At last, she steeled herself to go up the stairs again, and sit with her grandfather where he lay. He was decently arrayed in his best black suit, with pennies on his eyes and in a plain wooden coffin which Jack Alcock, the joiner, had knocked up that very morning. His face was set in a yellow mask, as though carved from some soapstone. She looked down at the sharp nose, the great forehead which hinted at the brain beneath, an aristocratic face, thin lips. Her old adversary, the man she had thought so hard, so unforgiving was now quite vanquished, with a look she had never seen before. How she loved that proud old man, kin or not. But it was too late to tell him now. In the best of all possible worlds, there might have been reconciliation. But this was just the ordinary world, where things left unsaid were left unsaid for ever, and there was no going back.

She sat beside her grandfather's bed in the little upstairs room for a long time. On the walls were the religious samplers which her own mother had embroidered in the long winter evenings, each one signed in cross stitch with her name. *The good man waiteth upon the Lord* hung above the bed; *Behold I am the way the truth and the life* was to one side of the window, and *Beware the righteous wrath* on the wall at the foot of the bed, where her grandfather could have seen it all the time.

Above his white head was one of her favourite pictures. A dark-haired Jesus, a crown of thorns on his head, standing by a shadowy gateway. He was holding up a lantern and beyond the gate there seemed to be a thick impenetrable forest. The lantern gleamed a little way into the darkness and showed the beginnings of the path. Underneath was written in gold letters *I am the Light of the World*. Was that where her grandfather was going now, through that gate into that deep forest?

Betty laid her head on the coverlet and wept. If she had only stayed. If she had only been there. She could have fed the beasts, and cared for them both. Her grandparents would have been here, at the homestead, getting better. Hannah would have been bustling about, singing hymns, and he might have been out back feeding his pigs, or in the tiny parlour, reading his beloved Bible. She owed so much to them both, especially to him, although it had been to Hannah she had always turned for comfort. He had had a hard life and since he had embraced religion so fervently, he had become harder himself, but underneath he had cared for Betty. Much of what she had become was due to him, the good and the bad. She knew that now.

She sat for a long time by the bed, thinking about it all. Gradually she began to see that they were very alike, she and her grandfather, even if they weren't true kin. She had always imagined she was like her mother, and perhaps she was, but she was her grandfather too: passionate, committed and angry. He had wanted more for her. He had seen what the world was like. He thought it a corrupt place, and that there were only two ways to find a better life: by religion, which gave you your soul and no man could touch it, and by education. Other folk were such lazy fools, they never bothered about learning till suddenly you were as good as them and they hadn't even noticed you getting there. He hadn't held with the idea of the Established Church and that all folk were assigned to their place on Earth and there was no moving them. He had seen that as just another lie, perpetuated by men of power, to keep poor folk in 'their place'.

Matthew was buried the next day beside his wife in the little graveyard behind the Meeting House. It was unconsecrated ground; holy enough for good Quaker folk, however. It was a bitter day. A thin wind funnelled along the valley carrying flakes of snow. Betty didn't cry, she just felt empty inside, all emotion rung out of her. Afterwards, Mr Arnison of Penrith read the will in the dim, cold parlour with its ticking clock. They were all astonished to hear just how much of a warm man Matthew Bowman had been. The seams of copper up at Brandy Gyhll had been very productive. Matthew and Hannah had worked hard too and been thrifty.

There it was, neatly set out. Matthew had left everything to her, in the event of Hannah's not surviving him; his farm, twenty acres of land in good heart, another cottage further up the valley, let on a tenancy, shares in the mine and all their possessions. There was also a tidy sum of money which she was not to touch till she was twenty-one, when, it was hoped, she would be in a sensible frame of mind to take care of it. To her amazement, Betty found that she was rich.

When everyone had left and Jinny had gone to milk her cow, Betty sat down by herself and tried to think about her life coherently. It was hard to fight her way through the numbing feeling of grief, towards some understanding. She was stunned by the events of the afternoon. The news of the inheritance would take some time to sink in, but more than anything else what stuck in her mind was that Matthew had known she was not his true kin, yet he showed by his will that he had loved her as much as if she had been his own granddaughter. That was what counted. Not some unthinkable moment on the back stairs at Bambeck Hall.

Yet she did think about it. Most lasses of her age who had been to school and mixed in the village were pretty knowledgeable about sex. Nonetheless, it was still a kind of mystery to her. She had accepted the changes in her body, although she missed not having a mother to talk to. She had been too constrained by the Puritan atmosphere in her grand-parents' house to ask her grandmother such questions. It was a dreadful thought, that a man could just pin you up against a wall and take you, and then you could have a child. Jinny had not spared her words. And to think that she was blood-related to such a creature, who would so casually ruin the life of a young lass in his house. Or were all men like that? Perhaps they were. . . .

In the evenings she sat by the lamplight, sorting drawers and cupboards, reading through letters and papers, their ghostly echo of past lives. And only then, gradually, did her own past and that of her grandparents begin to make sense. She saw in her grandfather's letters to Hannah, that fierce protectiveness which had inspired him to put aside his rigid beliefs and take her as a wife. It was all there, oddly affecting from that angry old man, who had been so stern with her, and whom she had only ever known as old, preoccupied with its own griefs, his own enduring bitterness. There he was, caught for ever in those faded pages, idealistic and vulner-able in love.

It gave her a strange sense of her own mortality, as though someone, sometime, might see her as a mirror image of Matthew, another angry, fierce creature who had put up barriers against the world. That 'old dragon' everybody went in fear of, outspoken, harsh, friendless, dying almost alone in an empty world. She didn't want that, but what then did she want from life? It was hard to know.

All this put her even more in turmoil. She wrote to her father every day, letters pouring out her feelings, although she never mentioned the truth about her mother. She was sure somehow that he didn't know. Had her own mother even known? John was not a great letter writer and although he was still in Carlisle, it could have been darkest Africa for all the chance of seeing him. He wrote that he would try to get home for Christmas, but otherwise he would be sure to come and see her before they embarked for France. They were doing a good job, the Colonel was a fine chap and Mr Fergusson was now a Captain. It was everyone's duty to stick it out, even though it was hard not seeing her for so long. She had told him about the legacy, and he was so pleased for her, knowing she would be well provided for if anything happened. How these words sent a chill through her! She was to look to Mrs Fergusson for guidance if she needed it, because she had promised.

She must understand he didn't have the words, didn't know how to put them down on paper like some folk, but he loved her always. She was sure of that. The thought gave her comfort.

Sometimes Old Jinny or Mrs Whitson would stop by in the day for a 'bit crack'. She had tried to talk to Jinny about what she should do. All the old woman would say was, that now Betty was to be a rich lass with a tidy sum to come in a year or two, she should settle down and farm her grandparents place and maybe find herself a good husband. Privately, Jinny thought the lass was a bit flighty still. The result of old Matthew putting too many ideas and too much book learning into her head, and there was some of the Fergusson wildness, no doubt.

A fortnight after Matthew's death, Betty sat up in bed in her little room at the farm, wide awake after a deep sleep. It was pitch black in the room and she had no way of telling what hour it was. Alone in the house, she was suddenly afraid. Maybe his ghost would come back! She thought she would die if it did. The memory of him lying there, in the next room, so dead, was bad enough.

Then it came to her, what she had seen in her dream. The dream had gone, but the thoughts remained, so clear they could have been written up in front of her.

Anger was a force which didn't die: a slow destructive force which broke down everything in its path. So far she had used it herself as a weapon to get her own way and to fuel her sense of independence. But would it always be like that, a useful, powerful thing? Matthew's anger had turned him against folk in the end, and he had died a bitter, friendless old man. He had carried his grudge against the Fergussons to the grave. There was wrong in the world. She had felt the lash of it herself. You had to put it right if you could. But did it have to sour all hope, all joy, all love? She knew how unhappy her grandmother had been in her last years when she herself was growing up. She had often found her in tears in the kitchen. And she herself had been driven away by his harsh rule, no doubt about it.

She thought back to that night when she had been told she would never return to school, after she had pushed Mary into the beck. Her grandfather had told her then that she had grown too wild, that her incontinent nature would be her downfall. And that from now on he would control her education, away from the harmful influences of the village school. She had sobbed and sobbed but it made no difference. At last she had shouted through her tears, rebelliously, 'It isn't fair! It isn't fair!'

He had stopped in the doorway on his way out to feed the calves and looked back at her.

'Life isn't fair, lass. You're a fool to expect it to be. You had better get used to that. There's no justice in this world and you'll need to be a site better to get into other one, lass. 'Twas always that way, since the Garden of Eden and Man's Fall. Do you not read Scriptures?'

And he had slammed out of the door, leaving her to cry her heart out at the kitchen table. Hannah was caught helplessly between the two of them, looking on.

Now she could see it as a cry from his own heart, though she hadn't known it then. The world had seemed a harsher place after that. He had seemed to say, 'There is no one here to save you. The world is dark. You have to fight on alone.' For a child, who desperately wants the world to be gentled into rightness, it was a lifeline snatched away.

She got out of bed, shivering as her feet hit the cold floor. Wrapping the patchwork quilt around her, she tiptoed over to the window, which looked over the back of the house, away up the fell. She pulled aside the drapes, which Matthew had always insisted on for modesty's sake, although there were nothing but foxes and rabbits to gawp at her. Outside, the moon had only recently set and there was an afterglow in the sky. It had been snowing on the fell bottom and there was a pale dusting of white on the bracken, gleaming against the dark boulders. Higher still she could see the outline of the fell tops, sailing away against a dark blue sky, the stars faint against the pale of the moonlight.

'I won't sell this place,' she spoke out loud without realizing. 'It's a part of me. But I don't want to live here. Not now. Perhaps never. I've got a new life of my own to make. All that is past is past and can't be helped.'

She spoke firmly as though to another person in the room. Indeed she had a strong sense that her grandfather was there, close by. But she was no longer afraid.

Melancholy washed over her and a sense of her deep dream. Then she remembered. She had been dreaming about that funny, cranky lad, that boy who always made her laugh and furiously angry all at once. Her instinct told her that she could help him. That without her he would drown in love and self-pity, a permanent invalid. His grandmother had seen it, and Betty had given her word that she would do her best. The old lady was right. In the end, no one else would.

There was something she had to finish. Or was it after all something which had to be started and wouldn't be finished for a long time? She couldn't quite explain what she meant. She had understood it all while she had been dreaming, but now the thoughts began to fade, and were hard to catch. But it was there, the conviction which she had in her dream.

She missed him, that old man. She would always love her grandfather, and respect him, but being dead didn't mean you were right. Oddly, she also missed that dark-haired, difficult boy and everything at the Hall. That lad had got under her skin, somehow. She couldn't just leave him like that, and besides she had promised. She would go back to the Hall, just for a while, rent the farm out to Sim and Martha in the village. Jinny had told her they needed a place. She would go back, just as though everything were the same. She would never breathe a word of all she had learned about her mother. It made no difference what she was, not in the real world, not now. Except that now she and Charles were sort of cousins. Perhaps that was why she cared so much. Apart from her beloved father, he was all the family she had left.

Shivering with cold, she ran back across the icy floorboards, and jumped into her bed, leaving the drapes wide so that she could watch the dawn. She felt she was beginning afresh. Everything was before her. It might be the back end of the year, and the prospect of Christmas with none of her own folk around her. But it was a new beginning. She would be different now. She would try not to be angry and difficult. She would turn over a new leaf. . . .

And with these great thoughts tolling in her head, she fell asleep.

CHAPTER 8

The last few mornings, when Charles came to see his grandmother, she had just lain there with her face turned to the window. She hardly seemed to be able to summon the strength to speak to him. But this morning, when Tom took him down after his studies, she greeted him with a smile, and his spirits lifted. Perhaps she was going to be all right after all.

'Did you ask in the kitchen? Is she coming back?'

Every time he saw her, she asked the same question.

'Yes, grandmother. Connie told me. She is really coming back. Both her grandparents died, you know. She's been left lots of money. I don't know why she should want to come back here. If I had my own money I would never come back. Except to see you, Grandmamma, of course,' he added hastily.

She sighed. 'She'll come back to keep her promise. Then I'll know you will be looked after. She has strength, and integrity. I knew it immediately. She promised, and she won't let us down.'

'Yes,' he thought about it. 'I think she would always keep her promises.'

'She is a fine girl. I want to see her when she comes. Don't forget.'

'I found out lots of other things when I was in the kitchen,' Charles burst out impatiently, interrupting her. 'I would make a good spy, you know, Grandmamma, like Kim! Do you remember when you gave me "Kim" for my birthday?'

'Yes, I remember.'

'I found out that Betty's grandfather, Matthew Bowman, was quite rich. He found this seam of copper up on the fell and he worked it for years till he got lots of money. . . .'

He stopped, alarmed. A terrible change had come over his grandmother's face. Her eyes were closed and she seemed to be gasping for breath. It was as though she had shrivelled up.

'Grandmamma! What's wrong? Please, open your eyes! Say something!'

Her hand reached out for his and clutched it fiercely. She was struggling to speak.

'Matthew Bowman! Did you say, Matthew Bowman?'

'Yes, of course, Grandmamma. Matthew Bowman. The kipper man told me. . . . He was having his dinner in the kitchen after he'd delivered some bloaters for Mama. He sometimes delivers over Stainton way and he knows. . . .'

'Some water, Charles. There's a jug beside you.'

Her face was deathly white, and her breathing sounded awful. What if she died now, this minute? What would he do?

He wheeled his chair across to the bedside table, and poured the water with a shaking hand.

'Grandmamma, what is it? Please. . . .'

'Matthew Bowman!'

'You wouldn't know him, Grandmamma. He was only a miner, after all. Fancy Betty inheriting lots of money. She will be even more unbearable, of course.'

'His grandchild. So that's it. Of course! The red hair! But who would have thought he could have produced such a fine child in the second generation. . . .' She was muttering to herself. 'How could it be? And John's wife, Violet, of course. I never saw her. She was his child. Did she ever know, I wonder?'

He was mystified by her. Is this what happened just before you died, wandering in your wits? Would it happen to him?

'Now!' She spoke with such violence that his heart began to thump, opening her sightless eyes wide and seeming to stare at him. For the first time in his life, he was frightened of her.

'Lean over to my bureau. That drawer there. The leather folder. There's an envelope. Open it.'

He did as he was told. The folder was lying in the front of the desk, as though it had been put there on purpose, ready to be found. Inside was an envelope and inside that a faded, hand-tinted lithograph.

'Look at the picture!' She commanded him.

'Yes, Grandmamma. I'm looking.' He was intrigued, his fear forgotten. 'I say, there's a painting of this place in the library. Isn't this where you and grandpapa went to live, in India, when he was in the diplomatic service?'

'Yes, yes!' Her voice was steadier now and she seemed to have regained her wits. 'On the borders of Sikkim. I loved it so much, although your grandfather never cared for it. I think of it often.' She leaned towards him confidentially, lowering her voice. 'Do you know that bungalow in the picture still belongs to us? I intend to leave it to you in my will when I die. The Raj takes care of it for us and uses it to accommodate travellers. But it is to be yours. I want you to go back. You must go back! It is on the main trail to Tibet. You can go on from there into the Himalaya. . . .'

'Grandmamma! How can you say such a thing? If you could see me . . . anyway, you know well enough! I will never go anywhere. It's one thing to dream. . . .'

'You *will* go!' Once again that claw-like hand found his, the nails digging into him. Once more he felt a shiver of fear.

'But Grandmamma, I'm helpless. You know that!'

'All the things I have told you about, they begin there! It is the first step!'

'But it's stupid! I won't. I can't!'

She leaned over him, her face, with its blind eyes, close to his.

'The girl will help you. She has the strength. I know it. She is bound up with you. I understand that now. It is fitting that she will help you. It will make everything right again. Don't you see?'

'Grandmamma!' 'He was exasperated. 'I wish you'd talk sense. You're frightening me. You know I can't even get up the stairs by myself. How am I ever going to get out to India . . . to that place? There probably aren't any roads!'

She laid back on her pillows, her face suddenly still, as though all the fight had gone out of her.

'The first steps are important; they lead to the last. I was told of a place, once, high in the Snow Mountains. Someone I once cared about was there. . . .' There were tears running down the old cheeks.

'I have never told you, Charles. Look! Look into the picture. What do you see?'

He looked again. Three faded figures stood stiffly on an unnaturally bright lawn, before a low white house with a green-painted veranda.

'Tell me what you see!' There was an urgency in her voice.

He squinted at the picture. 'I see a lady . . . in a white dress. She's young. That must be you, Grandmamma! You were really beautiful then! And there's a rather cross-looking man. He looks hot. He's wearing a white hat, and a white suit. He's got a moustache. . . .'

'Yes! Yes!'

'And there are flowers . . . beautiful flowers. The colours are wonderful. One is blue, here in the corner. And there is another figure, under the tree. He isn't an Englishman, is he, Grandmamma? He is dressed in yellow stuff and he has a funny hat. He has such a strange face. . . .'

'Yes, you are quite right, he is not an Englishman. That is Kensin Lo. He was a Tibetan Prince. A Shapé, one of the ruling class. He came to stay with us at the bungalow when he was on a diplomatic mission to India. He became our . . . friend. He came twice more to see us. The second time was when that picture was taken . . . just before he left!'

For a few moments, there was quiet in the room. Then, seeming to gain some extra strength from somewhere, she went on in a stronger voice.

'That very last time, as a gift, he brought me the Blue Poppy. It grows in Tibet. It was a rare species, never found before. Kensin Lo brought it for me. I loved flowers then, too. Blue was my colour. . . .' She was talking half to herself. 'It only grows in one place, on the mountain where the great monastery is. Kensin Lo was returning, that last time, to become its Abbot. Only there, in the whole of Tibet, does this Blue Poppy grow. It is the rarest and the strangest. Kensin was very well educated and he knew many languages. Even Latin. He had had an English tutor and had been to an English school. He told me this Poppy had never been named, but he would name it for me . . . Meconopsis Maudii! There! Others have been found, of course. The Abbé Delavey found one in the Yunnan and there were others. . . .I hear there have been others. . . . But never *that* Blue Poppy. It is special.' Her voice changed as though she were repeating something long-remembered. 'He told me it grows by the great Lake, the dark blue lake under the sacred mountain. It can be found on a path near the water. And where it grows, it loves its own reflection. That was how it was with us. We too loved our own reflections, as though we were each other. . . .'

He was only half-listening.

'What a wonderful story! Grandmamma! Why didn't you tell me before? A mysterious monastery in the mountains. A flower named after you. . . .'

'He was a great lover of flowers and he understood all those things. He said it was his way of making me immortal. But it has all gone now. It is only dust!'

She gripped his hand.

'Remember! You must remember! I have left the bungalow to you. Kadji's family took care of it for the government. I made my husband specify that they would always have that job. I owed them that. They

were my friends. Ask for him when you go back. He will know. He has
something for you. Then you'll understand why it matters so much. We
grew the rare Blue Poppy there, my poppy, but it flowered only once. You
can see it in the photograph. It flowered that year, like a blessing.'

He squinted at the picture, holding it up to the light.

'Yes, I can see it! It's beautiful. The colour is wonderful!'

'After that, it would never come again. I never took any seed. Now I
have only a memory.'

Looking at her old, worn face, he had a sudden urge to comfort her.

'I will find it for you, Grandmamma.' He said impulsively. 'I will find
the seeds and plant them. I will grow it for you.'

It was a child talking, but she half-wanted to believe him. For a
moment her face was joyful.

'I will bring some back for you to make you happy. We will plant them
here, in Cumberland. And I will be your eyes. I will tell you all about the
garden. I will do it for you.'

She gave a deep sigh. Looking down at her, he saw that her eyes were
closed. There was an expression of peace on her face. Whatever mysterious thing it was that had so distressed her, had somehow been
resolved. . . .

All that night his dreams were disturbed by hurrying footsteps and
hushed voices. When he awoke, he realized that he had been dreaming of
his grandmother. They had been walking up a stony track between narrow
banks. Behind them there walked a shadowy figure. And above them,
dominating the skyline, some high mountains hung in the impossible sky.
They were covered in snow. He had been filled with joy.

When Connie came in to him with his breakfast, she told him, gently,
that his grandmother had died in the night.

CHAPTER 9

Charles stared out of the window of the library. It had been an awful morning. His mother, in tears, had told him over breakfast that his father would probably not be coming home on leave for a while. There was so much to do at the training camp in Carlisle. That would mean John would not be home either. He missed John's comforting presence, his sheer physical strength, almost more than he missed his father.

His mother was always upset nowadays, and now his grandmother had gone, there was never anyone to talk to. How could she have left him all alone, just when he needed her most? And he missed that stupid girl. She had made him feel so alive, albeit just for a little while. It had been weeks since she had left, and despite her promise, she had not yet returned. Had he been so mean to her that she was never coming back? He needed her there to cheer him on. What a weakling he was! He had even tried a step or two on his own but had given up in depression and despair.

He was staring out of the window moodily, when he heard a hissing sound behind him. He swung round. A bright red head was peering at him in the doorway.

'Is it safe?'

He was torn as usual between laughter and irritation. That girl!

'Betty. You're back!' He was so glad to see her.

She came slowly into the room. There was something different about her, an odd mixture of shyness and confidence. She had grown up a lot in the weeks she had been away.

She came over to his chair, and, reaching out, she touched his arm.

'I'm that sorry about your grandmother, lad. She was kind to me, that time I met her.'

Charles sighed.

'I miss her frightfully. She was always there. But I'll keep my promise to her too, somehow. Some day, I mean to be a plant hunter, Betty! Just like Mr Kingdon-Ward! I don't know how I am going to do it, but I will! That's why I am studying so hard. And when I come back I'll plant a Blue Poppy in my garden in memory of my grandmother. So she'll live on for ever and ever!'

Betty nodded.

'That would be a wonderful thing to do for your gran. She would be that proud of you, Charlie. I were sad not to spend more time with the old lass. But I'll not forget I made a promise too. I've come back to get you off your backside and up them mountains. Then you can start your precious plant hunting! But it's one step at a time, mind. But I'll be there to help you like I promised, even if you hate me at the finish!'

He shook his head.

'I don't know if I really can, Betty. But I mean to try. For grand-mamma's sake. Just don't be too hard on me!' He hesitated. 'But there's something else. Would you help me, here. In the library, be my friend even? Like I asked before?' The words came out in a rush.

She grinned at him.

'I'll tell you what. I want an arrangement, lad. I help you with your books and you can help me with mine. Because I don't mean to be a kitchen skivvy all my life with Mrs Callerthwaite screaming blue murder at me. I'm going to be as good as you. So we'll have an arrangement. How about it? I'll help you and you can help me. Otherwise I'll get back to the kitchen and you can do for yourself!'

He felt a surge of crossness. How dare she suggest she could be his equal! Then he remembered how miserable and lonely he had been. It was worth the risk.

'Well, then?' She was looking at him as though she understood. How was it that whatever it was he was thinking, she seemed to know almost before he did. That was another irritating thing about her.

'My mother will be furious if she finds out.'

She turned and began to walk toward the door.

'You are the most infuriating person I have ever met,' he burst out. She had reached the door by now. 'Just because I'm helpless. . . .'

This time she turned back. Her eyes were blazing furiously.

'If you say that again to me, I'll leave you alone. You'll only be helpless when you're dead, pushing up the daisies and that'll not be for a while yet!'

His anger suddenly evaporated. He grinned at her. Slowly, the colour faded from her cheeks and she smiled back at him. The bargain was sealed.

Alice laid down Thomas's letter and sighed. She would write back and tell him he was loved, and they were all coping splendidly. She wouldn't tell him how much she missed him, and how hard it was. But what was she to do with Charles? She knew she wasn't good with him, although she gave him every care. She mollycoddled him and fussed him, that was the truth of it. But what else was she to do? It was all doubly difficult now, trying to run the house on a skeleton staff.

Now, the last straw! Charles's tutor had given in her notice. She was going to be married. Wasn't that astonishing? And so dreadfully inconvenient. How was she to find a replacement at the beginning of a war? All the suitable people were going, enlisting, or into war work. How was Charles to continue his studies? He had long ago outstripped them all, especially Miss Whatsername. In that respect perhaps it was a blessing in disguise. But what was she to do?

Now Cook wanted to see her in the drawing-room, a stiff little note slipped into the day's menu. Suppose Cook gave her notice, how on earth would they manage?

There was a knock on the door. Cook's rather disobliging face appeared.

'Ma'am?'

'Yes, Cook?'

Mrs Callerthwaite took up a stance just inside the doorway, took a deep breath and launched into the speech she had been preparing all morning.

'Forgive me, ma'am. It's about that lass, Betty. Well, ma'am, she means to be helpful, but you ask her do summat, though she's willing, her heart isn't in it. Always dreaming and reading books in the corner, that's her trouble. It's hard enough being short-staffed, without having to black the range myself on account of she's off in a dream with some book.'

Alice sighed.

'I'm sorry, Cook. What do you want me to do? You know she's John's child, and I promised to give her a position. Are you saying she isn't suitable in the kitchen? You know it's impossible to get staff at the moment. And you do have Connie to help as well.'

'With all respect, ma'am,' Mrs Callerthwaite continued after an awkward pause. 'It's all been put on me, like, since John and other lads went off to the war. That lad, Tom, is willing enough but he don't know how to organise the below stairs work, ma'am, and I find I'm doing it all. . . .'

Alice stared at her helplessly. If only Thomas were here.

'And I don't see how I can do a proper job without my proper staff. I need another willing lass with some training, ma'am. . . . Though even that wouldn't be enough for this big house and all the running of it, to tell the truth. I know the master's away and there isn't that much entertaining any more, but it's everyday matters coming to harm, getting behind like. I can't forever be chasing up to the library seeking out the lass when I want her to clean the pots. . . .'

'The library? I don't understand.'

'Yes, Mrs Fergusson.' Mrs Callerthwaite assumed her most put-upon expression. 'I'm not one to tell tales, but the moment you take your eyes off her ladyship, she's down with the blackleading and the job half done, and she off up them back stairs to them books of hers. I heard tell her grandfather put funny ideas into her head. He didn't fit her out for the real world, I'll say that, ma'am.'

'But the library is out of bounds to the servants, Mrs Callerthwaite. I'm sure you know that. I think you must be mistaken. I don't have cause to go into the library myself, I must admit, but my son takes all his lessons there. I am sure he would have said something.'

Mrs Callerthwaite's mouth set in a stubborn line.

'Well, I'm not saying any more, Mrs Fergusson. But I have a cousin who would oblige us by coming in and helping just to do a favour. It would help me. I don't know how I'll manage else, and maybe the lass could be useful with summat else. She's bright enough, I'll say that. But she just isn't suited for it, not that sort of work. She's more trouble than she's worth in kitchen, to be frank with you.'

Alice walked over to the window. Really, as if life wasn't vexing enough. Why was it that she could so rarely get the upper hand with the servants? She was aware that she was being manipulated, but what could she do? She would be in a dreadful pickle if Cook left, poached by one of her friends, who always, by hook or by crook, managed to maintain large staffs and a good table. Better to give in gracefully. And in any case, there was no doubt some substance in Mrs Callerthwaite's complaint.

'I appreciate your telling me. It may be that we can find other work for Betty. That is my concern. But yes, certainly, tell your relative to come and see me with a view to taking up a kitchen post. I will consider her.'

As soon as Cook had left, looking self-righteous, Alice hurried up the staircase and along the first floor corridor. The Fergussons had not been known for their scholarly pursuits in the past, preferring the less intellectual path of traditional country sports. Charles's own desire to go up to Cambridge and study the Natural Sciences was all the more surprising, given their family background. Thus the library was rather stuck away at the back of the house, reflecting its relative unimportance, occasionally useful as an extra room for entertaining. The best views had been given to the drawing-room.

She opened the door. Charles was in the far corner, hunched over the table as usual, books and maps and diagrams spread in front of him. And there was another figure in the room. It couldn't be Miss Hopkins. She had left three days previously in order to prepare her trousseau. But it was certainly a female figure. She could see that even in the gloomy light from the window. The person was up a ladder, leaning over at a dangerous angle above the upper rows of books and showing rather too much petticoat for modesty. Charles was leaning back in his chair, looking up and shouting peevishly.

'Not there, you foolish child. Further over. Under "D". Under "D", you nincompoop!'

Listening there in the doorway, Alice heard the reply with increasing disbelief.

'You're a great gowk, Charlie Fergusson. I've looked all over the shelf and there's nothing in this spot about your dratted sub-species. Himalayan foothills! You would do a sight better for yourself if you would get out on own fells for a breath of good Cumberland air! You're not so bedfast you can't do that! And if you're going to be bossing me about when I'm only trying to give you a helping hand, you can look for your blasted books yourself!'

To her further astonishment, Alice heard a peal of laughter echo around the dusty shelves. It was her son laughing. Not the effete chuckle that she might have expected from such a weakling body, but an uproarious sound, full of new-found joy.

CHAPTER 10

HQ
Blackhall Racecourse
Carlisle
20 November

Dearest Alice,
You were perfectly right to be angry. I agree! Where would we be if we allowed such familiarity to continue between the servants and ourselves? It is certainly true that Betty should be sent back to the kitchen for a while, and reprimanded severely for stepping over the line. But your description was so vivid it made me smile. Will you forgive me? And when you told me that Charles was laughing away in the way you described, I had to laugh myself. I had no idea he had so much mischief in him and I am much gladdened by it. Perhaps being away here and seeing how ordinary common men face up to the idea of the Front, and generally getting to know the fellows, who really are a splendid bunch, has made me change a few of my ideas.

And I have to tell you that Charles has written to me himself. Please do not be angry with him. I have already reprimanded him for it in my letter. He has become rather unhappy and lonely since I left and he feels he is a burden on you. This daughter of John's has only been helping him with his books, at his request. She is a rather cheeky young miss and must be kept in order, but if she is having a good effect on Charles, perhaps she could help him a little during the day, if it makes him happy. John has told me that she has been very strictly brought up by her grandfather who was most religious, and that she has been educated by him to a good standard. Don't be put off by her rough speech and her temper.

If she is only to care for Charles and cheer him up, I don't think she can do too much harm. Perhaps, with this awful war hanging over us, we have to shake down together. For my sake, my darling, try the girl out as a helper for Charles. Her difficult ways cannot harm him, and if she has some scholarship and good humour she may be a help to him, until we can find him another tutor. Charles wishes so much to have a companion, and he tells me she has been such a boon to him.

I think of you both and pray for you every night before turning in. John is jolly good at making cocoa!

With all my love.
Your Thomas.

She had been so sure that he would agree with her. Dear stuffy Thomas. What was the world coming to? Here they were, her husband and her beloved son, the two most important people in her world, going behind her back and conspiring against her. The tone of her husband's letter, although as usual, kindly, had contained more than a hint that he thought she was making a fuss about nothing. It implied that the world was changing and she was being left behind, even that she was being unreasonable. But he didn't have to deal with recalcitrant servants who, given an inch, would inevitably take a mile! She had, after all, always considered herself quite modern, quite an innovator, certainly not a tyrant. Was she so wrong to object to Charles and a servant girl giggling together in the library? There had to be some structure, for heaven's sake, or the world would fall apart.

She seemed to spend an awful lot of time nowadays just staring out of the morning-room window, at the unkempt lawn and the pasture beyond, where the prize Herdwick sheep grazed, now deprived of their lambs. She felt left behind. The world was moving on. It was becoming a confusing place. Perhaps she was growing old?

She sat and looked out at the November trees stretching up towards the distant fells, those fells where in the first days of their marriage, they had walked daringly together, she in a long tweed skirt which bunched and rubbed unbearably. They had been happy then, happy and free. The world had seemed full of promise. Now he was moving on and she was standing still. His letter lay on her lap, a mute accusation.

A chill wind sprang up and rattled the casement windows. The last red and green leaves from the maple tree by the corner of the house splatted wetly on to the glass, and then were whirled away. I hate this dark house, she thought. I shall be trapped here for ever. None of us will ever get away. Only Thomas, perhaps, with his wretched war.

Outside, in the wind, just out of sight of the window, Charles stood in front of his bath chair for the first time unaided. Looking out over the lawn, he fixed his eyes on the skeleton of the maple tree. Tom had been persuaded to bring him this far, and then Charles had told him to go away.

He had not spoken to Betty for days. She was being kept to the kitchen in disgrace. But her abrasive voice still echoed around in his brain. She was a funny creature. She made him laugh. Life seemed rather empty now that she had been banished from the library. He wondered if his letter to his father would have any effect. He doubted it. And now he had no one to help him with his books.

Betty's words came back to him. . . .

'If you want anything, Charlie, in this life, you've got to go for it yourself. I'm learning that. Your fancy background doesn't count for nowt. And don't you give me no old-fashioned looks, and tell me I'm no age to be telling you home truths. I may be same age as you, but I'm a world wiser. And I know one thing. If you ever wants to see that dratted blue poppy in them foreign fells of yours, it is only a step away. But you've got to get there by yourself. No folk will help you in the end!'

With her irritating, nagging voice in his ears, he let go of the chair and began to walk by himself towards the maple tree, one step at a time.

It was going to be an embarrassing interview for them both. 'After all,' thought Alice, 'I am going to have to back down.' The girl stood in front of her, eyes downcast, her collar all awry, still hot and flushed from the kitchen range.

'She is going to get her own way,' thought Alice. 'It's going to be hard.'

'I'm sorry, ma'am.' It was a pure voice, hardly a trace of dialect at that moment. She was a confusing child. Now she gave off none of the aggressive, alive feeling that Alice had sensed that day in the library. If she burned, it was with a light on a low flame.

'So you should be! It was a totally reprehensible way to behave. The library is out of bounds to the servants.'

Suddenly, in a quiet corner of her mind, she found herself asking why. Why, when hardly anyone ever went in there, should it be barred from anyone who cared enough to go?

'In any case, we have been through all this before,' she continued with renewed force. 'It's true we must all pull together. But I will not have you taking advantage of your unusual position. It is hardly grateful after all we have done for you.'

The girl looked up, with that sudden blue gaze of hers, and as quickly looked down again at the floor. But in that moment Alice was distressed to see tears in her eyes. She was stabbed by a sense of guilt. It was hard for the child. Not even the servants liked her being there, however much they put up with it for John's sake.

Alice crossed the room and looked out of the window, giving the girl time to pull herself together.

'However, in the circumstances, it is my husband's wish, and mine, now you have been suitably reprimanded' – she could feel the girl's gaze on her back – 'that you may be of some help to my son, in some limited way.'

She turned with a smile. The girl, whatever she was, was hardly paying attention. She was looking beyond Alice, out of the window, her eyes blazing. This rather untidy creature was transformed. She's formidable. I could be afraid of her, Alice thought suddenly.

The girl was half-running to the window seat, proper demeanour forgotten.

'Look, ma'am! Look out of window. Did you ever see anything like it?'

Against her better judgement, she was drawn by that thrilling voice and the pointing finger. She stepped forward to the window seat, and peered out into the dark day.

There, across the lawn, step by slow step, her son was walking into the wind. It was a wet, blustery day. He still wore a tartan rug round his shoulders after being wheeled out in the bath chair. Now it billowed around him like giant wings. That shock of black hair, which stood up so rebelliously from his forehead, had been blown up into a wild brush. His head was up and he looked out across the lawn, like someone who was seeing into a vast distance. Even through the blurred pane, she could see the determined set of his mouth. It gave her heart pain to watch him.

The two women stood together.

'It does your heart gay good, ma'am, doesn't it?' The girl said softly. 'Aren't you glad to see him? He's in fine fettle now. There'll be no stopping him.'

Something stirred in Alice, recognition, a shy, tremulous hope. But then, in a second, the old terrors came flooding back. She rounded on the girl.

'But he's ill! You don't understand? Any minute, the specialist said. It's all your fault! You turned his head.' That drowning feeling returned, that fear she had taken upon herself, a life sentence for them both.

'We have to stop him. My poor son.' She was half-hysterical, turning blindly for the door.

But the girl had her hand on her arm with an urgent pressure.

'For his sake, ma'am. He needs this chance. It'll destroy him else. He's that eaten up inside. Let him go free. Let him walk by himself!'

Alice turned back to her. The girl was standing white-faced, tears running down her cheeks.

'He loves you well, Mrs Fergusson,' she burst out. 'He wouldn't do anything to hurt you. But it's keeping him in a cage, just like them poor owls the keeper has in his hut yonder. My granddad did that to me too, kept me out of the free air. I never could abide to see a living thing kept like that. Look at him, ma'am! Turn yourself back and look!'

Alice stared at the girl, astonished and angry. This was the end! This was what happened when servants were allowed to step over the mark! But then, obeying some inner compulsion, she turned slowly and peered fearfully out of the window.

He was standing just below her, her son, his arms out against the wind, the rug half off his shoulders and flying out behind him, his face to the rain. She moved forward to open the window and caution him, to bring him inside, before he caught his death. But as she did so, the wind came roaring into the room, sending Thomas's letter skittering across the floor. With that rumbustuous wind came a scent of the fells and that unbeliev-able sound she had first heard in the library. The sound of her son laugh-ing for joy.

CHAPTER 11

By the time she had blacked the drawing-room grate and scoured the pans, all the while listening to the old skinflint telling her how hopeless she was, it was hours before Betty could escape from Mrs Callerthwaite. She ran up the back stairs to the library, worried that Charles might have finished for the morning.

Mrs Fergusson was out at some charitable day, in aid of the soldiers at the front. She was full of good works nowadays. Since she and Betty had watched Charles walking for the first time across the lawn, a kind of grudging warmth had grown up between them, though Betty was aware that she must not push her luck too far. She knew that Charles's mother resented her, and she still had to spend most of the day helping Mrs Callerthwaite with the housework.

Still, it was worth it to know that she was really, officially, allowed into the library, that is if Mrs Callerthwaite could 'spare' her for a few precious minutes in the day.

She skidded around the corner, in a scrow and out of breath, trying to fix her apron and straighten her hair on the run. The library door was open. Charles was watching for her, hunched up in his chair by the window, banging his hand on the arm.

'Where in heaven's name have you been? I've been waiting hours for you!'

'Ay, it's all right for some folk! Get up at near on noon. No grates to black! No bins to empty. No cats to feed. No pans to scrub. You don't know you've been born, Charlie. You doesn't, honest!'

Despite himself, his face broke into a grin.

'Mrs C. been giving you a bad time? I feel sorry for that woman, trying to keep you in order. Serves you right!'

It was as though they had known each other all their lives. Sometimes, however, they would remember the gulf between them. Sometimes she would step over the mark, and occasionally he would still treat her like a servant. After his upbringing, it was hard not to.

Most of the time though, they rubbed along together very well. He needed her, and, for herself, she would have gone through a great deal to keep coming into the library. It was the books she wanted, she told herself. But how was it when she caught sight of him, hunched up in that chair of his, she sometimes felt such odd feelings. She supposed she was really very fond of him. He was, after all, the only kin she had left, apart from her own father. Only Charles didn't know it.

She shut the library door and crossed over to stand by his chair.

'Come on and show me what you've been up to, Charlie, while I've been working my fingers to the bone.' Usually he showed her his books, and the writing he had done. But today he seemed too excited to settle.

'Oh, I haven't really done much. I couldn't concentrate. I had a letter today! I've been dying to show you. You'll never guess. Father's coming home on leave. Look!'

He waved the paper under her nose.

'The battalion are being moved to somewhere in the South, quite soon anyway. But he's managed to get two days leave. And guess what, he says he'll bring John with him! He is father's sergeant now, of course. He's put in for leave for him. So they'll come together. Isn't that the very best bit of news? Your father coming home too. I'm almost more pleased about that than anything!'

She could have hugged him. Her own father coming back to Bambeck! She would see him. It was too wonderful to take in.

'But you've got to help me!' He went on enthusiastically. 'I want to plan a surprise. We've both got to do it, otherwise it won't be any fun.'

'No mischief, Charlie! I can't afford to be in trouble when my father comes.'

'No, I promise. But how about this! I want to walk down the staircase to meet him, Betty! Don't you think that would be the most wonderful surprise in the world! I won't tell mother, of course. She'll only stop me!'

'You know you're not allowed, Charlie. In case you fall. It's such a long drop, too.'

'You can help me! I'm so much stronger now. And when we see the carriage coming up the drive, I'll be ready! Oh, you must help me! As father comes in the front hall, I'll be there at the top of the stairs. I can hang onto the banisters, if I have to. I've got it all worked out. But my legs are so strong now, I won't need any help. Not really. Just so long as we get some practice in! Oh, it'll be such fun!'

Betty shook her head.

'I think you should ask your mother. But it *would* be nice for your father to see. It's a grand idea. Just so long as you don't wear yourself out. You'll crock yourself up, if you're not careful. Then where will you be?'

'Oh, don't be silly, Betty! I'm not stupid. And what about you? We'll have to do something for you! After all, what have we been doing all these weeks, when you've been helping me? You've learned a lot too. I think you should recite something! Wouldn't that be just splendid! When your father comes to see you, you can learn a poem and recite it for everyone! I think that's a grand idea.'

'Nay, I'm not making a fool of myself like that. Folk would just laugh. . . .'

Betty tried to imagine Mrs Fergusson's face. She wouldn't be too pleased, she was sure of it. And she would get the blame for everything.

'I'll help you, Charlie, if you think you'll be all right. But I'm not reciting anything for folk to laugh at. Ay, I'll help you out, but don't ask me to do anything else. And listen now, we must be careful not to upset your mother.'

'Where's your spirit of adventure, Betty? I thought it was supposed to be me who was the milksop! But thanks, anyway. You're really wonderful. I thought we could start today. Mother's gone out for the day. Would you do that for me? Just the first time. Then I can manage on my own.'

Truthfully, he wasn't really so sure of himself. In fact he was really scared. But that made it all the more important to do. If only Betty had been more encouraging. She had started him off, for heaven's sake. It was her acid tongue, her taunting, which had got him walking in the first place. Now she seemed worried and, in those last few minutes, he had begun to worry too.

They made their way together along the corridor. He scorned the chair. Before he could get down the stairs he had to get up the wretched things. Well, if he could do that, he could do anything. Coming down would be nothing. Tom, the boy, had always half-lifted him up the stairs, and before that, John, but that was in the past. From today onwards, he would do it by himself, without any help. Right now he didn't want anyone else involved, unless it was Betty, and she didn't count.

He had tried really hard with his walking. After years of lying in the bath chair and hardly using his legs, he had been unnerved by their weakness. The muscles had never had a chance to develop, and he became frighteningly shaky after only a few moments.

Every morning before breakfast and again in the late afternoon, if it wasn't raining too hard, he had made Tom take him round the back of the house and leave him there for an hour. He gave himself that long walking on the flat, making himself go further every time. Only yesterday he had got as far as the stone steps, and actually climbed a few. But he couldn't bring himself to tell Betty that he had been unable to get the whole way up onto the top lawn. That a strange tightness had come in his chest and a little pain, and that he had been afraid. When Tom found him, he had been sitting on the sixth step from the bottom, dizzy and breathless. He had made Tom promise not to say a word.

That pompous old fool Nelson didn't help. He had heard from Alice, who told him with a mixture of pride and fear, that Charles was walking about by himself. Nelson had lost no time in telling them both exactly what the prognosis was. Sudden death. The heart could give out at any time. Such was the nature of the irregularity – Charles could exactly imitate that pompous voice in his head – that the patient could drop dead at any time.

But if that were true, did exertion make any difference? He wished he had had the courage to interrupt Dr Nelson's sermon and ask. If it were going to happen anyway, he might as well die outside the prison, even if it were only a few yards beyond the bars. That was his private pact with himself. It was what kept him moving. Half of him knew that was the only way forward, but the other half was simply afraid.

It was no good denying it. Somehow Betty, with her cheerful irreverence, made him forget the awful death sentence he carried with him. It made him less afraid. He could almost laugh at his fears. Almost. But when he was on his own, it was a different matter.

Now, standing in the hall in the quiet house, looking up at the broad sweep of staircase above him, he almost turned from it. He was suddenly very aware of the deep stairwell, with its ornate banisters sweeping up towards the roof, the pale sunlight from the cupola filtering down in dusty light. Echoes came to him from the house itself, Connie somewhere, singing as she polished, the clatter of the distant kitchen where luncheon (just for him) was being prepared. Betty would be summoned in a minute to fetch the tray. They must be quick.

The stairs loomed above him. They reminded him of the giant steps in *Jack and the Beanstalk*, which he had read in the nursery. He had a sudden vivid memory of the coloured picture, which showed Jack, in a green cap like Robin Hood's, trying to scale the enormous stone step at the bottom of the giant's door. And there above him, was an enormous sandaled foot, waiting to crush him into dust. Suddenly he felt as frightened as a little child. He couldn't go up. It would kill him. He just couldn't do it.

'Come on, Charlie!' Betty was gripping his arm. 'I have to go for your dinner in a minute. Just imagine now, if you're scared stiff, it's just no more than a little fell. Each one of those is no more than a little one of them precious foreign mountains . . . and right up the top, there's one of them blue flowers you're always cracking on about! Believe me, it's not so far!'

He shook her hand off his arm.

'I'm not scared, Betty. It would take more than that to frighten me!'

He put his foot determinedly on the first step, and then the second. It was just a question of getting his muscles working. After all, they had never had the chance. But what if he had a seizure while he was climbing? Dr Nelson had said he must never, never climb the stairs. The strain on his heart would be too much. Charles heard again that awful doom-laden voice in his head.

'If the patient' (why did he always refer to Charles as, 'the patient' in that sepulchral tone, just as though he were some hopeless, terminal case?) 'If the patient must walk a little on level ground, I suppose it is acceptable, as long as there is assistance near. A necessary evil, ma'am.'

He had never spoken directly to Charles. It was as though his very presence was a thorn in Dr Nelson's side. Charles was convinced the good doctor thought he was mentally retarded and would not understand what he was saying. Why else would he be so tactless?

He was getting breathless already.

'Careful now. Just don't do yourself a mischief!'

'Just walk behind me, Betty, in case I slip. But I'll do it on my own.'

Suddenly it was much easier than he had thought. He managed the first ten steps with no trouble, congratulating himself on having practised on the stone steps in the garden. He was on the first landing! But by the time he had got there his thigh and calf muscles were aching, and he was very breathless. Was this the beginning of it? He could feel that Betty was behind him. He could catch the occasional faint scent of lavender. How did he know her hair always smelt of lavender when he had never been that close? The thought drifted irrelevantly through his mind.

By the second landing he was almost finished. Pain had begun in his chest. He was frightened. But something else was overriding the fear. The picture of Dr Nelson's smug, red face staring down at him, with those bulbous eyes, condemning him to spend his life in that wretched chair. . . .

'You know my views, Mrs Fergusson. The patient would be much better off immobilised in his chair. But it is nonetheless my duty to emphasise that he must never, never exert himself with any climbing. Apart from anything else the heart will be irrevocably damaged.'

He had proved that pompous old fool wrong by even living, let alone by walking, and he would do it again. Pain or no pain, he would get there.

He had made it. With hardly anything left, he crawled up the top step, and lay there panting on the carpet. His legs felt like one of Mrs Callerthwaite's floppy jellies that she still made for his birthday. He had no strength left. The pain in his chest was awful. He closed his eyes. Was this what dying was like? Hot, black darkness.

'Betty. Where are you? I'm dying! I really am!'

He felt her hand patting his back.

'No, lad.' She was close to him now, sitting on the step below him. 'Don't carry on so. You're only out of breath. You've come a long way. And for more than fourteen years you've hardly walked a hand's span. What do you expect?' His breathing was getting easier. He opened his eyes. Above him, closer now, the cupola filtered stained-glass light onto his upturned face. It was like a church. So quiet. He could lie there for ever. A great gratitude flooded over him.

'Betty, when I grow up, I'm going to marry you! I don't care what mother says.'

There was a pause. He didn't dare to look at her, but just concentrated on the light from the cupola.

'You made me get out of that dreadful chair. You made me do all this! Without you, I wouldn't have had anything. I owe pretty well everything to you.'

'No, lad. You'll change your mind when you grow up a bit. When you go away, you'll find many more lasses to love.'

'You don't take me seriously, do you?'

The breathlessness had quite left him, and he had no more pain.

'I know what I want. I really care for you. And I think you really care for me. The world is changing, Betty.'

He sat up and looked at her. She was sitting on the top stair now, her

'It's time I was going,' she thought with sudden insight. 'This'll never go away.'

He came down the last flight of steps all of a rush. Without meaning to, instinctively protective, she held out her arms to him. His breath was coming in great sobs and he was trembling. She could feel him against her like fire, he was so hot. Then, self-consciously, they broke away from each other, but not before they had both registered the touching, the feeling of each other's bodies, as though they belonged. Betty felt it was branded on her for ever, that map of him.

He took her hand then, and pulled her along the corridor.

'Come on, Betty. I want you to do something for me!'

She was struggling with strange, new feelings.

'No! I only came to tell you I can't stop. I'm glad I saw you come down the stairs. You've done really well by yourself. I'm that proud.'

She had to distance herself from him. Once again she felt that she was years and years older than him, that she had to protect him.

'Oh, come on Betty. Just for an hour. I know Mrs C. is having forty winks. Come on, you did promise. . . .'

'Promise what?' She was apprehensive.

'You promised you would recite a poem for your father. You know, when he comes. I'm going to read some Tennyson to you and then you can choose.'

'Charlie, I never promised. I never said I'd do it, to be laughed at. . . .'

So he hadn't felt as she had after all. That closeness, that rush of love, that moment in the quiet hall. And his words of the morning had been forgotten. He really was no more than a child, and she was so very old. She should have been relieved that his words had just been innocent gratitude. But somewhere inside her, she was terribly sad.

CHAPTER 12

He had taken a book down from the shelves, made her sit by the window, and had started reading to her. The sun slanted in through the library windows. She was still full of strange feelings. He was reading with some magical lilt in his voice. She had been spellbound. She was caught. It had been as though someone held her in quicklime by the feet, like the poor birds the keeper trapped. She looked out at Bambeck Fell, distant and misty on the horizon, and she saw it all, all the pictures the words were saying to her. All laid out in her head, in the garden with the mountains behind, magically there.

At last she was aware that he had stopped. There was a deep silence in the room, and neither of them spoke. She stared out at the window, willing the pictures to stay.

'Ay, Charlie,' she said at last, 'that was better than Miss Little, with her thumping voice.'

The village schoolmistress had read poems to them, smacking at the front desk, and catching their knuckles with her ruler to make the words go in. She had hated poems ever since.

'Alfred, Lord Tennyson. He wrote that. Don't you think it's good? He came to stay in Cumberland you know. Not far from here. Down by the Lake. They say he used it in one of his poems.'

So he had been here, come to look at the Lakes all the way from London. Funny to think she had lived in this spot all her life and she had never seen those great stretches of water for herself. They might as well have been on the moon.

'I'll tell you what, Charlie. If I learn the poem for you, will you take me one day? Up one of the hills, so we can see one of those Lakes? You can do it now, lad. Now you've started, there's nothing to stop you. And I'll be there, helping you on. There won't be anything to be afraid of. I'll read one of them poems for you, I promise. The one with the lass who was all sad when her lad had gone away, and about the beautiful river? But you'll have to promise too. . . .'

'*The Lady of Shalott*! I could teach it to you. Then you could recite it when your father comes tomorrow. What a surprise that would be!'

She shook her head.

'I'll learn it for myself, Mr Know-it-All. I can read as well as you can. But you'll have to keep your promise too. No backing out, mind.'

He grinned down at her, his face transformed in that way which so turned her over, as though there had been a fire lit inside her.

'If I weren't going to study the Natural Sciences, I would be a poet, Betty.'

She nodded slowly.

'I fancy that, myself. Making up thing just out of words, and then getting rich by it! No skivvying over grates and the like. Just words and dreaming. Maybe I'll be a poet, too!'

'Oh, Betty, you're hopeless!' He laughed.

She shook her head.

'I might be famous one day, Charlie. What do you think? After all, if you can get up them stairs the way you did, I can do anything too. . . .'

She put the old book down carefully, balanced so that it wouldn't fall off onto the dairy floor. It was a beautiful thing, smelling of fine leather, with the pages gold on the edges so when you put them together they made a wide band, all gold. She didn't want it spoiled. Charles had lent it to her. She hadn't liked to take it, but he had said his mother would never notice. In any case she would be glad to see the books used. Betty wasn't so sure. But then the words had cast such a spell over her, she thought it was worth a telling-off. It wasn't the first poetry she had read, not even Miss Little reciting some dry old stuff she had long forgotten, just remembering how boring it was. Her grandfather had read her 'Paradise Lost', in that voice he used for his preaching. She had only liked the bad angels, the rest were a sapless lot, like rag dolls with no stuffing. Now she was reading for herself. It was like a secret power. She was supposed to be churning the milk. Every time she forgot where she was and got absorbed by the words, the churn would stop. No wonder the butter was taking so long.

She felt a stinging slap across her head. The book went flying, landing upside-down in a puddle on the stone flags, with all its fine gold pages crumpled up.

The humiliation of it. To have to stand by while Mrs Callerthwaite catalogued her crimes.

'I'm sorry to have to say this, Mrs Fergusson, but the lass is simply not suited, as I said before. She never has her mind on the job and I'm forever chasing her to do things I've asked her to do half a dozen times. It wears a body out! And this is the last straw!'

Triumphantly, Mrs Callerthwaite produced the sodden book from beneath her apron, like the conjurer producing a white rabbit out of his hat.

'I caught the lass reading while she was supposed to be turning the butter!'

Betty kept her eyes down, trying to avoid Alice's look. If only Charles were here to explain, though in a way that would have made her embarrassment worse.

'Do you have any explanation for this?'

The voice was cold. She looked up and she and Alice caught each other's eyes for a moment. She was certainly for it!

'Then she threw the book down in a temper. . . .'

This was too much for Betty.

'I did not!' She said indignantly 'It dropped out of my hand when you slapped me, Mrs Callerthwaite. I were taking good care of it till then!'

'And you will hold your tongue, miss!' Cook gave her a furious look.

They were both glaring at her now. Alice was as angry as a skep full of mad bees.

'I'm that sorry, Mrs Fergusson. I know I should never have took the book but I were taking care of it. I had meant to give it back.'

'Steal it more like!' Mrs Callerthwaite snorted under her breath.

'I think it is time I spoke to Betty alone, Mrs Callerthwaite. Thank you so much for bringing this matter to my attention. You may leave now.'

Deprived of the sight of Betty getting a telling-off, Mrs Callerthwaite bustled virtuously out of the room, though not before giving Betty a final glare.

'As I've said before, Mrs Fergusson,' she said, turning back in the doorway. 'I have that cousin who would be glad to come in and help. She would be a sight more willing, and she wouldn't expect no favours. Not like some folk!'

'Yes. Thank you, Mrs Callerthwaite.'

There was a brief silence.

The door closed and they were left alone together.

'Did you intend to steal the book, Betty?'

'No, ma'am.'

They looked at each other for a moment. Alice sighed, trying to calm the irrational anger which always seemed to come to the surface when faced with the girl. If only she would keep out of the way and not forever be so . . . obvious! This would have to happen just as her husband was expected home. John too would be with him, and she would look like a hard taskmaster if she punished the girl. But what was one to do? Instinct told her that Betty was telling the truth, but nevertheless, the gall of it! She picked up the book with finger and thumb.

'Did my son have anything to do with this episode, by any chance?'

'No ma'am! It were my own idea. I just wanted to read about the Lady of the Lake.'

The girl was probably protecting her son. The thought made her crosser still. How dare the little minx!

'I have to think of an appropriate punishment, but now is not the time.'

As though to echo her words, there was a commotion downstairs and a sound of running footsteps.

'Thomas!'

Alice gathered up her skirts, and Betty was temporarily forgotten, as she swept out of the room. As she reached the top of the stairs, an amazing scene was spread before her in the hall below. Her husband was standing there, still in his greatcoat. He was holding out his arms and laughing, his expression a curious mixture of surprise, pleasure and anxiety. His attention was fixed on a point halfway up the stairs.

Alice followed his gaze, and gasped in disbelief. Her son was walking down the stairs, by himself! Step by unsteady step, his eyes fixed on his father's face, his frail little legs trembled as each foot groped for the step below.

She heard a sound behind her and swung round. That wretched girl was standing there, her hands clasped together, such a look of pride and proprietorial joy on her face that Alice longed to slap her.

'You!' She choked, 'It was you! You have done this. This is all your fault!'

'Father! Father!'

Her son had reached the bottom step, and with his last strength he ran haltingly across to his father.

Laughing, Thomas held out his arms to him, and lifted him up high.

'Aren't you proud of me?' Charles looked up at his father as Thomas placed him gently back on the marble floor. 'Betty helped me do it! We're friends now. And I've taught her a poem. I lent her a book, and she's going to say a poem for John. We wanted it to be a surprise. It was all my own idea, but I couldn't have done it without her.'

So it had been a plot between them after all! And now they were all smiling, the servants looking on. Thomas was looking so proud that she would have to smile too and pretend it was a success, while anger raged inside her. She felt betrayed, left out. It was too awful!

Thomas was holding out his arms to her. She had waited so long to see him and now it was spoilt. That brat had spoiled it all.

'Come down, Alice! And is that Elizabeth there, hiding at the back? Come down, my dear!'

The creature was coming down the stairs behind her. How dare she!

'Where's John?' Charles was pulling at his father's sleeve. 'Is he outside? Betty's been waiting for ages. We have to do the poem. It was part of the bargain.'

Alice had reached her husband. Constrained by the presence of the servants, he did not embrace her, only taking her hand and kissing it. She thought, with a spasm of pain, how thin he had become. How she longed to hug him to her!

Then Thomas was looking past her. Betty stood, hesitating on the bottom step. Alice had a moment of insight. The girl was neither fish nor fowl. Standing there, with that strange elegance she always had about her, however untidy her clothes (and they often were), standing on the staircase the servants never used except when they were polishing the banisters, half in the servants' world, and half in theirs. Her husband was oblivious to the tensions between them, intent on drawing the girl into their world. For a brief moment she almost felt sorry for her, despite everything.

'I'm afraid Betty is in disgrace, my dear.' Her voice was colder than she had meant. 'I was in the middle of reprimanding her. She had taken a book out of the library, and now it is quite spoiled.'

But no one was listening.

'Come here, Elizabeth.' Her husband was speaking gently. The girl came down the last step, her eyes downcast. 'I am so sorry. Your father was put on extra duties this weekend and he has been unable to come. There are so many of us who have been given leave that there is rather a shortage of volunteers for the important tasks. And you know your father. He will put himself in the way of everything. He's too conscientious for his own good. I've brought a letter from him. I'm so sorry, Elizabeth. I know how much you must have been looking forward to seeing him.'

Alice glanced up at Betty's face. What she saw there made all the anger drain away. Tears were coursing down the girl's face. She gave a little curt-sey. Then, blindly, without asking leave, she turned and ran, stumbling back up the stairs which Charles had so triumphantly walked down a few moments before.

CHAPTER 13

Betty raised her swollen face from the pillow and felt for the letter. She knew every word by heart, and had cried over it many times. Yet to read it again, imagining her father's voice, gave her some comfort in a dark world.

HQ
Blackhall Racecourse
22 January

Dear Elizabeth,

This letter is written in haste. I know this will be by way of disappointing you, but I have been given duties and cannot come with Captain Fergusson. It is what happens in the Army, and after all we are fighting for King and Country. But in my heart I wish I could see you, it being so long, and if we go to the Front in the spring. I will ask the Captain about you when he comes back. He says that you have been a good lass and have been of service to his son. I am proud of you to be spoken of so well.

Carlisle is not so far away, and the Captain has promised to try for some leave for me before we embark. You would be proud of your old father. We are fine fellows now, fitted up very well by Lord Lonsdale. He is a good chap. You should have seen us at the beginning in our flat caps and Sunday best. Billy Bleamire, who farmed beside your grandfather, his boots were three sizes too big and he had on a queer bonnet a lass could have worn. Now we all have a uniform made up specially in a kind of dark-grey stuff. German cloth, they call it!

You know lass, that I care for you. I know I'm not much of a one for writing down my feelings. This is all my own work except the spellings and some pieces which I have done by a friend and with the Captain's help.

I hope you like the ribbons I am sending. A peddler came round the racecourse with his tray. I chose the best blue ribbons for your eyes, and also the lace shawl to wear about your shoulder on Sundays. I am glad you are well set up with Mrs Fergusson. Work hard, my lass and be a good girl always. I am that proud of you. . . .

In the last few weeks, she had been given an attic room at the top of the house. It was very much better to have a room of her own, away from Connie, who was good-hearted enough but was always whining on. And Connie hadn't been so clean, always leaving her dirty stockings on the floor and not washing, although it was hard enough when the water had to be brought so far. Betty had been strictly brought up in matter of cleanliness. Even though her bootlaces were always undone and her apron creased and marked, she was sure to be clean underneath.

Now, in this little room, with its sloping walls under the eaves, she was making a spot of her own, with bits and pieces gleaned from the storeroom next door. Mrs Fergusson never came this far upstairs, so Charles had said it was all right. She kept reminding herself that she would soon be rich enough to buy anything, a proper quilt with a lace cover, a little porcelain lamp she had seen once in Penrith market, whatever she wanted. Soon there would be money from her grandfather's will, so Mr Arnison said. Even though most of her legacy was in property, there would be more than enough money to live on.

Yet even those little privileges, like her own room, had made her more unpopular, and had made the 'trouble' she had been in with Mrs Callerthwaite that much worse. It was so unjust. Lying there in her bed, clutching her father's letter to her and staring sideways into the lamp, she let the hot tears dribble backwards down her face, onto the pillow, making rainbows on her lashes as she watched the light. They were quite pretty, the coloured rainbows. When you crinkled your eyes up, there were spears of gold and silver shooting out of the sides, spears of light like Jesus's lamp in the painting of her grandfather's, the room misty and soft like a dream.

Jesus probably wouldn't like her getting angry, but it made you feel you could conquer the world. She had felt real anger returning to her as a kind of power in those last few hours. She knew it was a destructive thing, but maybe just now she needed it. You couldn't be a milksop all your life. Surely He wouldn't like that. He had got angry in the Temple, after all. It didn't do a bit of good just giving way to folk. They would march straight over you, as though you were nothing more than a slug on a path, waiting to be squashed. Perhaps when she was old and had won her battles, she would ask forgiveness of Him. But just now she hoped He would understand.

For the twentieth time she smoothed the blue silk ribbons her father had sent her, laid out now on the faded quilt. They were a wonderful, brilliant blue. She would have liked to have seen them against her nightdress, but there was no mirror in the room. One day she would have a mirror of her own, though there had never been one in her grandfather's house. He had said that such things were ungodly and would lead to vanity. The first time she could remember seeing herself properly had been here, at Bambeck, in the great hall with the black and white squares. There had been a big gold mirror on the wall (Mrs Fergusson called it a 'looking glass'). She had glimpsed herself there, a scruffy dishevelled little creature despite her best pinafore.

Since then she had returned many times to the mirror to gaze and dream, when she was supposed to be polishing the marble tiles, or blacking the hall grate. She had decided that she was odd-looking, her hair so bright she had often thought of putting the blacking on it to tone it down. How she had suffered for that hair, the bane of her life since schooldays! Ay, her hair was definitely queer, although Charles said it went back to the Vikings, that colour, like his own family. She had been rather embarrassed and had changed the subject quickly. She had very bright eyes too, a funny blue colour like the cornflower in the barley field. And now, at least, she had a bit more of a body, sticking out in places, and her face was rounder. She hoped she was all right below the waist. She hadn't been able to see, even standing on tiptoe. Perhaps she had a big backside. It would be awful to have a big backside. She might not get anyone at all to marry her, whatever Charles said. Nay, not even someone who was grateful to her or felt sorry for her. In fact, the awful thought was, would anyone ever marry a girl with hair as red as a cockerel's wattle, and no folks of her own? She pushed the idea aside.

What if she tiptoed down the back stairs, now everyone was asleep, and into the great hall, and looked into the mirror? Then she could see how the ribbons looked. She knew it was foolish, but they were so pretty. And she needed cheering up. Perhaps if she wore a blue ribbon in her hair it might make up for the big backside. And the lovely lace her father had sent. It must have cost him all his pay for a week or more. She would never dare to wear it around her shoulders. Well, perhaps on her afternoon off with her good frock. But she could hold it up against her cheek, and see what it looked like in the mirror. She could be like *The Lady of Shalott*. Then she could write back to her father and tell him how well his presents looked. Perhaps he would be comforted in that lonely place.

It must be very late now. She had no clock in her room. Mrs Callerthwaite would always wake Connie, and Connie would come along to Betty and try to get into her bed to warm her feet. Connie's feet stank.

Now she had apologised to Mrs Callerthwaite, she was to be allowed back into the library tomorrow. It had stuck in her craw to do it, and Mrs Callerthwaite had smirked unbearably. But there, it was done. She supposed she had been let off lightly, but she felt so humiliated. They were all glad she had been put in her place, no doubt about it.

She got out of bed very quietly – there was only a thin wall between her and Connie – and opened the door.

CHAPTER 14

'Rats! Rats! Come on, chaps! Behind you!'

She wondered if she should call for Nelson. Perhaps he was delirious. He could have caught some disease in those dreadful living conditions up in Carlisle.

Then he had woken suddenly and, reaching out, had made love to her with an intense, concentrated passion. They had laid together in the darkness, he with his arm around her and they had talked about Charles. It had been easier then, in the dark.

'You know, there is a terrific spirit in the boy,' he said. 'I realized it when he walked down those stairs towards me. Should we have been mollycoddling him all these years? It's John's daughter who has brought the character out in him. I'm sure of it. What a lot she has done for him!'

She had almost cried out, in resentment, 'What about me? What about all I have done, before that little minx came in and spoiled it all?' But some instinct kept her silent, and she only said,

'She has encouraged Charles. I do agree. Although I am not at all sure the specialist would approve of all this exertion. In fact, I think he will be horrified. You can be sure Dr Nelson will reprimand him. Remember his advice to us! And she does rather get above herself. You don't have to manage this house! It's not easy while you are away, and she causes trouble with the servants. Look at the business of the book. Can you imagine, in the dairy! No wonder Mrs Callerthwaite was put out.'

She heard him sigh in the darkness, and immediately regretted her words. Anxious that she should not have spoiled their intimacy, she reached up her hand and stroked the arm around her shoulders.

'It must be hard for you, Alice,' he said at last, 'but do try to let go a little. I've seen so much in the past months. I don't suppose the world will ever be the same again after this war is over. It's changed the way I look

at things. I felt so bad for Elizabeth standing there. I couldn't help thinking of John. The timing couldn't have been worse. I felt responsible for
it.'

'What would you have me do? Let the girl take books out of the library
willy-nilly? Throw it open to the servants?' Despite herself, she could feel
her anger rising. Why did any mention of John's daughter always catch her
on the raw?

He was silent for a few moments. She wished she could see his face.

'I know it isn't easy for you, Alice. I have left you with a great deal to
manage on your own. The discipline in the house must be very difficult.
You do a wonderful job. . . .' he paused, 'but does it seem wrong to you
that books we never read should give pleasure to someone, even a servant?
And, after all, she is rather special. I owe a lot to John. He's looked after
me through thick and thin. And let's not forget, what happened when
Elizabeth was born. I will always feel badly about that. . . .'

She couldn't believe he was speaking to her like this, dear stuffy
Thomas. But once again, she swallowed down the irrational anger she
could hardly explain. They held each other in the dark, and she spoke
sweetly to him. Then he had slept again, peaceful at last. He was due to
leave in the morning. Never had those hours seemed so precious. So she
lay with him, listening to his breathing, blessing the fact that he was there,
safe beside her.

But she couldn't sleep. Their conversation had stirred something in
her. Why couldn't the world stay the same? It had once been so safe and
reliable, everyone knowing their place in it. And here it was, turned
upside-down. Men were dying every day, for some dreadful war which
some people, even here in Cumberland, said was unnecessary and could
have been prevented. Servants thought themselves masters in the house,
and women were shouting political slogans at the hustings. It was all too
difficult.

She sighed, and turned over in the bed. She knew she was being unreasonable about Betty. What sort of selfish creature had she become? What
was the matter with her? Thomas was right. It was John's child who had
been visited upon them. If it hadn't been for Dr Nelson being so preoccupied with Charles, John's wife might still have been alive. Now the girl
was trying to help her son. Yet the fact that the girl was helping Charles
made it worse instead of better. That was the trouble. How dreadful to
have to be beholden to that self-confident little madam!

There it was and at least she had the grace to be a little ashamed. The girl had given her son something precious, some life-giving force which in its turn had given him the power to resist her. It was driving him beyond her reach. He was no longer the white-faced little invalid he had been. But why did that frighten her so?

She saw herself, suddenly, down the endless corridors of some dark future, hovering on the edge of their lives, her husband's and her son's, watching while they grew away from her. Was she behaving badly? She asked herself. Suddenly she couldn't stand lying there any longer. She would go down to her little sitting-room and make up the fire. Connie would have banked it up for the night. She wouldn't call anyone. There was some whisky on the side table. She would have a small glass, as she did sometimes before retiring, and maybe then she would be able to sleep.

There was always a lamp lit in the hall downstairs, so Alice was not surprised to see a gentle wash of light lapping up the stairwell. But she was astonished to hear, in the silence of the house, a voice carrying clearly onto the top landing, so clear that she could make out every word. She hurried to the top step, apprehensive. It was a girl's voice. For a second, foolish thoughts of ghosts flitted through her mind. She pushed them aside and stood at the top of the stairs, holding her bedside lamp, looking down.

There was an astonishing scene below. On the black and white marble floor, John's child was standing in front of the looking glass, quite absorbed in her reflection. Her hair was bound about with bands of some brilliant blue. She had caught it up somehow, so she looked quite different, almost stately, the red hair standing out against the chessboard of the floor. She could have been some exotic chess piece herself, standing there in a faded cambric nightgown with her hair bound so, and some floating stuff around her shoulders. Not a pawn though, Alice thought suddenly with a flash of intuition. More of a queen. It was an odd thought to come into one's mind about one's servant. With a sense of righteous indignation verging on rage, she began to walk down the curved staircase.

Still, the girl did not notice her, quite self-absorbed as she moved about in front of the looking glass, lit by that smoky, buttery light from the lamp. Her voice came clearly up the stairwell. . . .

She left the web, she left the loom,
She made three paces through the room,
She saw the water lily bloom,

She saw the helmet and the plume
She look'd down to Camelot
Out flew the web and floated wide. . . .

The lace was flung from the girl's shoulders and thrown in the air, landing behind her on the marble floor. Alice came to a stop despite herself, suddenly unwilling to break the spell.

The mirror crack'd from side to side. . . .

An arm was flung out towards the looking glass. . . .

The curse is come upon me, cried
The Lady of Shalott!

With a wild cry and a dramatic twist of her body, the performer fell to the ground. Alice stood transfixed. Nothing in her experience had prepared her for this. A servant in her house behaving so! It was impossible, unbelievable. Yet she was stirred too by the power of that voice, the vision of the girl. It would have been delightful yes, moving even, if it had been anyone else but that creature, invading a world where she didn't belong. A thrilling performance by Miss Ellen Terry in the drawing-room after dinner! But not by a servant in her own front hall! She took a deep breath and marched to the bottom of the staircase.

The child had certainly been rather carried away by her own performance. She hadn't moved from where she lay. A hysterical temperament. Hardly a fit companion for Charles. Here at last she had reason enough, and more, to dismiss her, John's child or not! But where had it come from, that wonderful dramatic sense? It *had* been thrilling in its way, and yet utterly infuriating.

Then, seeing the child lying on the marble floor, anxiety crept into the edge of her fury. The figure on the floor suddenly seemed rather small and vulnerable. Alice came swiftly through the hall, clutching her nightgown, and made her way to the still form, where it lay in the lamplight. The red hair had come out of its ribboned binding and was loose about the face, startling against the white cheek and the white marble beneath. A nightgown billowed about her (not entirely decently). The lace now lay on the black tile beneath her shoulders, where she had flung it before she fell. It was beautiful gossamer lace, such as a lady might wear. With a spurt of suspicion, Alice wondered where she had got it from. You could never tell with that little minx.

The face was so still. What should she do? Lowering her own lamp she looked down at the child. A strong face. A strong nose, a fine chin. Too much character perhaps. The collar of the nightgown was up. The still figure seemed almost timeless, Elizabethan, something like those frozen marble effigies in Bambeck church. She saw in a little moment of sympathy, that the material had been badly turned. There was much evidence of darning, clumsily executed; in some places the cloth had been bunched up crudely to cover some worn part. Alice had some skill with the needle. For a moment she felt a strong urge to take the child up and put it to bed, to take its nightgown to be finely mended, unpick the rough darning, make it right again. How foolish!

Had the girl had some sort of a fit? She must ring for someone, but Thomas mustn't be disturbed. She looked closely at the face. Why did she feel as though they were on the same side, as though they shared some grief, or love. The girl had been crying. There were grubby tear stains on her face. And above, on her forehead, Alice saw with sudden horror, there was a terrible, black bruise just emerging from the white skin. . . .

CHAPTER 15

She was a striking creature, with that red hair. Alice sat beside her in the quiet room, watching her face, that awful savage bruise standing out against the pallor. It was the first time Alice had ever really looked at her. Yes, she was a beautiful child, now almost a woman. Alice felt ashamed. The girl had been entrusted to her care. It was painful to have to admit that she had treated her with real hostility. But she was so infuriating! The girl had come into the house, turned them upside-down, preached rebellion to her son, had even got Thomas on her side. That hurt most of all. And all this without really doing *anything* one could really punish!

To be truthful, Alice had been glad to see the back of her. When she had gone off to her grandparents farm, it had been such a relief. Responsibility fulfilled. Promise kept. And this annoying, red-haired creature kept away from their ordered lives.

But then she had come back, and things had got worse. Alice had sensed that Charles had become less pliable. If he danced, it was to a different tune, and the fact that he seemed happy only rubbed salt into the wound. The episode of the book had been the last straw. But she had to acknowledge that she had been too harsh. She hadn't meant that the girl should suffer, she truly hadn't. She should have handled this whole thing better. Mrs Callerthwaite was a malevolent creature, after all.

Later, in her sitting-room, she stabbed away at her embroidery, concentrating on the orange marigold in the centre of the circular frame. It was to be a little cloth for Charles's tray. How she had loved to make his tray pretty in the days when he was so dependent on her. A little vase of flowers on the snowy linen, a surprise toy smuggled into the napkin. And how appreciative he had been, holding up his white little cheek to be kissed and squeezing her hand. If only those days would come back again! She sighed. How much easier it had all been when he had been hers, absolutely. He had been such a good child, taking his medicine without complaint, looking to her for everything. Now his talk was full of dreams, dreams which didn't include her. Horrible talk of climbing in the fells, going away to school, even of going up to Cambridge, for heaven's sake. Just as though he were normal! And it was all that girl's fault. She had started it, and now there was no stopping it! Like some great engine, it would end up out of control, crushing them all.

Seeing Betty standing in the great hall, with all her striking beauty, Alice had felt all this very deeply. A sense of being set aside, useless, unwanted, in the face of the dreams of youth. It was too awful. Then the wretched girl had fallen, and suddenly she had seemed no more than a child, lying there helplessly. The anger and the fear had vanished, and, alone in the dim hall, something in Alice had responded to the motherless girl. Perhaps she was needed, after all.

Alice laid her embroidery down and tiptoed over to the bed. Betty still seemed to be sleeping too deeply. Had she woken at all? Dr Nelson had said she must wake soon or she might never wake again. Surely it couldn't be that serious?

There was a slight sound behind her. The door opened and Thomas came in quietly. He was in his uniform. With a start, Alice realized that he was due to leave that morning. All the business of the girl had quite put it out of her head. She had left him still sleeping, exhausted after his restless night.

'Cook told me,' he whispered as he came into the room. 'You should have woken me. You shouldn't have to cope on your own.'

An acid retort sprang to her lips, but she swallowed it. Cope on her own! What did she do every day, for heaven's sake!

'I wanted to let you sleep. After all, you were so tired.'

He sat down beside her and took her hand. 'How is the child?'

'We sent for Dr Nelson immediately of course. He rather frightened me, muttering on about brain fever. But as long as we keep her quiet. . . .'

Thomas sighed.

'What on earth am I to tell John, poor man? He will be distraught. I will have to tell him.'

They sat side by side, looking at the girl. Her red hair was laid out on the white pillow. As they watched, she turned her head restlessly, whispering something in her sleep. Alice had secretly dreamed of having a baby girl, but the congenital heart problems which the specialist had diagnosed had prevented her from having more children. Now this girl lay defenceless and alone. She was all mystery, yet in some ways her life had been entwined with Alice's since the beginning.

Almost involuntarily, Alice leaned over and touched the pale cheek. She was very cold.

'I wish we could have done more for her,' Thomas said quietly.

She sensed a mute criticism in his words, and bit back tears. It was all so unfair!

The girl turned her head once more on the pillow and gave a little cry.

'Perhaps we should wake her,' Alice whispered at last. 'I don't think it is right to let her sleep so deeply. She should have woken by now. Dr Nelson, of course, could hardly be bothered, as he regarded her as only a servant.'

The weight of her words hung in the room. Thomas was looking down at her, a strange expression on his face.

'It won't be long now, Alice, you know,' he said softly. 'And we mustn't let anything happen to John's child.'

She was chilled by the prescience in his words and gave an involuntary shiver, pushing the dark thought aside. Nothing would happen to him. Surely he would be safe! The war would, after all, be over very soon. Then, looking down at the sleeping girl again, that curious tenderness stole over her. It would change to irritation as soon as she woke. She was bound to say something contentious and then they would begin again. If only she could have stayed where she belonged, in her proper place. How much easier it would have been, for everyone.

Thomas stood up, and put his hand on her shoulder.

'Well, my dear. It's time I was going. I came to get you so we could have breakfast together. Then I must be off. I think you should have a rest. Let the girl sleep. Leave it to Nature, Alice. She's a strong girl. But if she is still unwell in a few hours, we must call the doctor again. Meanwhile, I will have to tell John, but we must try not to worry him too much.'

CHAPTER 16

When Betty woke she was in a strange room. Even the quality of the light was different. In her own little attic room, the only light came from a skylight set in the roof. Here, there was light everywhere, huge slabs of it, winter sun illuminating the chair opposite, placed between dark blocks of shadow created by half-drawn curtains.

She began to focus, but her head felt swimmy and it was hard to see clearly. She was almost sure that she recognized the grate in the corner, which she could just glimpse by turning her head very slightly, although it hurt to do so. Yes, she was sure that was the grate she had so much trouble blackleading. Those twirly bits on the corner she remembered all too well. She recognized that little chest of drawers and the foreign screen in one corner by the bed. She was almost sure this was a guest room in the east wing of the house, down the corridor from the main staircase.

In a panic she tried to sit up, but waves of sickness overcame her and she put her head back on the pillow. But before she lay down she caught sight of the embroidered chair by the bed. There were her clothes! Someone had brought them from her room. They looked so shabby against the silk roses and the gilt of the chair. The sight of them made her feel even more disorientated. Her things in this room! What was she doing here, in this place, where she didn't belong?

Perhaps she had sleepwalked into this room, this bed. She had some vague memory of walking down the back stairs towards the main hall. Yes, that was it. But how had she ended up here? Now there would be a terrible fuss. She would have to leave Bambeck Hall in disgrace. Her father would never forgive her. It was one thing to leave when she felt the time was right, but quite another to be thrown out. Her mind was working slowly, but somehow she was sure she had done something terribly wrong. If she didn't do something quickly, they would find her here. Forcing down the sickness, she pulled back the covers in a feverish terror, surprised to see that she was not in her usual shabby nightwear, but a white lawn nightdress! She was almost sure it was one of Mrs Fergusson's. She had pressed it that many times. Oh, dear God! What had she done?

There was a quiet knock on the door. She froze in horror, her feet halfway out of the bed. There was nothing to be done. She would be out on her ear in no time. Falling asleep in the guest room bed, in Mrs Fergusson's nightdress!

Charles's head appeared round the door.

'Oh, you are awake! I've been sitting next door with a book waiting for you to wake up. You've been asleep for ages.'

Betty stared at him, too astonished to speak. Then in a fever of activity, she got all of the way out of bed, modesty forgotten, and placed her feet on the floor. She had to get dressed and out of there before Mrs Fergusson arrived. Maybe then she would get away with it.

But as her feet touched the floor, it began to climb up to meet the wall. The little chest of drawers, in some mysterious way, seemed to fall upwards and upwards, without ever getting there.

There was an awful pain in her head. And she felt she was going to be sick. That would be the last straw. To be found being sick in the guest room.

'Get back into bed, you idiot. You've had a bang on the head.'

Somehow Charles had come right into the room. What if they were found together? And she only in her nightdress, or someone else's nightdress . . . oh, what did she mean!

'Charlie, you'll have to get me out of here! If your mother finds me, I'll be for it.'

Her voice sounded peculiar, as though she had been at the ale pot, like Tom on his evening off.

'It's all right, Betty. Oh, for heaven's sake, get back into bed, or I'll have to call someone to make you. Then I'll be in trouble, too. I'm not even supposed to be in here. Mother is looking after you. She doesn't know I've been sitting next door for hours, hoping you'll wake up. She thinks I'm in the library.'

'What? What are you talking about?'

Her head hurt so much and she was definitely going to be sick. Perhaps she would after all lie down for a while, just so she wouldn't be sick. Just for a moment. With difficulty, covering her knees with the nightdress for modesty's sake, she manoeuvred her legs back into the bed.

'That's better, you foolish creature!'

Charles was as embarrassed and uneasy as she was, standing close to the door, ready to rush out at any moment.

'Did you know you've had a brain fever? That's what old Nelson says, anyway. Mama's been very worried about you. She called him in the middle of the night. I was asleep, and didn't know anything about it. You've been out cold since she found you.'

'Have I been ill then?'

Even with her eyes closed she felt herself swinging and swinging about.

'You were knocked out, I suppose. Mama won't discuss it much. By all accounts, she found you unconscious downstairs in the *main hall* with a great bruise on your head. Mama, would you believe, has been nursing you most of the night. She's having a rest now. . . .'

'But how long have I been here, in this room?'

She struggled to sit up, regretting it immediately.

'Oh, just since last night. I say you do look awfully white. I ought to get someone. You aren't supposed to move, you know. Not at all. It might give you brain damage.'

She put her hand up to her head, and for the first time felt the bandage. Then, opening her eyes again, she noticed the ribbons and a folded square of lace, laid out neatly on the seat of the embroidered chair. Suddenly it was all there, the full awfulness of what she had done.

'Oh, no!'

'What is it? What's the matter? I say, I'm sorry I came in and made you move. I didn't mean to, really.'

She closed her eyes again, the better to focus. She was suddenly aware that Charles was standing by the bed.

'Does it hurt? It looks awful.'

'Ay, it does. Don't ask daft questions.' Some odd feeling made her sharp with him.

'Can't you remember how you did it?'

The image of herself in the mirror came up before her eyes. Yes, she remembered now! She had been talking to herself, but what then? What a daft cow! She had been so carried away. Now God had punished her for getting above herself. It wasn't the first time. But try as she might she couldn't fathom what happened after. What if Mrs Fergusson had spotted her carrying on like a clocky hen. She might be ill now, but as soon as she was well, then she would be for it, no mistake.

'I have to go now, Charlie. I've made a right fool of myself. You'll have to help me get my things together.'

'No! You've got to stay there, Betty. For God's sake, stop being so stubborn.'

He leaned over then and pressed her down into the pillow. She felt an uncomfortable sensation. She had touched him, but this was the first time he had ever touched her. Even in her weakened state, she felt it strangely.

'You know, you've been very good to me, Betty. I can hardly bear to see you lying there, looking so ill.'

His voice sounded very far away.

'I say, do open your eyes! You look as though you're going to die. I can't bear it. Look at me. Go on, look at me!'

With difficulty she opened her eyes. He was spinning up the wall in a very unnerving way.

'I can't. It makes me sick. It's all right, Charlie, I'm not going to pop my clogs just yet!'

A long way away, she felt him get hold of her hand where it was lying on the coverlet. She was glad now that her eyes were closed.

'You know, Betty. . . .'

She was aware of his closeness just by the bed.

'I did mean what I said the other day, about how much you have helped me. I'm sorry about that other sentimental stuff, it must have embarrassed you. But really it is thanks to you that I can walk about so well now. Of course, Dr Nelson keeps telling me I could drop dead at any time if my heart fails. I mustn't exert myself and I mustn't climb the stairs! Mind you, he'd be the one who'd have heart failure, if he knew how many times I've been up here in the last few hours. Oh, and I must have a rest in the afternoons, all that sort of stuff. But I *am* walking about. And Betty, I do feel it is making me stronger. My legs are getting better so quickly, and it's all because of you. Mother knows that too. So don't go away now, just when I need you most. Anyway, you're too ill to get up, so I won't help you.'

She felt slow tears begin to squeeze through her lids on to her cheeks.

'Ay, I know all that.' She spoke with difficulty. 'But you're strong enough now not to need a wet nurse. You'll have to fight some battles on your own. I have things of my own to do. I want to go and see my Dad before he goes off to France. I've got to see him, Charlie. He gave me the ribbons, and the lace too, and I want to say thank you. You have to understand. I can't be at your beck and call for ever. I've my own life to lead. And when you walked downstairs for your father, it was the first step.

Now you'll take others on your own. I've a bit of brass now and I want a life of my own! I only came back after my grandfather died because I care about you. And I'll always care for you, wherever I am.'

Because her eyes were closed it didn't seem to matter that he could see her crying. She felt his hand holding hers very tightly, but she couldn't, wouldn't, open her eyes.

'I've been so selfish, Betty. I should have realized what it is like for you. But now I'll do something for you. We'll go to see your father together. You can't possibly go on your own. As soon as you're better. I promise. I'll go with you. I can see my father too, at the camp. It'll be an adventure. I'll tell mother today!'

Again it came to her how young he was. How old she felt now, listening to him. Years and years and years older than him. It was a gulf she felt she could never cross.

'By Jove, I shall protect you. It will be a knight's quest. I will be your knight in shining armour! Do you remember *The Lady of Shalott?*'

'Ay. . . .'

She remembered everything so clearly now with all its terrible embarrassment. Clowning about in front of the mirror reciting that daft poem! Did he know?

'Oh, I do love those lines. How does it go now?'

'I can't mind it at present, Charlie, I just want to lie down, quiet like. . . .'

But it was no good. He would go on.

'Yes, I remember. In the library when I read Tennyson to you and you read back to me. You looked as though someone had just put a spell on you. How could you have forgotten?'

The sun came dazzling through the leaves
And flamed upon the brazen greaves
Of bold Sir Lancelot!

'I will be your Sir Lancelot, Elizabeth! I will take care of you. Your every wish will be my command! You wait and see. I will get a chariot fit for a queen, well, the pony and trap anyway, and a fast steed! And we will away to Carlisle!'

It was wonderful. Wonderful to be spoken to like a lady. But again she felt the gulf between them. How very young he was! It was for her to protect him. Not the other way round. She shook her hand free and buried it under the covers, still not opening her eyes.

'You're a daft bugger, Charlie! Your mother will never let you off her apron strings. Not even for a day! Just you wait and see!'

Yet she felt herself smiling at his foolishness. He might confuse love with gratitude, but he would always be her best friend. The world seemed to have stopped spinning for a little while. Encouraged by feeling better, she opened her eyes. His face was very close. That pale, intense face with its sad, brown eyes. A funny feeling came into her belly again.

Hesitantly, he leaned forward over the sheets and kissed her very softly on the cheek. Then, his colour flushed up, starting at his neck and mounting all the way to his thick hair, and he turned from her, rushing from the room.

CHAPTER 17

As soon as he had left the room, she made herself get out of bed. It was hard at first, keeping her balance. Once or twice she had to stop and hold onto the carved bedhead while the room swung about. She felt so sick she had to swallow hard. But she was determined and, before long, she got herself going again.

It suddenly seemed more important than anything to get away from Bambeck. She knew she would be in trouble with Alice about the foolish business in the front hall. That was bad enough. But there were worse things. Ay, Charlie. That was what was worse. It was all getting muddled up and difficult. Her head was so muzzy she couldn't sort her feelings at all. But she was sure about one thing. She had to leave straight away before she got more tangled up in it. Something in her was speaking quite clearly, telling her what to do.

It was difficult putting on her stockings. Once or twice she fell back on the bed, and all the time the wall swung about in that daft way, so she couldn't keep her balance. But in the end she just fixed her eyes on one spot and concentrated. After that, it wasn't so bad.

She was in a terror that someone would come. Charles would come back maybe. And Alice might wake and come in to see her at any time. The thought of that put her into a real panic, and she snagged her stockings in her haste, so she looked even more of a scarecrow than usual. There was a little mirror high up above the fireplace and she managed to look in it, though with feeling so giddy she all but fell in the fire. Somehow, she tied the blue ribbon in her hair and the bit of lace round her shoulders. After all she was going to see her Dad, and it was important to start off right.

She would not have any spare clothes, nor any money. Not even a coat. But thank heaven for that thoughtful person (was it Connie?) who had laid out her clothes and placed her shoes under the bed. Still, she would be cold. Yet somehow that voice was saying, so clearly she could almost hear it, that she would find her Dad, and then everything would be all right. Like a sign, she felt in the pocket of her apron and found the two pennies she had saved from her last week's wage. If she could get down to the Carlisle road, she would have something to pay the carter with.

Alice had wrapped a shawl around Betty's shoulders while she slept. It was only January and the room, even with a fire, was cold. When she had got out of bed, she had taken the shawl off and laid it on the bed. Seeing it there now, folded up, gave her a pang. They had taken her in and been kind to her in their way. It hadn't been all bad. Now she was repaying them by leaving the lad to cope by himself, when he had always been on her side. For a few seconds, her resolve wavered. But then she took a deep breath, and gathered up the shawl. She would send it back as soon as she reached Carlisle, with a note, just to say thank-you. She opened the door.

Looking out into the corridor, she realized she had been right. This was the guest bedroom in the west wing. How grand! To have laid abed in a fine room like that, even if it were only for one night. Again, for a moment, she thought of how lovely it would be to be cosseted and fussed over until she was well. But she knew it wouldn't really be that simple. It never was. Bitter experience had taught her that. She might put off the evil day until she was well enough, but sooner or later she would get her come-uppance from Alice. On top of all that, the muddled feeling about Charlie would get worse and worse. Then there was her Dad. Hadn't Charlie told her that very soon the battalion was to be moved? Ay, any day now he could be sent to France. There was no time to lose. She would have to go now!

She took a step or two out into the corridor and closed the door softly behind her. The wall swung away from her alarmingly. What had Charlie said about brain fever? Nay, she was being soft. There was nowt wrong with her but a bang on the head, and that would mend soon enough. She'd had plenty of those in the past, climbing trees, with her dress tucked into her drawers.

She walked as quietly as she could down the empty corridor. The whole house seemed at rest, the ticking of the grandfather clock on the first landing made it seem more silent still. Eleven o'clock. They would be having elevenses in the kitchen, with Mrs Callerthwaite's ginger biscuits. A tray would have gone upstairs to Mrs Fergusson, at three minutes to the hour. A wave of something like homesickness washed over her. But no!

Connie with the tray would wake Alice. This was no time for soft thoughts. She must hurry! It was all behind her.

Perhaps she should have left a note to say goodbye, but it was too late for that. Hanging onto the banisters for grim death, she fought off the giddiness which threatened to send her pitching down the stairs. Only a few days ago she and the lad had sat here together, on this top step, and he had told her he wanted to marry her. She had thought it was real, like she felt for him. But she had grown much older, in these last few hours. Now she knew it was different for him.

Ay, she could see clearly now. His feelings for her were like any bairn might have for his nanny. She knew that, but for a few moments she had almost been fooled.

She made her way down the staircase as silently as she could, trying not to notice how much the stairs and the walls were swaying about. It must be like that for Tom when he had been at the ale pot. She wouldn't have this sickening feeling by choice, not for anything. No wonder her grandfather had been against strong drink.

The front door was open, the whitened step wet where Connie had been scrubbing. The brush lay face up on the floor surrounded by suds. She would be for it when Mrs Callerthwaite spotted that! But Betty suddenly realized she wouldn't be there to see it.

Delicately, like a lady, she stepped down the soapy steps and on to the crunchy gravel of the drive. Just a few more yards and she would gain the shadows of the hedge. Then no one would be able to see her from the house. The wintry sun was shining on the bare trees and the distant fells. She could see the drive stretching away, empty towards the road. The dizziness had almost left her. She felt only a great exhilaration. She was free!

CHAPTER 18

Charles was distraught. He wouldn't rest until she had rung for the boy and told him to ride down to the Plaskett house, in case Betty had taken refuge there. Alice was furious. The brat! And she had taken Alice's shawl! How typical! Tom had come back and reported that Nellie Plaskett had not seen Betty for days, and Charles had looked then as though he was going to have one of his turns. He had got it into his head that the girl could have gone off to see her father. They had talked about it, together! Whatever next? But to calm him down Alice sent Tom off again, with instructions to take the cart along the back lanes towards the Carlisle road. As if she would try to walk to Carlisle racecourse! It was almost twenty miles. Still, Charles was in such a state of distress, she didn't like to cross him. . . .

She had sent Connie down for Dr Nelson. They had interrupted his luncheon and his bedside manner was notably absent. The girl, he pointed out smugly, had already shown signs of concussion, and should have been watched. She could become unconscious at any time. As if he cared!

Charles was pacing about the room, occasionally flinging himself onto the chaise lounge. Dr Nelson felt his pulse and, looking grave, ordered him to bed. Alice had only to look at the expression on Charles's face to know what was coming. There was an awful scene. He was quite wound up, like a clockwork doll. Charles told Dr Nelson he was a silly old fool and that he would refuse to be treated by him ever again. Alice had found herself having to make excuses to the odious man, as an unspoken question hung in the air. Why was her son so concerned about a servant girl who had suddenly upped and left? Oh, she could see what he was thinking!

At the end, Charles stormed out of the room, refusing to apologise. Alice had to summon Connie with a luncheon tray and a glass of whisky before Nelson could be mollified. It was all extremely vexing!

Secretly, Alice was afraid. In all the years of their life together she had never had to discipline Charles. He had always been such a good child. After the doctor had left, she went through into the library where she guessed Charles might be. He was sitting with an open book on his lap, but his face was turned to the window. In the distance the bluish misty outline of the fells rose up into the sky.

She put her hand on his shoulder, but he didn't stir.

'Charles, I really feel we should have a little talk.'

He didn't speak.

'I can understand how worried you must be about this girl. After all she is a servant in our house. It is our responsibility to take care of her.'

Alice paused again, but again he didn't reply. 'You must admit I did try. I put her in the guest bedroom.'

Without turning towards her, he started to speak in a distant, flat voice which frightened her more than anything.

'She is John's daughter, Mama. And John is looking after Father. Is it too much that we should look after Betty in return?'

'Yes, yes, I know. Of course she is John's daughter, and she has given you valuable help. . . .'

She tried to remember her feelings of the early morning, when she had looked down on the sleeping girl, and felt ashamed.

'And I admit she has encouraged you to be more independent, to start walking by yourself, which one supposes must be for the best. . . . if it makes you happy.'

It was hard for her to say, but she was determined to be fair.

'Yes. It makes me happy.'

That cold tone again which struck a chill through her. Where had her darling child gone? He was certainly not there beside her. In his place, there was a stranger.

'Yet we must be sensible. We know from Dr Nelson that your heart could give out at any time. . . .'

'I don't want to hear this, Mother.'

'But you *must*. By walking about, even going *upstairs*, you are directly contravening the doctor's orders. At least you must face the consequences if you decide to go against medical advice. . . .'

He had turned to face her. She was shocked by his appearance. He was very pale, and his eyes, in their deep pouches, looked quite black. Instinctively she leaned forward and put her hand on his arm, but he shook it off.

'She taught me. . . .' his voice was choked. 'She taught me to stand on my own feet, to fight my own battles. You . . . you . . . and Nelson, you're suffocating me. I *will* die, mother, I *will*, if you don't let me be free. It's *my* decision. Don't you think I know? It's *my* life. Let me make up my own mind! Otherwise I *will* die. I couldn't go on. Don't you see? I feel like some crippled bird in a cage, which has never tried its wings.'

She was reminded, in that shocking moment, of the girl standing just so in front of her, white-faced, tears running down her cheeks, and her vehement defence of Charles.

'It's keeping him in a cage, just like those poor little owls the keeper has in the hut yonder. . . .'

For the first time in their lives they were on different sides, she and her beloved son. Fighting! All that anger she could hear in his voice – how long had that been there without her noticing? Oh, how she wished Thomas were here. He would know just what to say. She had been left to cope with all this. It was too much!

'Please, Mother.'

His tone was gentler now.

'Betty taught me, you know. I have to stand on my own feet. Grandmother always told me that, but Betty taught me how to do it. She's a strong girl. She's had to be! That's why I'm so worried about her. She helped me, and now she's gone off and she is ill, lying in a ditch somewhere. You heard what Nelson said.'

'You called Dr Nelson an old fool not half an hour ago.'

She couldn't resist saying it, but immediately regretted it. His face took on that closed, stony look again.

'Look, Mother. I know it's hard for you to understand, but I owe a lot to Betty. I do know how you must be feeling.'

Did he know? Did he even begin to understand how it was for her? To see her own son taken away. To see him take such risks when at any moment. . . . She wished she could tell him how it felt, but she never could. It was dreadful, all this raw emotion, almost indecent. They had never talked like this before. Things had always been decently hidden, like the legs of the table in the dining room, swathed to the floor in red velvet. She began to dread what might come next.

'And I have grown awfully fond of her, Mama.'

There it was! What she had dreaded, since the wretched child had come into the house. She saw it all now. This was what the creature had done. Inveigled her way into her son's affection, taken over his love, so that there was none left for her!

'I have never heard such nonsense. She is *only* a servant. I will not have you talking like that. What would your father say?'

She was screaming. Heaven knows, the servants were probably listening. She must get herself under control. But how could she have let this develop right under her nose? All her tender feeling of the morning had evaporated. The scheming little minx!

'I will send her away! I will send her away! You're not even fifteen, for God's sake! What's gone on between you? Answer me!'

She was beside herself. He watched this screaming woman in horror. She clutched at his arm, but he was staring at her in an awful way, as though she had betrayed him.

'Is that why she fainted at the bottom of the stairs? Have you been . . . *answer me?*'

Suddenly he was not looking at her any longer. He raised himself out of the chair, walking past her as though she didn't exist. It wasn't until he got to the door that he turned and looked at her, his face still set in that dreadful expression.

'I wish to be sent away from here, Mama. I had been meaning to talk to you about it. Betty and I discussed it.'

That creature! That snake in the grass!

'I wish to be sent away to school. I need to perfect my Latin and Greek so that I may take the entrance examination for Cambridge in two years time. I intend to go up to study the Natural Sciences.'

'Don't be ridiculous. You're a sick boy. An invalid. Pull yourself together. You will stay here.'

He was so far away from her. She would never get him back.

'If you don't let me go away to school, I will write to Father. I am sure he will support me. In the meantime, if Tom returns without Betty, I am going out with him again. We will search all night if we have to. It is the very least we can do. After all, you are quite right, she is a servant of ours. We have a responsibility towards her.'

'Wait!'

He walked out of the door. She heard the faint scurry of feet on the bottom stairs. That wretched Connie would have been listening, and it would be all over the house within an hour.

'Wait! Do you hear me! Come back in here, this instant!'

The door closed quietly leaving her staring helplessly at the panelling, wondering if she had lost him forever. . . .

CHAPTER 19

It was a cold, bright day, but with a thin wind. It wasn't long before Betty regretted not having taken a coat with her. She had turned left at the end of the drive and taken the road which led up to the top of the fell. Surely, this must be the way. It meant going past Tommy Atkinson's farm, but it couldn't be helped. She knew he rented it from the Hall. If he saw her, there would be no getting away, but she would just have to risk it.

Determinedly she set her feet on the track. A fresh wave of dizziness overcame her. If only the road would keep still! She skirted cautiously round the stone wall of Bambeck Hall Farm. She peered over the red sandstone wall. She was in luck. There was no one in the yard. Only a pair of gimmer lambs penned by the gate. The Longhorn bull glared at her out of his pen. What a life for a bull! Shut away from fresh air and light, in that stinking place. She shuddered. All she had to do, unlike that poor creature, was to put one foot in front of the other for a few miles and she would be free. Once she had seen her father, all would be clear. She couldn't think clearly beyond that.

There was a flurry of barking. She caught her breath. Tommy's dog had caught sight of her. He came dashing across the yard, making a dreadful racket, until his chain caught up with him and he was brought up short. Betty put her head down and hurried past, dreading the sound of the back door opening and Tommy or his wife calling to her.

Were all folk and all creatures chained to something for their whole lives? It was terrible to think of it. It might be all right for the fell sheep always returning to the *heaf*, that place where they were born. But it wouldn't suit her. She would be chained to no one and no place. Excepting her dad maybe. But too many folk to love meant you got hurt. She had done her bit for the lad. Now she was going to set herself free.

At the top of the fell she turned and looked back into the valley. There was the Hall, its turrets just visible between the great elms. The rooks were flying up. Someone was about. Perhaps they had found out already that she had gone.

It wouldn't be long till dusk, though she had walked no more than an hour or two. Already the sun was sinking below the line of the fells. How far away was it to Carlisle? Without a coat and with no food, feeling as ill as she did, she wouldn't stand much chance out at night. It would grow colder still. Just for a moment, she thought wistfully of the Hall, with her own little spot under the eaves, the fire crackling in the library hearth, Charles poring over his books. Nay, a safe haven could also become a prison. You could get trapped like that, and never get away.

Why hadn't she thought to ask how far it was to Carlisle? All she knew was that the carter went there and back in a day. If only her head wasn't so muzzy, she could have worked it out. Once she got there, it would be easy enough. Everyone would know where the racecourse was. All she had to do now was to get to the road and wait for the carter to come past.

The road seemed very steep. Surely, she must turn soon for the main road. She had never been this far up into the fells before. Any errands she had run had been down into the village. It was really quite wild and strange up here. She stopped to get her breath and turned again to look back. From this high up she could see the village itself, with Nellie Plaskett's cottage nestling by the road, and there, next door, the roof of the house where she was born.

Ay, in less than two months she would be fifteen, and so would Charlie. Was that why she felt so old? She shook her head, trying to banish the awful thumping pain which had developed at the back of her skull. It was strange that the bruise didn't hurt at all, only the back of her head, and now she was beginning to feel very sick. She bent over at the side of the road and retched painfully on her empty stomach. Of course, she hadn't had any food. Why hadn't she thought to sneak down to the pantry and fill her pockets? Dizziness overwhelmed her, and she was forced to sit down by the side of the road. She mustn't be sick again. It hurt too much. What on earth had possessed her to run away? She could no longer remember clearly. She could just as easily have left when she had had time to get really well. But that would have meant facing Alice, and worse still, seeing Charles. Ay, that was it. And what about her father? He would be leaving soon, and she would have to hurry if she was to catch him.

The fellside stretched down into the valley, a tracery of grey dry-stone walls, and green fields. They had been spreading manure to bring on the spring grass. She could smell it on the wind. She had a farm of her own now. Maybe one day she could farm her own place. Not necessarily Hannah and Matthew's spot. But somewhere. She would be her own boss, in the fresh air. No folk to tell her what to do. Only the seasons and the beasts to be her masters.

Beyond Bambeck village, looking back, the highest fells of the Lake District loomed against a darkening sky, catching the last light on their western faces. They looked romantic and far away, like those dream mountains of Charlie's. She would explore them all one day, and beyond. It would be a good life. She would be her own mistress. It was all a matter of just putting one foot in front of the other, and you would always get there in the end.

Perhaps a little rest would do her good, though she mustn't stop long. She was so tired. If she missed the carter she would have to walk on alone in the dark and the bitter cold. It was very still now and growing colder. There would be a frost tonight. With an effort, she got to her feet and started again, plodding upwards on the road. First lambs were finding their mothers to lie down with, and the dale was alive with their calls, echoing through the dusk. It was a peaceful place. She loved it. She didn't want to leave. How wonderful to have a warm mother to run back to. Inexplicably her eyes filled with tears. The grey stone walls against the fading light, thorn trees on the skyline, the softening winter dusk, all conspired to make her sad. She must be in bad fettle to start blabbing so easily. She was going away. She was going to be free. She was going to see her father. But something insistent, nonetheless, was trying to pull her back. The farm dog on its chain. She shuddered.

She *would* break away. She would travel and learn new things and how to speak a little better, like Mrs Fergusson, but just because she wanted to. Not because any folk told her, and not forgetting her own native speech, which was real to her. Then maybe, when she had done with seeing things, she would come back and farm her own land. She would make other folk do her bidding, but not unkindly, like some masters did. After all, she had been a servant herself and she knew how hard it was. She might even go away to college. Charles said there were women students at Cambridge. Not many yet, but a few. The world was changing fast. She could study the new ideas. Travel a bit, but keep her own spot, a place where no one could tell you what to do. Perhaps when the War was over . . . Ay, she would do all those things and make a home for herself and for her dad, and they would be happy together. . . .

But daydreaming wouldn't get her to Carlisle. Her father would be leaving soon. She must hurry. She had told Charlie often enough to get off his backside, and stop building castles in the air. Now it was her turn. If she was determined enough she would get there, and regrets for things done and lost wouldn't change a thing.

She wrapped the shawl around her, and set her face to the brow of the hill, where the last light gleamed.

CHAPTER 20

It had been a long day at market. A thin wind blew through Widow Jackson's shawl, making her arthritic bones ache. She was getting too old for this game. Even the collie was getting stiff in his joints. If only Mr Jackson hadn't popped his clogs, life would have been so much easier with two of them to cope on the farm.

It was the grey end of a bitter winter's day. She had sold her eggs, a couple of thin chickens, and a few leeks from the vegetable patch. She had thought about buying a pig, but the problem of getting it back home, all alone, was too much for her. All she wanted now was her bed.

The old horse plodded down the last long stretch of road between the stone walls, before he turned off, as he always did, onto the little lonnin which led up to High Greenrigg. Then, the collie, without warning, leapt down from the cart and shot across the road, barking furiously. Widow Jackson whistled and called, but Jock had his nose buried in a deep section of hedge, his plumed tail waving furiously, and he would not heed her.

She pulled the old horse to a halt, and left him to stand half-asleep in the shafts while she clambered down, grumbling to herself. The dog still had his nose stuck in the hedge. She had to pull up her skirts and wade through the frosted tussocks at the road edge before she could get to him. As she grew closer, she saw that the dog was nosing and licking at a bundle of clothes. To her astonishment, she saw the bundle was a girl, a young lass lying under the shadow of the hedge.

How long had she been lying there? She rushed forward, heedless of her old bones. The lass looked half-dead, her red hair scattered around her, her face so white, with a bandage on one side. Widow Jackson put her arms around the girl's shoulders and tried to lift her, the dog trying to lick the bairn's face. The lass's eyes opened, and she looked up at the Widow

117

Jackson.

'Am I in Carlisle yet? I'm going to see me Dad.'

'By heaven, what you doing, lying out here? You'll catch your death and you've not even a proper shawl on. I'd better take you home and see what we can do with you, you poor lass.'

Betty was hanging out the washing on the line in the orchard at High Greenrigg. Thanks to Widow Jackson's tender care, she was now fully recovered. The two women had formed an instant bond. Widow Jackson's husband had died some years earlier. In the manner of the fell women, she had carried on, uncomplaining, running the farm single-handed. In that hard world, you 'just got on with it', and there was nothing more to be said.

Betty, brought back to the farm on the cart, had been rather sick in those first days, wandering in her wits. A sort of unspoken understanding had come about in that time. Betty would stay on for a bit and give a hand to Widow Jackson. Widow Jackson had a son William, who had been a grand help on the farm, but he had decided to enlist in the first days of the War, thinking it his duty. It was the same for so many folk who relied on the lads to give a hand on the farm. The men were going away and the old women were left to grieve, and to cope as best they could.

Widow Jackson had shown her great kindness. They had begun to grow fond of each other. As her health improved, Betty took to giving the widow a hand in the dairy and around the house. Somehow it didn't seem so bad when you were helping out a friend and not being a servant to anyone.

As she hung the washing on the line, she thought about Bambeck, not for the first time. How she'd run away, because she'd been afraid of such unfamiliar feelings. When she was fully recovered, maybe, she would go back and see them, to explain. . . .

Widow Jackson, who seemed to know a lot about what was going on, had told her that it might not be too long before the Border Regiment was sent to France. Now she was better, she must get to see her father. When Widow Jackson went to market on Wednesday, Betty decided she would go with her.

As she hung the last of the snowy white sheets on the line, her fingers numb in the cold breeze, she looked over the line and saw a figure coming in through the gate. She gave a little cry and dropping the last of the pillowcases onto the wet ground, she ran through the orchard towards the gate.

Father! Could it be possible? Sat as large as life at the table in Widow Jackson's kitchen, behind a mound of teacakes and muffins and a big jug of cream. It was a miracle. They couldn't stop smiling at each other. And it was all Widow Jackson's work. Without saying owt, she had taken herself off to Carlisle, and somehow found her way to see the Colonel over at the racecourse. Once there, she had poured out the whole story, how the poor lass was lying sick, having tried to get to Carlisle on foot, and how she might die of a broken heart if her father didn't come to see her. So there he was, smiling and laughing as though he had been there for ever.

Thanks to the persuasive powers of Widow Jackson, John had been given three days compassionate leave. He and Mrs Jackson got on straight off, and she gave him the little room under the eaves with the deep feather bed and fine pillows. It was William's room, kept ready for when he came back.

John had arrived a weary man, worn out with strain and worry about his daughter. Three days at Widow Jackson's with fresh food, fresh air and the joy of being with his beloved daughter, worked its own transformation. Betty was able to see her father at his best, a laughing, happy man, the way he had been when he first courted and married her mother.

Betty was strong enough now to take some short walks. On the last day they borrowed the pony and trap and drove down into Lakeland, to Bassenthwaite Lake and Keswick, which Betty had never seen. It was a magical day. They stood on the shores of Derwent Water together, watching a pair of wild swans fly up into the still snow-covered fells as they called to one another, their voices echoing around the lake. Betty's eyes had filled with tears. It was such a precious time, and they had had so little of it.

Later, they walked the green lane down to Grange and round the border of the lake, stopping for a dinner of bread and cheese and a pint of ale at the inn. Then they fetched the pony and trap from where it was stabled at the Keswick hotel, and made their way home to the Widow Jackson's.

Betty could not afterwards remember what they talked about on that day. It had been on the tip of her tongue many times to tell her father about her mother's real birthright, but somehow, something always stopped her. It would be opening up old wounds, and today, she felt instinctively, was a time for healing, a day for memories.

They had sat up together by the dying fire until long after midnight, talking of this and that. She kissed her father goodnight outside William's room, knowing that in the morning they would have to say goodbye.

'Thank you, Father.'

He had smiled and put his arms around her. 'Don't forget, lass, there will always be folk to take care of you, even if I'm gone.'

She shook her head violently.

'Dad, you'll come back to me, I'm sure.'

He made a wry face.

'I feel much better now, lass, knowing there's the Widow Jackson to take care of you. She's a fine woman. You have a bit of independence now with your money, thanks to Matthew. And you can live here and take care of Widow Jackson if that's right. But don't forget your little lad at Bambeck. Mrs Fergusson is a bit of a dragon, we both know that, but she has a good heart underneath. She's had a hard time with that lad. You have to be a bit forgiving, Betty. Promise me now, you'll keep a contact with them. They promised me they'd take care of you and they won't let me down.'

She nodded mutely, quelling the rebellious feeling which had risen up at his words. 'Yes, father I'll do it for you. I'll make up with them at the Hall. But my place is here. I can be useful and I'm happy.'

In the morning they were up before dawn. John had hitched a lift with the carter from Carlisle three days before. Now he would wait at the end of the lonnin for the carter to come past again. There were many things that Betty wanted to say, but none of them would come into her mind. She wanted to hug him and never let him go. She contented herself with bringing him the new bread and a crock of butter, cooking him a dish of eggs and making him a big pot of tea. She made up a bait box with a slab of bread and some fat bacon and a couple of last year's apples from the orchard, so that he had something to keep him going for the journey into Carlisle.

They walked together through the orchard, towards the gate. In the first early light, she saw that a clump of daffodils in the long grass were breaking into bud. Widow Jackson had told her that the orchard daffodils were the first daffodils to bloom on the fellside. They were famous for it. She had bent down and broke off a handful of stalks, their pale greenish-yellow buds just bursting, and thrust them into her father's hand.

'Find a crock to put these in, and think of me.'

The carter was coming up the lonnin. In a minute, her father had climbed up. She had handed him his bait box, wiping her eyes on her apron.

He had turned at the corner and waved to her. She could see, even from this distance, he was crying too.

CHAPTER 21

Military Hospital
Etaples

16 July 1916

Dear Mrs Fergusson,
I felt I had to write to you and express my heartfelt sympathy for
your loss. Your husband did not count the cost to himself, but led
his men forward with his head held high. He showed true devotion
to duty at the head of his men, in the honourable tradition of the
Lonsdales which he done so much to create.

I sign myself one who served alongside your husband and held
him to be among the bravest of the brave.
With the greatest respect,
Sincerely,
Lieut. A.R.

The girl stood on the ridge, looking out over the great space of the Eden
Valley. A warm wind blew across the Lake District fells, hazy now in the
strong summer light. With that wind came the call of sheep, and the clatter of the horse-drawn baler, working all hours to get the harvest in.

Her red hair, half-freed from the bun at the back of her head, was
lifted behind her, and streamed in the wind. She stood very still, her
white apron flapping unfastened as though it would take off and sail away
to the summit of the fell, to be pinioned there against the blue sky. Every
once in a while she would tug at it and, with an impatient gesture, would
push back her hair.

It was a set face, very white and stern with signs on it of recent tears, as she concentrated now in the lonnin which wound its lazy way up to the old sandstone farm. It was all too slow for the watcher, who took a step or two down the path and then, undecided, turned and took up her position again. For someone was climbing the fell road, pushing a bicycle, slowly and laboriously. Her sharp eyes had seen the figure ride a little way up the track and then, as though easily exhausted by the gradient, dismount and begin to push. From the slowness of the figure's progress, and from his effort to climb the fell, the girl had guessed who this might be, and she was afraid.

He had written to her. That was a shock, that 'they' should know where she was. She supposed her father had told then after all, meaning to protect her from some unknown harm. It was too late to ask him about this now.

Ever since the day when the telegram had arrived from the Records Office in Preston – *'The War Office regrets'* – her world had changed forever. It seemed that something inside herself had died. It was hard to feel anything. Anger, perhaps, but that was all. She had been sorry for Captain Fergusson when she heard that he also had been killed; she was sorry for Charles; she was even sorry for Alice. She felt for all those women she had never met, wives and daughters and sweethearts, who would have had the same words to cope with, but she could not be sorry for herself. Some kind soul had posted the pages of *The Times* up outside the Post Office in the village, for every village had lost someone. They were all Cumberland men. In some villages every able-bodied lad had been lost.

She couldn't weep with those women, in the village street who cried into their skirts, and wore black. They were there every day, giving and receiving support. The whole village mourned. But she was alone. That was the sum of it. They had mothers and aunts and children in that tight knit community. They could share their grief. But if she had to cry, even a little, she would cry alone. It would be a badge of faith.

He had written. 'I am coming to see you'. Just a note scrawled on a card, slipped in with his mother's letter. Alice had been kind. She had invited Betty back to the Hall, but she would never go. Now he was climbing up the fell towards her. Much as she wanted to, she couldn't run away.

He looked up, half-perceiving a figure there, in his short-sighted way. After fumbling with his spectacles, he had at last put them on and seen her properly. She hadn't moved, and he had made no sign of greeting.

What after all was there to say?

They stood and stared at one another. Then she found her voice.

'You're a bloody fool, Charlie, corpsing yourself to get up this fell. It puffs me out just to look at you. You'll give yourself a heart attack.'

'I do much worse things at school,' he said stiffly, stung by her tone. 'Don't start that.'

She shook her head, pushing down those protective feelings which always came upon her when she saw him.

'I don't know why you put yourself out to come. There's nothing to say and I don't need no sympathy.'

He sighed. 'I came to . . . tell you something, and to bring you this. . . .' He fumbled in his pocket. 'It's a letter from someone in the battalion. . .' His voice failed him for a moment and he looked down. Seeing how close to tears he was, she felt a queer little pain, tears welling in her own throat. 'Someone who knew your father, and mine. You know.'

She swallowed, not trusting her voice.

'Do you want me to read it to you? I will if you want.'

'No I don't want to hear it.'

'I say, but you must. They were frightfully brave, all of them. Do you know, the Colonel came up to the front of the men, they were supposed to capture some farm, then of course all Hell was let loose. The Colonel came up to lead them and they just kept going forward. I say, you should know. It was the bravest thing you could imagine. Your father and my father, shoulder to shoulder. I think you should know!'

She turned away and began to walk back up the hill. He ran after her and caught her arm.

'Don't you want to hear?'

She turned on him savagely.

'I'd had a letter of me own, thank you, Charlie. I don't need you to tell me anything. Ay, and I wrote back, straight off. Do you want to see the letter? It came back just this morning!'

She felt in the pocket of her apron and pulled out a crumpled envelope, holding it up to his face. Across the front of it, stamped in black, were the words 'DECEASED. RETURN TO SENDER.'

She turned away again, but not before he saw the tears in her eyes. How foolish he had been to think of coming. It would be worse now, for them both.

'I'm . . . I'm awfully sorry. I say, I didn't mean to upset you even more.'

'Just leave me alone! I'm that sorry about your father and I'm even

in the kitchen, to see the obvious affection between the two of them. It was cool and dark in the kitchen after the bright day. A huge wooden table stood under the window with a collection of brown crocks on it. Betty's feet slapped backwards and forwards across the flagstones in her pattens, putting down butter and new bread. He was tempted to ask if she had made them both, but he didn't want his head bitten off. She never looked at him once, he noticed, but served him at the table, her eyes averted. And she served him, not as a servant might, but with simple courtesy as she would any guest, even though he could tell she was still angry with him for being there at all.

He attempted to answer the questions Mrs Jackson put to him. He had never been able to talk on equal terms with farmers over at Bambeck. There was always that invisible barrier. But here, Mrs Jackson was as easy and straight with him as though he had been her own son. In this kitchen he found that those barriers no longer existed.

'I'll go now and finish in the washhouse,' Mrs Jackson said at last, after Charles had worked his way through several of the scones. 'Betty'll look after you very well.'

They were left alone in the kitchen, the two of them. She was at the far end of the long table, the bright Pennine light filtering in through the deepest window, buried in its thick wall. Pools of sunlight slept cat-like on the green slates of the floor. There was the smell of freshly baked bread. A great longing swept over him, for all the things he had known so little of in his life.

Betty came and perched on the far side of the table, looking at him properly at last.

'Cheer up, lad. You never did mind my sharp tongue, and there's no need to start now! I'm sorry I was in a rage with you. Truth is, I've tried not to think at all of my past life. It's gone and done with. I'm happy here.'

'I'm sorry too,' he said at last. 'About everything. I didn't want to rake over old coals.'

They were talking for the first time as equals. There in the dim kitchen, the only sound was the crackle of the range and the slow tock of the grandfather clock in the corner.

'No,' she shook her head. 'It was good of you to come. After all, we were friends, weren't we? And we've both lost folk. I do think of you sometimes. You know how it is.'

'Yes, I do know. I haven't forgotten anything.'

She looked at him and smiled.

'We never did anything else but go at one another like a pair of banty cocks.'

'You helped me through, Elizabeth.' He spoke softly into the half-dark, but if she heard him she gave no sign. She stood up, brushing her apron down.

'If you'll excuse me, Charlie. It's washday, you know. The clothes don't wash themselves.'

He swallowed nervously.

'Betty. I just wondered. . . .'

'What is it, lad?'

'I might be going away for a bit, and I just wonder, would you be able to spare a day to come out with me? If I came to fetch you with the pony trap? Just before I go away. Would you come and walk with me in the fells? Just once! I've got it all planned. I could get a picnic basket from Cook, and we could just have a day together, just friends, saying goodbye.'

He tailed off.

She looked at him uncertainly.

'Well, I suppose it wouldn't do any harm. But could you walk that far, Charlie? I saw you panting away coming up the hill there. . . .'

'That's just the point!' He broke in eagerly. 'I know I still get out of breath a bit, but I have been trying very hard to get fitter. We could walk up Bambeck fell together. You know how I used to dream of doing that! I have been almost to the top. I could see the summit, Betty! What do you think of that? I suppose it's rather foolish, but I stopped just before I got to the summit. I wanted you to be with me when I got there, like going up the stairs, do you remember?'

'Ay, I remember, Charlie.'

'Well, if Mrs Jackson could spare you just for a day, we could get up to the top, together! It'll be just right! You would be proud of me, Betty.'

She was looking at him.

'I'm proud of you now, lad.' She said softly. 'Don't you know that? Ay, I'll do it for you, Charlie, for the sake of friendship. But I'll bring myself if you don't mind. I've my own transport now, and I don't like to be dependent on other folk. I'll meet you on Thursday morning at The Sportsman, down the bottom of the fell on the other side from Bambeck. We can go up that path. But mind, it's only one last time.'

He grasped her hand. 'It means so much to me, Betty. I know this will probably be goodbye. You've made it clear you have your own life,' he paused, and then went on in a rush, 'but I owe you so much. . . .'

She shook her head, turning away and withdrawing her hand.

'No lad. If you're going to get sentimental, I'll not come. For old times' sake, only that. And then we'll bid each other goodbye like sensible folks, and get on with our lives. Is that a bargain?'

CHAPTER 22

What had come over her, to behave so foolishly? Before she had seen him, it had all been so clear in her mind. She had her own perfectly satisfactory life. He was getting on very well without her. Why was it then that the memory of him, embarrassed and ill-at-ease in Mrs Jackson's kitchen, so often came into her mind, knocking her arguments for six like a row of skittles? Now, here she was, dressed up like a dog's dinner in a bit of fancy stuff, which Mrs Jackson had made her buy in Carlisle market, gallivanting down the fellside with the old horse and trap. What if the day turned clarty? So far it was a perfect summer morning, but here in Cumberland the weather was notoriously fickle.

Yet, despite herself, her spirits lifted. The hedges were frothing with meadowsweet, and spires of purple willowherb overtopped the stone walls. Dog roses tangled in the hedges. Swallows darted around her, and everywhere, above the fellside lanes, the curlew's bubbling call echoed into the watching hills. It was good to be alive. Nevertheless, she reminded herself sternly, the whole enterprise was just too daft for words.

He was waiting for her already, although she too was early. Sitting on the wooden bench outside The Sportsman, looking eager and sad at the same time (how she could read his mind!). He sprang to his feet, helping her down from the trap as a gentleman might help a lady. She couldn't help being impressed, against her will.

'I'm not in my dotage yet, Charlie. I can fetch for myself.'

'You look beautiful!'

He was staring at her. Immediately she regretted the muslin.

'Come on now, Charlie. 'Tis only a bit of stuff from the market. I would wear it for the milking!'

True, she had been quite pleased with her appearance, prancing about in front of the mirror. Cream muslin with tiny sprigs of green flowers. Mrs

Jackson had a good eye. In a moment of hesitant pride she had almost thought herself pretty, staring in the old mirror, ducking her head under the beam, and twirling about a bit. She had always had a weakness for fine things, and it did go with her hair. For a few moments, she had been transported. But then she had come down to earth and given herself a good talking-to. Her only other concession was to tie her hair in a bit of green velvet ribbon which Mrs Jackson had got for her from the pedlar weeks back as a seventeenth birthday present. So, she conceded, she looked respectable. That was quite enough.

They stabled the horses at the inn, and took the steep path. Even Betty's legs were feeling leaden until she got going, and she was used to walking the fells in all weathers, looking for cragfast sheep. She could hear Charles panting behind her. He had such determination. He just kept going, too breathless to speak. She was anxious for him, but some instinct kept her quiet.

Very soon, the busy world had fallen away. It was always the same in the fells, as you climbed higher. How quiet it became, with only the sound of water from the rushing beck which ran beside them in a ravine. They stopped once or twice, to watch the tiny waterfalls run through the mossy rock into clear pools which caught the sun. While Charles got his breath, Betty picked some bleaberries which they shared. Once or twice, she experienced a burst of pure joy which even common sense would not quite extinguish. That first constraint between them had fallen away, as the world had. They were just together, here, walking in the fells in the sunshine.

It was a long climb on the steep path. By the time they got halfway up, Charles looked done for. But though she suggested they stop for their dinners (they were sharing the carrying of the picnic basket) he would have none of it.

'I want to get to the top, Betty. Then I'll stop!'

Betty felt her legs must give way soon. She could hear Charles's laboured breath. He'll not get there! She thought to herself. Looking up at where the little clouds seem to skim the line of the hill, she saw to her relief that ahead of them was the jumble of rocks which led to the summit cairn. But Charles flopped face downwards in the heather, and lay as though he were dead. She came scrambling down, her heart pounding with panic.

'Are you all right?' She squatted beside him. 'This is a daft thing, Charlie. You don't have to kill yourself to prove anything to me.'

He rolled over, his face very white, his breath coming in great gasps. Against her will, she was near to tears.

'You're a daft bugger! I should never have let you start out at all! It's my fault. One of us should have a bit of sense!'

He didn't answer. She leaned close to him and touched his cheek. His eyes were closed.

'Tell me you're all right! Say something, you great gowk!'

He opened his eyes then and gave her a smile of such sweetness that her belly turned over.

'I . . . just needed to get my breath, Betty. Don't worry. I was like this last time. It's just weakness. Look, we're nearly at the top and this is the first time I've had to stop!'

'You're a bloody fool!' she exploded.

'No, Betty, I'm not. I know what I'm doing. Don't you realize I live with this every day? It isn't my heart. If it were I would have a pain, just here. This is just breathlessness. Really. It gets less the more I do. Just give me a chance, please!'

She sat beside him while he lay in the heather. It was colder up here, a sharp wind blowing across the face of the fell. She shivered, and drew her shawl around her. When she turned back he was sitting up, grinning.

'See!'

'I see nothing but a fool!'

'Oh, be quiet, Betty! You sound like my mother. I'm perfectly all right. Let's go on. I'll go first this time!'

She followed him up the last steep slope, the heather springy underfoot. There were great boulders here, scattered like a game of jackstones abandoned by giants. They were nothing but ants in this vastness; scrambling across the huge blocks of stone which had been in this place for some unimaginable time, their lives nothing but the passing of cloud shadows over the hills.

Then at last they were standing on the summit, where previous travellers had each placed a stone, one by one as they reached the top. Now there was a small cairn to mark the spot. Charles bent down and found a tiny chunk of granite in a crack in the rock and threw it up onto the cairn. She did the same. Then he stood, breathing heavily, facing into the wind, looking out into the blue distance.

'He will get wherever he wants to go,' she thought. 'And he can do it on his own. He doesn't need me now.'

The thought brought with it a sudden, unexpected sense of loss.

He turned and smiled at her, stretching out his hand.

'Come and stand with me! It's so wild here, Betty, I feel free. I can't tell you what it means to me, to get up here, to the summit of Bambeck Fell! After all these years just looking at it from that horrible bath chair. Somehow, whatever else I climb, and I know now that I can climb anything if I set my mind to it, this is the most important mountain of all for me!'

'Ay I know, lad. I was there at the beginning, remember?'

He clasped her hands, pulling her up onto the summit cairn. They stood, facing each other, trying to balance against the wind. She looked back towards the Pennines, across the great plain. She could see, reflected in his eyes, the higher mountains towards the Lakes, where they receded into mist. She knew, with a sudden certainty, that she had lost him now.

'I'm going away, Betty.'

'Ay, lad.'

'This is a good way to say goodbye.'

He leaned down. When had he grown taller than her, and she hadn't noticed? Brushing her hair away from her face, he kissed her gently on the mouth, first hesitantly, but then again, with more assurance. Some deep thrilling, forbidden feeling ran through her. He stopped and looked down at her.

'Do you mind?' He touched her face. In his deep eyes, she could still see that reflection of mountains and, at that instant, a bird flying past against blue sky.

'Nay, lad. I don't mind.'

'I love you, Betty. I will come back, if you want me to.'

'Nay, lad.' She shook her head, fighting down that strange, drowning feeling. 'Yet I do love thee. We always were like kin after all. It'll be hard, like, to say goodbye.'

What had happened to her, to take away her will, to fill her up with such soft feelings? She must be turning daft in the head. Yet in that free wind, close to the summit of the mountain, it seemed they were out of the world. There was a sense of ancient forces she could only guess at.

She had never kissed a lad in her whole life, and certainly nothing else neither, being strictly brought up. So how was it that they seemed to know the map of each other so well, that it was like coming home?

It was late on that perfect summer's day, before they made their slow way down the fell path. A light mist was lying in the valley. Stopping near the base of the hill, they turned and looked back. The sun was just slip-

ping behind the great bulk of Bambeck Fell, outlining its darkening silhou-
ette in a momentary halo of gold. Shadows from the adjacent mountains
stretched towards each other like imploring hands across the face of the
fell.

'You didn't ever say where you were going. But I know. I always could
read your mind.'

'I'm sorry Betty. I know it's foolish, but I have to. I owe it to my
father.'

'You're a daft fool. You don't have to. It's a waste of a life. And you've
only just got your own life back. There's been enough dying already.'

'I know all that.'

'You always were that stubborn.' She was exasperated.

'Do I have to keep my promise, Betty?'

'Ay.'

'Even if I come through all that?'

'Ay. It wouldn't make any sense. It never made any sense.'

'But we do love each other, don't we?'

'I thought you would have known that by now, Charlie.'

'Yes. I'll never forget.'

'Well, then button your gob and get on with it, if you must. I'm going
now!'

She turned away abruptly and strode away down the path. As she
walked, tears ran unheeded down her face.

He stood at the bottom of the fell, in the shadow of the mountain, and
watched her go.

CHAPTER 23

So he had gone away to the War, that foolish lad of hers. She had been powerless to stop him. She had heard the news from Ollie on market day. Now, every day, it was as though half of her was there too, in that unimaginable hell.

One black day, at the back end of winter, William Jackson came home. When the pressure of beds at the Infirmary grew too great, Betty and Mrs Jackson took the farm cart up to Carlisle, wrapped William in rugs and brought him back to High Greenrigg. The Helm wind, that mad wind which drove folk crazy, had been blowing for days. A straight line of menacing cloud lay across the Pennines, leaving a dreadful gloom from morning till night. The two women struggled to keep William warm in the freezing air. Both of them knew they were bringing him home to die.

They struggled with him that first night, trying to help his terrible breathing with kettles of water, a great fire in the old sandstone chimney. The doctor came in the small hours. But William's ravaged lungs, destroyed by deadly mustard gas, rasped on with no relief, the sound seeming to fill every corner of the old farmhouse. There was nothing to be done.

Then, the following morning, the Helm wind died away. The first week rays of February sunlight struggled through the window, and William rallied. Betty had been sitting with him all night, holding his hand. About six o' clock he opened his eyes for the first time for hours and smiled at her.

In those first weeks, she found in herself a gentleness and compassion which surprised her. She could not reach out to Charles in that terrible place, but here and now, there was someone who needed her. William saw her as an angel, though she knew she was anything but that. He called for her constantly, wearing her to a frazzle. He was often difficult and petu-

135

lant and got on her nerves when his breathing became bad and he retched for air. He had been a spoiled child before he went away, and sometimes, when childishness returned with fear and pain, she saw that spoiled child again. There were many times when she longed to snap at him. But she also saw the other things, the terrors of the trenches, the memories of dead friends. In those dark hours it was doubly painful to bear the thought of that other lad still out there, alone, without her beside him.

Miraculously, William was well enough by late Spring to be taken outside. He would sit for a little while, in the brief spring sun, looking out towards the Eden valley with its softly curving river. In those last weeks he had begun to believe that he might recover completely, and at last had plucked up the courage to speak to Betty. . . .

'Now then, Betty! How about we get wed, thee and me?' They were sitting outside in the sun. 'We would jog along well enough together, wouldn't you say? And you've been a gay kind lass to me. I'm mending fast, thanks to thee. Will thee wed me?'

Why not wed William? She owed a great deal to Widow Jackson, and William would need care for a long time. It was the least she could do for them both. Overcome with pity and a protective feeling which was almost love, she agreed. Only Widow Jackson, sharp as a pin, looked at her sideways.

'You know I love you like my own daughter, lass. I'd be glad to see you marry our William, though he can be a difficult lad when he's in bad fettle. . . . But you and I, we know how it's going to end. You're a young lass with a life before you. I know you want to give him comfort for his last little time in this world, but you could have years of nursing without me to help you. I'm an old woman now, and I won't always be here.'

There was a pause. Betty was at the sink, washing the crocks. Mrs Jackson could see from the set of her shoulders that she was in determined mood. She turned and leaned against the board. Try as she would, the old lady could not read her expression.

'I've told our William he don't have to take notice of those doctors.' Betty said at last. 'We both know he was sent home to die, and that's as maybe, but look at him now! If he has us both to care of him he might have a happy life, and live to a good old age, after all.' She hesitated. 'Anyways, it's the least I can do, all things considered.'

The old woman sighed and shook her head.

'Ay, maybe. But I'm telling you, lass, much as my own heart wants it to be, I know it's nothing now with William but a remission, same as doctor says. And what about the other lad, out there still? You mind how you care for him. If he comes back alive, you'll want to be with him. I'll not forget your face when he was here, in this very kitchen. He's a bonny lad and he loves you too. It does no good at all to marry for pity, and maybe gratitude, because I gave you a home when you needed it.'

Betty stared out of the deep-set window, at the hills outlined against the summer dusk. She cried out, inside, with everything in her, to know that Charles was safe and that she might one day see him again. He was hers after all. But it was no good wishing. Even if he came back, there could never be a future for them together. They had promised. She took a deep breath. No looking back.

The last dish clattered into the stone sink, slipping from her fingers.

'No!' She said firmly. 'If William wants me for his comfort, it's the least I can do. There's no one else!'

Poor William. It had been a voyage of discovery which had transported him away from pain for a little while. She had felt very old and experienced. That first night she had cradled his poor head and wept, for all that might have been. Gently, softly, she had taken him into her. It had hurt a little. Will was doubled up with coughing after. She held him in her arms all night to keep him safe. Only in that dark hour before dawn, while he slept beside her, did she allow herself to think about Charles, how they had loved each other that day on Bambeck Fell. All over now. Those things weren't meant for the harsh world. They were best not thought about. Yet, unbidden, bitter tears did come, for all that might have been.

Poor William slept. She was glad of it. There was so little peace in his life.

Tonight she would be boiling kettles on the fire again, in that stuffy room, so that the steam might give him a little relief. But the truth was, there was no relief. Not for him: nor for her. Yet she was ashamed to think of her situation in this way, to think that she was in a prison. How she screamed out inside herself to be free of that sick room, of the smell of phlegm and blood, of the endless washing, of the windows tight closed against the summer breeze, lest he should catch a chill.

And the worst thing was that he sensed her feelings. He would hold her hand and look at her, as she mopped his sweating brow or changed his covers. He would stop her then and smile wearily up at her. And once he had said.

'You are a butterfly in a prison, my lass. I long to let the window wide and set you free.'

Another time he had opened his eyes when she had thought him asleep and said softly.

'It won't be long now.'

How she pitied him, that poor lad, how bitterly she castigated herself for her selfishness, when he was going through such pain, and all she could think about was herself. That petulance she had seen in him in those first weeks had been burned away by pain, and there was only sweetness left, the very best of him. She could not help but love him now.

Yet with a part of her, she longed to put it all from her, run and run, out into the green woods, where life beckoned. How she longed for someone else to do all the work, to take it from her, to smooth her forehead and say, 'There! There!'

It had only been a remission, after all. The doctor had been right.

She must get on with it, get off her backside and not twine, because William needed her now more than ever. Mrs Jackson had become so stiff in her joints she couldn't get up the stairs. There were no folks about to care for him, but her. There was no one but her to wash the blood from the sheets, time after time, to boil up the calves' feet to make the jelly which might help him rally, to supervise the milking and the haymaking and give the men what for when the job wasn't done right.

For all her idealism, she was drained by the drudgery of her life, and other folk always turning to her as though she were strong. The truth was, she was as weak as water.

She would twine on for a bit like this and then she would look down and see Will sleeping, his blond hair falling across his white face, the sound of his breathing harsh in the hot little room. She knew he loved her, and that made her feel even more helpless. She would sit by him and watch him sleeping, and think what a whining lass she was. If she couldn't be grateful for her health and strength so she could help other folk out, she wasn't worth a brass farthing.

She had tried resolutely not to think of Charles, out there somewhere in that unimaginable country of the War. She had heard nothing for so long. Wouldn't she have known with her whole being if anything had happened to him? Yet just when she had begun to believe that he must, after all, have died in that terrible place, a letter had come with a French postmark.

She would tell William when he woke, and he would be glad for her, but for now she just wanted to sit by herself somewhere and read it, to deal with the terrible joy which threatened for a few moments to overwhelm her. Of course she couldn't reply. He had no right to be sending her letters, but it was that bad over there, if the newspapers were to be believed. Maybe he just needed someone to talk to, and how could she deny him that?

Now that Will was sleeping, she set a wheelback chair outside on the grass just outside the door, where she could hear the slightest sound from William. It was good to smell the air blowing straight from the fells, after the stifling odour of the sickroom. She longed to open the window and let the sharp Pennine wind blow through the room, but the doctor had forbidden it. He had said it might cause stagnation of the lungs, so she had bowed to his judgement, although her instincts told her he was wrong. All that camphor and wrapping-up and fires in the room couldn't be good, even for a healthy body. But then she was blessed with good health, always had been, and no weather ever defeated her, even in the depths of winter when she had to go out onto the fell in a blizzard.

Sitting outside in the evening air, she began to read.

My dearest Betty,

I know you told me not to write, but how could I not? I have nothing to hold me together now, other than the memory of you. Forgive me. I know how angry you will be. Here, in this place, the dream of you burns in my mind, when I'm afraid. If anything gets me through without going mad, it will be that dream of you on that day – your eyes reflecting the sky, the dusty smell of heather all around us where we lay. I climbed my hill, didn't I? It was all for you, in the end.

I wish you were here to tell the rats how to behave! Did I ever tell you how afraid of rats I used to be? Now I have a pet rat. He comes every night and I give him bits of mouldy bread and cheese.

I am sorry this letter is rambling. The truth is, I am almost asleep, but every time I drift off, another thumping great shell goes boom and I get a faceful of dirt.

Maybe I will dream of you, that we are standing above the terraced garden at Bambeck. One day I will plant my own Blue Poppy there, beside the sundial. I can almost hear the call of sheep in the fields beyond. All is peace.

I know what you said to me, but it doesn't make any difference, in the end.

For I am yours, for ever,
Charles.

CHAPTER 24

Betty buried her nose in the fresh daffodils, breathing in their green, haunting scent. She had begun to feel alive again for the first time for many weeks. William had been buried in the little churchyard under the fell, on a sharp autumn day when the first snow flurries had blown into the grave from the hills above. Poor Mrs Jackson's arthritis had grown bad that winter, worsened by the shock of losing her son. It had been a dark season for them both. Now, as the days at last began to lengthen, Betty was gathering a bunch of the best wild daffodils from the orchard to bring in to Widow Jackson; a touch of spring, bringing light into a sad house.

She looked up and saw that someone had come into the orchard. With a shock, she realized it was Charles. He looked so changed that she had hardly recognized him. Alice had written to her that Charles had been wounded in France, but she had been too numb to feel much, too preoccupied with William's dying.

Charles was standing looking out over the valley, so caught up in his thoughts that he seemed to have forgotten where he was. For a moment she was disturbed by a sharp memory of her father. He had stood in just that way, so many years ago, before he had gone away to be killed. In those few moments she could read in his half-averted face some terrible emptiness, like a shell of someone who had once been there.

She straightened up with the bunch of daffodils and walked quietly towards him. With a start he seemed to come back into the world and turned that white face towards her, the eyes even more deep-set, oddly blank. He looked straight at her without smiling, as though seeing a stranger. He was still in uniform. She wondered if he had been home.

'Betty, I had to come. We came through on the train, but I got a lift up. I've left my kit bag at the bottom of the lane. Would you give me a cup of tea? I just need to talk before I put on a face for Mother.'

It was as though they had never been away from each other, as though they could say anything without the normal boundaries. It was a frightening feeling. That was what she had run from, after all. She would tell him everything. After all, they had been friends. She wouldn't turn her back on him. But then she would send him on his way.

She forced herself to smile.

'Come on and see Mrs Jackson. She often talks of that day you came to the farm, before you joined up. She's that poorly nowadays she'd be glad of a visitor. I'll make you a big pot of tea.'

Widow Jackson was delighted to see him. The presence of a third person in the room forced them both into being cheerful. Charles sat at the big table supping tea. Gradually some of the emptiness, which had so chilled her, seeped away from his face. She could only guess at its cause, but, shuddering inwardly, she shook away the feeling of dread it had inspired in her.

Charles went to sit beside Mrs Jackson. She held his hand in her twisted one, looking at him intently.

'You've been through a bit then, young man,' she said at last. 'I can see from your face you're in bad fettle.'

Betty watched them both from the other side of the room, as she was laying the table.

'I was holed up in a French hospital.' Charles said at last, looking down at the floor. 'We got trapped in No Man's Land. It was a bit tricky for a while.'

Mrs Jackson nodded.

'Ay, Elizabeth told me you're to get a medal, so your mother wrote.'

The colour came and went in Charles's pallid face.

'Well . . . it's never quite what it sounds like in despatches. You're there and you're stuck in a situation. There were three of us. We had to get the other chap back somehow. You have to do something, however frightened you are. Believe me, I was very frightened!'

Mrs Jackson nodded again.

'Ay, I understand, lad. And our Betty, she's had a bad time too. It's just as hard to stay behind and care for a sick lad the way she has. . . .'

Charles looked across at Betty, who was standing by the table waiting for them.

'Yes,' he said at last. 'You're quite right. It's easy enough to play a hero when you haven't any choice. It must have been so difficult for you both.'

Mrs Jackson clasped his hand tighter.

'You know our William's dead? He died last back end.'

Charles glanced again at Betty.

'I didn't know. You never said, Betty. I'm very sorry.'

'Ay', Mrs Jackson sighed heavily, 'It were a bad time, the poor lad coughing his guts up. Now I'm in bad fettle ever since the cold spell last Christmas, and that poor lass is taking care of me too. She deserves a bit more of a life, don't you think, than taking care of an old woman. After all, she has her own life to lead.'

Betty shook her head vehemently. 'Don't talk so daft. I wouldn't want it any other way, except for you to get better. I'd be glad of that.'

'Ay, you're a gay good lass, but I know how you chaff against it. You never say anything. Mind you, lass, you're better at butter-making than you was when you first came to High Greenrigg!'

She and Betty glanced at one another. The old woman had a twinkle in her eye. Betty grinned.

'Ay, well. I'll tell you, Charlie, we've begun a new idea. We worked it out between us. To keep me occupied and out of mischief, and it brings some money into the farm, now Mrs Jackson can't get to market. I've started to take butter and milk down. I found there were other farms where the old folk didn't really want to drive to market every week, so I started taking their butter and milk too. Then we started up a class here last wintertime. Since January, milkmaids have been coming from the fell-side farms and we've had a lad from Newton Rigg teaching us how to make all sorts of fancy stuff with dairy products. What do you think about that?'

Charles shook his head, and smiled. 'I see you two have got it sewed up pretty well.'

Betty grinned at him.

'We don't sit on our backsides waiting for the world to come to us, naming no names, Charlie. The funny thing is, it isn't the butter and the eggs and the skimmed milk that's the real attraction. I've started taking bunches of daffodils down to the market. This corner up under the fell grows the best daffodils in Cumberland and they are the first out by a long way. It's a warm spot, always has been, I believe.'

Mrs Jackson nodded agreement.

'She's got a lot of ideas in that noddle of hers. There's no keeping up with her.'

'Townsfolk will pay a lot of money for a bunch of good flowers,' Betty continued. 'Mrs Jackson and I are bringing on summer flowers in the garden too. I think there could be quite a demand from the towns. A lot of them miss the countryside.'

They finished their tea and Charles stood up.

'Betty, if Mrs Jackson could spare you for a few minutes, would you come and have a walk up the fell with me? I need to stretch my legs. I've been on that train all day.'

Mrs Jackson looked up at him.

'We're right glad of the company. Why don't you stay on for a night? Get yourself in good fettle to face your mother? You don't want to go down to her with that white face of yours upsetting her. As I say, we'd be real glad of the company. Now then I'm having my nap now, and you'll excuse me! You two bairns can go off and have a walk and catch up a bit. She works too hard, that lass, and she never twines. It's time she had a bit of joy in her life.'

Now it was Betty's turn to colour up.

'I'm not sure whether I can spare any time to go walking today. I've a list of jobs to do before milking.'

'Oh, nonsense, lass. There's always time for a bit of a crack. You drive yourself too hard, and it's a job you don't even like that much!'

They walked on through the orchard, through the young daffodils and under the old apple trees, out of the iron gate at the back which opened straight on to the fellside. The new grass was just pushing through, but there was still the red-brown of last year's dead bracken, although the first curled shoots were showing.

'Are you sure you're all right, Charlie, going up hills, I mean?'

There she was worrying again, fussing over him like a mother hen. When would she ever let him stand on his own feet? She gave herself a mental shake.

'I'm all right, Betty,' he puffed as the path grew steeper. 'Just pretend I'm going up the stairs at Bambeck Hall.' He grinned as best he could while catching his breath. 'Before I went away I got . . . quite good at walking. I'd been up a fell or two by then.' He paused. 'Don't you remember?' She didn't reply, and eventually he went on. 'When we were in France it was pretty flat. I got this bit of a nick in my side where a bullet got me. It took a long time to heal. I want to try to see if I can still get up the hills. I don't want to go backwards now, after all that effort.'

'Right, lad, we'll go up to the top. Then we'll go on to Dufton Pike. It'll just about give us time to be down before dark. Then I've my jobs to do.

I don't mind you staying over, but don't fuss round me. I've got market in the morning so I'll have to be up early.'

There was a pause while they concentrated on their feet thudding on the path.

'Tell me about the War, Charlie.' Betty said, at last.

He stopped and looked out over the valley which was spread beneath their feet, caught in the late afternoon light.

'I don't want to talk about it any more, Betty. It'll haunt me for a long time. Maybe later I'll want to talk about it. For the moment I just want to shut the door on it, to concentrate on the future. I've been thinking a lot about it. I'm determined to go up to Cambridge if I can pass the entrance examination, to study the Natural Sciences. I think that's where my career lies. The only thing I'm worried about is Mother. From her letters, she seems rather lonely. She needs something to occupy her mind.'

Betty, who was striding ahead of him, turned for a moment and stopped.

'I feel bad, lad, that I never went to see her. Maybe one day, Charlie, but I've my own life to lead now. I'm happy in this spot. Let's just let bygones be bygones. It's not your fault, but I can't help feeling that your family has only brought sadness into my life. Some of the reasons are best not talked about. Let's not hanker after the past, Charlie. We'll have a bit of a walk now and straighten you out to see your mother, but let's say goodbye like sensible folk and get on with our own lives. Mrs Jackson's my own folk now, and you have your own too. That's the way it should be.'

When they got back to the house, Mrs Jackson was just preparing to light the lamps.

'Now then, Mr Fergusson, have you cleared your head a bit with all that good Cumberland air?' She smiled at him. 'You've got some colour in your cheeks, if nothing else.'

'Mrs Jackson!' He came over to her and took her hand. 'I really ought to go now. I really shouldn't leave it any longer to go home. It will only take me an hour or two to bicycle to Bambeck. If I leave now before dark it won't be too bad. I know the way well enough. You've been so kind, offering me a bed and giving me such a grand tea. I feel so much stronger now.'

Mrs Jackson glanced from one to the other. Betty walked over to the stove and started stirring one of the pots.

'Leave that, lass! You bairns haven't had a scrap now, have you? I'll be right cross if you have been quarrelling. Elizabeth can be a difficult lass.'

Mrs Jackson twinkled at him, taking the sting out of her words.

Charles smiled, shaking his head. There was a pause.

'Well, I had best be going. . . .'

She turned round, her eyes suspiciously full and wet; her colour high.

'I'll see you out Charlie, on my way to the milking.'

Together they went out into the dusk, down the path and through the little orchard. The daffodils lifted their faces like stars out of the green dusk. Above them, the rising, bubbling call of a curlew echoed across the fell.

They stood together by the gate.

'Betty,' he said at last. 'You're crying.'

She shook her head.

'I was thinking of me Dad, and how I said goodbye on this very spot. I gave him his bait box and some daffodils to take, to remind him. And I never saw him again.'

She made a little choking sound, turning away.

'Betty! I'm so sorry, for everything. I just wish. . . .'

'Don't say anything, lad.'

'But I. . . .' He put his hand on her arm.

She broke away from him. Running back into the orchard, she flopped down on her knees in the damp dusky grass, reaching out her hands and picking at the daffodils. He came up behind her.

'Betty, please. . . .'

'You always did stir me up, Charlie, and make me cross. Go away! Leave me in peace. I've a good life. I'm not afraid of anything . . . except. . . .'

He knelt down beside her and looked into her face. She thrust the daffodils at him. The scent of them came up to him, sharply, like a feeling of something lost. He felt tears of his own welling up.

'I love you,' he said.

She shook her head violently.

'Don't ever say that. Don't you ever!'

'But I do! I always have. Even if you don't feel the same. Don't say goodbye like this!'

'No!'

Suddenly overcome, not really knowing what drove him, except the huge emptiness inside him, he reached across and took hold of her shoulders, scattering the flowers on the grass.

'Now look what you've done, you great gowk.'

He kissed her full on the mouth. The shock of it knocked them both back on their heels.

'Don't ever . . . ever . . . come near me again, Charlie. Don't ever, don't even write. Keep away. Please keep away.'

Her voice was full of anguish. She struggled to her feet, stepping on the corner of her apron, almost falling. He clutched at her elbow but she shrugged him off. Before he could say another word, she had turned and fled back into the house, the door slamming behind her. He was left standing alone in the dusk.

BOOK II

THE HOLY MOUNTAIN

Have you beauty, that leads the heart from things fashioned of wood
and stone to the holy mountain?

The Prophet, Kahlil Gibran

CHAPTER 25

Sir,

I have been instructed by Mr Forton and Professor Thompson to extend an invitation to you to accompany our autumn expedition into the remote areas of the Himalaya in search of new seeds for the University collection, to be undertaken in conjunction with The Royal Geographical Society.

In particular we shall be seeking further specimens of rhododendra. Your assigned task would be to assist in seed collection and classification, and in the collection of data on flora of the Himalayan uplands. The exact itinerary will be dictated by political events. However it may be possible to extend research beyond Sikkim and the Indian Himal into certain areas of Tibet. This depends of course on the political situation pertaining at that time.

In view of your excellent research paper on Alpine Flora, which was read with interest by the University Botanical Society, we feel you would be a worthy candidate for a place on our expedition. . . .

Charles stood holding the letter and staring out of his window of his college rooms, into the courtyard below. Two black-robed dons scurried by, huddled against the bitter Fenland wind.

He had read the letter from the University Botanical Society time and time again. It was hard to believe that here, at last, was his great chance, that his dream might become a reality. To walk among the great snow-covered peaks of the Himalaya, perhaps even to glimpse a blue *Meconopsis*. Perhaps to find a rarer specimen still than Captain Bailey had brought back, and Kingdon-Ward had named. Rarer even than *Meconopsis Betonicifolia*. Out there, somewhere, he was sure his Poppy grew, the colour of the Tibetan sky at dawn, struggled shyly into the light on some remote hillside. It was waiting for him. Perhaps one day he might even find the Blue Poppy his grandmother had grown in her garden in Sikkim, given to her by a Tibetan prince.

He shook himself from his daydream. He was a serious scientist, and there was no place now for such dreams. They had served their purpose, but he had put them aside with his sickly childhood. Summers collecting specimens, and college expeditions to the Alps had convinced him that he had little to fear. He was no longer troubled by the weakness in his legs, even though years of muscle wastage had left their mark. Only rarely had that queer pain in his chest come back again. Would he be wise to take such a risk? To put the others in the expedition in peril? What if after all these years, the gloomy predictions of the specialist, Mr Ashington, and Dr Nelson came true after all?

As though she were there beside him after all these years, he heard Betty's voice over his shoulder.

'Stand on your own pins, lad, and bugger the rest!'

She was right! He looked at the letter again.

The expedition will set sail in late August. We hope to take advantage of the seed-setting period. This will involve walking in through the latter stages of the monsoon. . . .

There was a knock at the door. Still deep in thought, he opened it and took the note the college servant handed him. It was from Dawson, one of the archivists, in response to Charles's own note asking for data. Dawson wrote that he had uncovered something which might be of interest on Himalayan Flora. He pulled on his gown and hurried down the stone steps.

'Ah, Fergusson!' Dawson was huddled in his frayed jacket against the draught, sitting behind a dusty pile of documents. They had become friends, in an oddly formal way, drawn by their enthusiasm for Alpine Flora. For both of them too, the common experience of the trenches was an unspoken bond.

'Wait till you see what I have uncovered for you. A bit of a find!'

Charles followed Dawson through the ranks of reading tables. One or two men raised their heads irritably from their books and buried them once again. He didn't acknowledge any of them. He had become even more of a loner just lately, especially since his Fellowship.

Once through into the storerooms at the back of the library, they squeezed through narrow shelves bulging with papers. The musty smell of old vellum, and mice, wafted across to him, borne on the damp draught. It took him back to the library at home where he had spent so many lonely hours. Lonely, that was, until Betty came and turned his life upside-down.

There was a cleared space at the back where a table was laden with papers, and a number of wooden flower presses. Dawson leaned over and patted the top press on the pile.

'When I got your note about Himalayan Flora, I remembered these. If I hadn't gone looking I would never have found them. Never been catalogued, would you believe! It just shows you. What could be hiding in here in this place is anybody's guess. We haven't even begun to sort it out. Short-staffed, that's the trouble since the war. Must have just been left here at the end of one of the college expeditions. There isn't much here, just a few unnamed specimens, but I think you'll find them of interest. . . .'

Dawson paused and lifted the first of the latticed presses so that it was facing them. There was a label tied onto one side, written in capital letters, faded but still clear. *EXPEDITION FLORA: EASTERN HIMALAYA 1898–99.* He leaned over and lifted the latticed wooden frame off the pile of pressed blotting paper.

'Just look at this!'

Dawson removed the top layer of blotting paper. Inside was a 'flimsy' – a double sheet of tissue. With great delicacy he opened up the tissue. Charles peered over his shoulder. There, pressed onto the white paper was a rose-coloured primula, the colours still fresh. Even as he looked, the flower in the dim light seemed to fade, yet not before he had caught a faint aroma, some indefinable scent drifting up from the paper, so different from the smell of old books and dust which permeated the library.

Dawson was carefully replacing the flimsy and the blotting paper. Did he feel it too? Charles wondered to himself. For a few seconds, it seemed as though life had been let into the dusty room, whispering of adventure. It stirred his blood with excitement. He could go there! He only had to grasp it with both hands. His big chance. He had worked so hard for so long to escape from the half-life of a delicate child, the cloying love of his mother, the darkness of that house. For so long he had been trapped by the morbid fear of death which he carried with him. Now, suddenly, if he didn't grasp this chance, he would be forever trapped here too. Scholarship would become a risk-free substitute for life.

A bell tinkled at the far end of the room and Dawson bustled off, squeezing once more through the narrow shelves, releasing yet more dust and the smell of age from the piles of overhanging papers.

Charles sat down at the table and stared at the pile of presses, finger-
ing the wooden frame which Dawson had laid aside. He smoothed the
stained blotting paper. He could feel it at his fingertips. That passion for
exploration, for high places, for knowledge, which had driven explorers to
the furthest corners of the earth.

Softly, reverently, he lifted off the next layer of blotting paper. There
must be twenty or more specimens in this press alone. A yellow primula,
a deep purple aconite pressed upon the page, a field sketch of a scarlet
rhododendron, with a faded leaf. . . .

He sat for a long time, carefully going through the presses with his
fingertips. At last, almost at the end, he found what, intuitively, he knew
was there. There was a flash of blue in the dim light. He caught his breath.
Yes. It was here, as he had known it would be. Faded a little, but indisputably here. The violet of the Tibetan sky. Faded to a tissue paper thin-
ness, yet glowing with colour.

He looked more closely. It couldn't be *Meconopsis bailii* . . . *betonicifolia*. . . . Look at the leaf. . . . Was it new? As yet undiscovered? He struggled to read the pale scrawl at the base of the page, no more than a field
note. The collector would never have had a chance to catalogue his specimens properly and hadn't named this one. Charles remembered that the
first blue *Meconopsis* wasn't named until the Abbé Delavey in 1886 found
a specimen in the Yunnan and named it for the betony-shaped leaf. Major
Bailey had rediscovered it in 1913, Kingdon-Ward had carried on the
quest, and was the first to collect seed. It was rumoured that the first
flowers might be seen at this year's Chelsea Flower Show.

In the dim light he squinted at the faded brown scrawl. . . . *'Eastern
Himalaya 14,500 ft'*. . . . Then in a different ink, a faded green, someone
had written: 'Tibet – possible?' Had the collector meant to go into Tibet
and hope to find another specimen? Perhaps he had never returned, leaving others to bring back his box, which had lain unsorted for so long in a
corner of the archives.

He looked again at the flower. There were strange spiny leaves, a single
crown of blue. And that colour! Even in this light, filtered through a small
window, it was the blue of the Madonna's robe in the great window of
King's chapel when the sun shone through. Something out of this world.
An unearthly blue.

He sat alone with the dusty presses. There were a few other specimens, dried-up things after all this time. Most of this collection would
never have been looked at again. In a small battered box, which Dawson

had put on one side of the table, Charles found some seed pods, a canvas bag of seed, unlabelled, a magnifying glass and a spare pen nib. There was also a notebook labelled again, 'E. *Himalaya Expedition: 1898-99*'.

He leafed through the notes, struggling to read the faded writing. On the third page he found what he was looking for. . . .

14,500 ft Tibetan border. Sharp wind today. H. C. down with stomach pains. Myself quite well now. Walked alone cataloguing plants for the first part of the morning. The coolies are slow. Much rain in early morning. Too high for leeches, thank God. Found a blue flower, quite the most beautiful thing I have ever seen. Took it to H.C. who agrees it is a *Meconopsis* – but unnamed species. A small blue flower, singly on a long stem with a rosette of leaves, quite perfect colour, a little like the yellow *Meconopsis Cambrica* which grows on our walls at home, but a much larger flower head. Such a blue I never saw before. One of the coolies says he has seen this 'by a lake many many flowers, like the lake itself, and you see it in the sky.' This sounds very fanciful. I question him further and he says over the Snow Mountains. I think this means in Tibet. . . .

Tibet! How that name rang in his head. He felt a tingle of excitement.

In that hour in the library without even addressing the problem, inexplicably everything had become clear? A dusty box in a cold little storeroom at the back of the college library, a few scrawled sentences, a flower which brought a touch of magic into this dusty world. Here was the romance of life, an indefinable excitement, a thrill of discovery. That world was out there, a book not yet opened. And somewhere was his Blue Poppy.

CHAPTER 26

Betty wondered uneasily if this visit was such a good idea. There was no need to have anything to do with the past. Betty was her own woman now. She had no need to hark back to the bad old days of Bambeck Hall. Willie was gone and Mrs Jackson had died, and she only had her own future to consider.

Her mind touched on those last months with poor Widow Jackson, in agony from her arthritis. Betty had been glad of her own strength. It had enabled her to lift and turn the helpless body (Widow Jackson was still a heavy woman) causing her as little pain as possible.

Life was without mercy. Why was it that the good suffered so? Matthew Bowman had been right. There was no justice in the world for gentle creatures. She had thought that, after William, nothing could hurt her again. Seeing Widow Jackson, that spirited old lady, die in such a way, had been almost the worst of all. Right till the end, the old woman had kept her sense of humour and courage.

There was an emptiness now. They had shared such plans. Now it was left to Betty to do it all alone. Widow Jackson had told her she was leaving her the farm and all the stock. She knew it would be in good hands.

For a while Betty had felt quite lost. For the first time for so long, there was no one left to care for.

The butter-making business was doing well. She had set it up in a barn, a year or two back, when she'd been tied to the house with William. It was a natural extension of her market business.

After Widow Jackson's death, she had gone down to Newton Rigg and done a butter-making course, finding to her surprise that the skills were not so difficult to master. Now she was involved with the outworkers on the farms, and employed five dairy maids. It provided an additional income for many of the farmer's wives and daughters. The business was expanding fast. There was a great interest in fresh butter and milk from Penrith, a market town which was growing year by year. She had a dairy shop of her own now, on a prime site in Penrith.

And of course, there were the flowers. What had started with a few bunches of early daffodils from the orchard, had grown into a flourishing business supplying fresh flowers to shops as far away as Preston, using the railway for deliveries. She had put up a couple of glasshouses in that sheltered spot in the orchard, at Mrs Jackson's suggestion. How the old lady had loved those flowers! Although they could never compete with Covent Garden and the warmer South, local folk seemed to prefer her hardier Northern blooms, especially as she could deliver so quickly. She had bought a little motorised van, the first on the fellside, to help with deliveries to the markets and shops.

Oh, she would have a future. She had nursed, and cared for folk for far too long. It had left its mark. Now she was a wealthy woman, she could go away to College or University. She could do anything. The world was opening up for women. She could be one of them.

So what was it that drew her back to Bambeck Hall? She had spent years trying to avoid even thinking about it. Nothing had changed. No good would come of going back, of maybe seeing Charles again. He had taken her at her word. She had never heard from him again. Folk said he had made a successful career at Cambridge University, and had even written a book. For all she knew, he might even be married, though happen she would have heard of it. She was glad for him anyway. She had her own life to lead.

Yet now she was in a dilemma. A letter had come, from Alice herself, imploring her to come and visit, with a date and time, as though there could be no argument about it. How arrogant the upper classes were! The world had hardly seemed to change for them at all, despite the War. The letter was couched in the warmest terms, and it would be ungracious to refuse. She had heard that Alice was ill. And it was true that there was something left unfinished between them. She would go back one last time, to sort out those last things. Then her conscience would be clear.

So, when the orders had been processed, and she had sent them off with Mary, her new assistant, she put on her best black and did her hair just so. She opened the wooden chest which stood under the window, and lifted out the shawl which she had taken so long ago to keep her warm during her flight from Bambeck Hall. So many times she had blamed herself for not giving it back to Charles. Why had she not? It would have been one less thing to prey on her mind, to bind her, however tenuously to the Hall. But there, she had not, and it was no use fretting.

She drove herself down the fell towards Bambeck in her shiny, new car, her only indulgence since she had come into her money. She prided herself on her tough existence, getting up for the milking at five, working all hours, pushing herself hard to succeed. If you were weak, if you showed a soft side, you would go under and no one would weep for you. Had anyone wept for her father, apart from herself, or for William, dying a slow agonising death from mustard gas? And for all her care, she had not been able to take Mrs Jackson's pain from her. The gentle, quiet people left the earth without trace. A lesson to be learned.

She had no one left in the world. Not even a child. And that was a mercy, after all.

Suddenly, it was there, that imposing entrance, the iron gates open to the world, now that there was no longer a lodge keeper. Those sandstone bulls, on great pillars either side of the gate, stared back at her coldly, their faces blurred by years of weathering.

She drove steadily up the front drive between bare trees. It was spring, but the buds were barely on the branches, held back by bitter winds and late frost. She had once thought this long drive enchanted when she had come there as a little girl, on that spring day after her tenth birthday. But that was past and gone.

As she approached the house, winding her way between the lower gardens, she registered, in passing, that it all looked very different. In those early War years, when she had been a servant here, so many of the staff had gone away to the Front. The gardens, once a feature of the Hall, had begun to decay. The glasshouses became so run down that, in a season, the beautiful, neat vegetable beds were overrun with weeds. But here, on one side, were new glasshouses flanking the hill, and on the other, unfamiliar plants and shrubs already making their mark on the landscape.

Had Charles been responsible for all this? He had once written to her about how he would change everything when he came home from the War. She allowed her mind to touch on him briefly. How would he seem to her now? She hadn't really thought of him for so long. Deliberately she recalled him as a rather spoilt invalid boy just struggling to make his way in the world. Until that last time, when she had sent him away for ever.

The house stood at the end of the drive, brooding over the valley, its windows blank in the morning light. She felt that same familiar dread. Some sense that this place had power over her, and could stop her being the person she wanted to be, however hard she fought to break away. She gave herself a mental shake: this was fanciful thinking. She had come of her own free will. Nothing had power over her now.

Connie opened the door.

Betty had prepared herself for this. She opened her mouth to say, 'How are you, Connie? Do you remember me?' but Connie's face wore a dreamy, abstracted look. She hardly looked at Betty, only standing back to usher her in. Betty struggled to hang on to that self-confidence which seemed to have deserted her. It was as though all this, her smart clothes, her elegant hair, successful businesses of her own, was in itself nothing but a dream, a dream which Bambeck had the power to dissolve.

She hesitated on the step. Connie waited impatiently, her right foot itching her other calf. 'Her feet are bothering her again!' Betty thought suddenly, with understanding. 'She can't wait to get back to the kitchen to put them up! I *know* what that's like.'

'Mrs Jackson of High Greenrigg, to see Mrs Fergusson.'

She walked across the black and white parquet floor, following Connie. Connie in her pattens, slapping her feet as she walked. What memories! She pushed them away. Connie hadn't even recognized her! Betty felt a surge of confidence.

Connie looked back at the tall, graceful young woman in a fashionable bombazine dress, the hair swept back. A face that was only vaguely familiar. She wasn't much interested anyway, dying to get back to the kitchen to put her feet up.

'Mrs Fergusson's having tea' Connie whispered in a conspiratorial tone. 'I forgot, who did you say?'

'Mrs Jackson of High Greenrigg,' Betty repeated. Connie still had a head like a sieve!

She walked into the drawing-room. At first it seemed empty. Then she realized that someone was lying on the long sofa under the window. She drew in her breath sharply. Once Alice's presence would have filled the whole room. Could this be the woman that she remembered, this white-haired, frail creature?

'She's been in bad fettle lately,' Connie whispered behind her, as they stood in the doorway. In a louder voice, she announced. . . .

'Mrs Jackson of . . . High Greenrigg.'

Connie closed the door behind her, and Betty walked towards the figure by the window. She held the shawl before her in its tissue paper, like a shield, a comforting thing in a frightening world.

CHAPTER 27

'My dear! It was so good of you to come.'

The voice was faint. 'Do forgive my not getting up. Come and sit down, here, beside me.'

Betty was aware of many things in that room. Up till now she had always had a kind of underneath view of the place, and of Alice, a view of a servant looking across at her mistress. It was the view of someone who had cleaned the grates, and blackleaded the hearth. But now, subtly, it was all different.

Betty sat down. Alice extended her hand, and grasped it, not letting go. Betty was forced to look straight at her.

'Let me look at you. I said to Charles, I'm sure that young lady will have made something of herself. And she will be quite striking, mark my words.'

Betty looked back at the white face, seeing the lines and puckers of recent illness. It was difficult to reconcile Alice's frailty with the memory that Betty had of her. Yet it was true that, although they had always clashed, there had been some strange affection between them. She felt it now.

'You are so grown now, perhaps I should call you Elizabeth?'

'Betty will do very well for my friends.'

There was a challenge if ever there was one.

'Betty, then! And you must call me Alice and we *shall* be friends.' The pressure on her hand was so affectionate, that in that moment Betty's defences fell away.

Betty looked across at her, noticing again the white face, the dark shadows under the eyes.

'Ah, it does me good to see a young face around me for a change. I can't tell you how lonely I am here, Betty. Connie doesn't do quite as well, and

158

Charles ... well, he is so often away, as perhaps you know. We are such foolish creatures, cutting ourselves off from the world because we think ourselves above it, don't you think?'

Betty was too startled to reply, but after a moment's thought, she took a deep breath.

'Well, yes! As a matter of fact I agree. In my work I see how the world is changing. But there is no need to be lonely ... Mrs Fergusson ... Alice. There's a lot of folk out there would be glad to be sociable. You just haven't to be too. ...' she was going to say 'high and mighty' but recollected herself in time. Friendship begun was one thing, but downright rudeness another. She was too used to speaking her mind.

She just hoped she looked respectable enough to be sitting in the drawing-room at Bambeck Hall. She had taken half an hour swearing at her hair, doing and re-doing the pins until she was satisfied. And the dress, although a plain black one, had been made by a good tailor in Penrith. Somehow, it mattered. It shouldn't have, but it did.

There they were, sitting opposite each other, almost equals. In an instant she had been made to feel at home, as though she had never been away. Only it was different now. Perhaps now she was a woman of property in her own right, she carried some different sense of her own worth. Alice in her own way seemed as nervous as she was, so fragile that she might be blown away by the first angry word.

Alice laid her hand on her arm.

'I have heard so much about you. You wouldn't believe how the gossip gets around, even to me! Ollie goes into Penrith to collect my shopping. He tells me you even have a shop in that little square. Not that I ever go myself, you understand. He came to your shop one day for some butter, and he was astonished. How well you have done for yourself! I have told Charles all about it. He was most interested.'

Alice smiled across at her.

'Now let's have some tea, shall we? Would you mind? Could you just pull that wretched thing by the fireplace? We still have the old bell system, although most of them don't work now. The whole house needs an overhaul, I'm afraid. Charles wants to put in the Electricity! Can you imagine! Some of my friends have installed these extraordinary new-fangled devices. I don't see any point in change just for change's sake, do you?'

Betty remembered only too well the tyranny of the bells. Once she would have been on the other end of them, being summoned peremp-

torarily. She would never have bells in her house. She had a housemaid
now to help her with the chores, but she hoped she would never treat her
in that way, as though servants weren't even human beings with feelings.
But she must remember, most folk had known no other way. If they had
seen it from below, they would have a different view entirely.

She brought herself back with a start. Alice was talking to her again.

'My dear, I was so sorry to hear about your husband. How perfectly
awful it must have been for you. Married for so short a time, too. After
that dreadful, dreadful tragedy with my dear husband and your dear
father. Oh, dear! The world is sometimes too much to bear. I do know
how you must have felt. I really do!'

There were tears in Alice's eyes. Betty felt any lingering resentment
melt away.

'Ay, it were a bad business, but it's done with now. I have to make a life
for myself. I'll not grieve any longer. But he was a good husband, and a
brave one. I've no regrets, except that I would have wished his pain away
and changed the manner of his dying. Not meaning to be cruel, Alice, but
it would have been better for the poor lad if he had finished hisself off on
the battlefield, rather than have that suffering. It's a terrible thing to see.
And I couldn't do anything for him.'

'I understand,' Alice said gently. They looked at each other.

'I brought back your shawl,' Betty went on quickly, 'I should have sent
it before. I don't know why I didn't. I haven't used it at all . . . just kept
it wrapped up in a chest. Only on that first day I was glad of it. And it did
keep me warm. I hope you will forgive me for taking it.'

Alice shook her head.

'Please, do keep it. Really! I'd like you to have it. I'm just glad we were
able to give you something back. There was precious little warmth in this
house for you. No wonder you ran away. And to think you might have
died out there in the cold.' She hesitated. 'I feel . . . I . . . was so unkind.
It's been on my mind ever since. But I was too proud to approach you . . .
until now.'

Betty looked across at her, taken aback once again by the directness of
her words. Then she shook her head vehemently.

'There was nothing to reproach yourself about. I've made a new life for
myself, as I say. You gave me a home and a position when I needed it. I
don't bear any grudge. It's just . . well, I have my own life now, and you
have yours. You and the lad. You're getting on fine without me, and that's
just grand. If I'd known you'd been fretting, I would have been down here

to sort you out.'

Alice smiled warmly across at her.

'You haven't changed, Betty! It does me good to hear you. You always did have wonderful commonsense. I could do with some of it! You know I really would like us to be friends now. The world is changing, isn't it? I never thought I'd say it, but I'm rather glad it is. Somehow, the war, and Charles going away, I don't find the same things so important.'

There was a knock and Connie came in the door with a laden tray.

'Did you remember the muffins, Connie? Ah, yes. How lovely! But you have forgotten the jam!'

Connie was unabashed.

'Sorry, Mrs Fergusson. We're that pushed on kitchen side.'

As soon as Connie had closed the door, Alice leaned forward, and took hold of Betty's hand again for a moment.

'My dear, as well as sorting out things between us, I asked you here to talk to you about something very important. As you can see my health is not good. That dreadful Nelson called for a specialist. He really is too senile to be of any use to anyone, but he refuses to retire. He has told me that I don't have long to live. He may be talking a lot of nonsense for all I know, but—' She held up her hand to stop Betty, who was about to protest. 'I know what you are going to say, but I really am so tired nowadays. Perhaps the doctors are right.'

She broke off. Betty noticed that her hand shook as she lifted the teapot, and a little tea spilt onto the tray cloth. She stopped herself from offering to help.

Alice began again, with some urgency in her voice. 'Now, I'm so afraid for Charles! At one time we thought he might just . . . that his heart might just . . . stop. It was what I always feared, as you know. It's so difficult. I need someone who understands. . . .'

She felt in her pocket and, taking out a letter, she handed it to Betty.

'Please, do read it out loud. I haven't my eyeglasses to hand. Then you'll see what I mean. It's brought back all my old fears to haunt me. I don't have anyone to confide in now.'

Betty slipped the letter out of its envelope and stared down at it. The sight of Charles's writing affected her strongly. They had not had any contact, since that day he had come home from the war. After what she had said, he must have realized how pointless it was. But there had been times, if she were honest, especially when things were bad, when she had caught herself wanting with all her heart to hear from him again.

'Dearest Mother,' she read aloud, in as normal a voice as she could manage. 'Just a short letter to let you know I have decided to come and see you for Easter after all. I do want to see you especially. I have some excellent news. I have had an invitation from my college to go overseas on an expedition. We will be away for some months, perhaps years, in Sikkim and possibly in the regions of the high Himalaya. Don't worry about it, though. I am so well these days you wouldn't believe. . . .'

She paused for a moment and looked up at Alice. Alice was looking at her intently. She felt her colour come up against her will. She stood up and went over to the mantelpiece, warming her hands before the fire.

'Please . . . do go on. . . .'

With an effort, Betty resumed her reading.

'In case you are worried – and I know you do worry – you may be reassured to know I have decided to take Dawson with me. He is the archivist I told you about. A thoroughly good chap. He is dying for a chance to go. I will look after him and he will look after me!

Please ask Ollie to meet us with the carriage at Penrith for the afternoon train on Friday.

Your loving son . . . Charles.'

There was a silence in the room as she finished reading. Friday was today! Betty was acutely aware of the ticking of the grandfather clock, the hissing of the wet wood on the fire. They would be arriving back at any minute. She mustn't see him. It would be too dreadful.

Alice spoke at last.

'I know it was rather wrong of me to ask you here like this, almost under false pretences. I do so want you to give me some moral support. You will see from the letter that Charles will be arriving this afternoon. Of course you must leave, if you feel it right. I had no wish to embarrass you, but I so wanted someone beside me to help me persuade him not to go. You were always so strong. I know you have his best interests at heart, although it has been rather hard at times for me to admit that. And more than anything else, he used to listen to you. I thought if we had a little talk first, then we could stand together, do you see. . . ?'

With difficulty, Betty swallowed down her anger. So this was what it had all been about! Just as she was beginning to trust Alice's overtures of friendship! She was to be used as a pawn to persuade her beloved son not to risk his precious neck. After all this time, she was still being used.

Alice stretched out her hand.

'Please! I can see you are angry. It really isn't what you think! I have been wanting for months to write to you. Then this letter came, and I thought I had to talk to someone who understood how afraid I am, who would support me. I have been so alone since Thomas died. Please try to understand.'

She sat for a moment, looking down at her hands in her lap. Suddenly all Betty's anger evaporated. It really wasn't time for hurt pride. She drew her chair up beside Alice and took her old, thin hand. Alice looked up at her.

'I can't tell you how nice it is to see you. You always were such a breath of fresh air in this awful house. It wasn't till after you left that I realized it. And Charles missed you so! I found that hard to accept at first. Later, I became wiser.'

Impetuously, she leaned across and kissed Betty on the cheek.

'You are such a good girl!' She exclaimed. 'I do admire you!'

Betty was dumbstruck. To be kissed by Alice, with every appearance of affection.

Alice sat up straight.

'Now then! We haven't much time. If you really *don't* want to see Charles, you shan't. He will be here within the hour, so let's just have our tea. I must tell you all the things I want to tell you. Then you must go on your way, if that is what you want. It was quite wrong of me to embarrass you. And there will be other times. I feel that we will be friends now, whatever happens. I hope I am right. I feel I treated you badly in the past, but I would like us to put all that behind us, if you will.'

There was a knock on the door and Connie came in. There was a little silence while she set the jam down among the muffins on the tray between them. She seemed to take an age. They waited while Connie clattered about, fussing over the tray, as she poured more tea for Alice. In reality, Betty was glad of the interruption. With Alice's kind words, and the affectionate kiss which had so taken her by surprise, tears had begun to sting her eyes.

When Connie had left them alone again, Betty leaned forward. For a moment they looked at each other.

'There's never been real bad feeling between us . . . Alice. If you had known it, we were really on the same side, caring about that lad of yours. You've no need to fret yourself about the past. You were kind to me. You gave me a home. I can't say I look back on my time at Bambeck Hall as entirely happy, but I do always think of you as meaning to be kind.'

She saw then that there were tears too in Alice's eyes.

'Look, you don't want to go listening to those doctors,' Betty went on, all of a rush. 'You'll get better soon. We'd all give up if we listened to them. Look at Charlie. . . .'

Alice shook her head.

'Somehow I know they're right about me, and for all I know they are right about Charles too. We will never know until it's too late. My poor boy!' She paused and wiped her eyes with a lace handkerchief.

'What do I do? Now he wants to go off on this wretched expedition. How can he think of such a thing? You see how ridiculous he is being. I shall have to speak to him.'

Betty shook her head.

'No you mustn't. You must let him lead his own life. He's got to make his own mistakes. You mustn't keep him in a cage. That will kill him as surely as anything. I know it's hard, but you have to let him go!'

Alice clutched at her hand.

'But he is all I have.'

'He'll love you the more for it. Believe me, Alice. Give him your blessing and let him go his own way. That way you'll never lose him.' She stood up. 'I really mustn't see him. I wouldn't know what to say.'

Alice kept hold of her hand.

'Sit down! Have some tea, please. They won't be here yet. You must tell me what I should do. I'm in such a quandary!'

Betty sat down reluctantly, her heart beating fast as she took a cup. If he were to come in and find her here, after everything. It was too awful to think of. But Alice was distressed. She would have to stay.

'Alice, listen! He only has one life, however long or short. He knows all the risks. Don't stop him living. He has to have the same chance, the same dreams, as other folk.'

Alice dabbed at her eyes again.

'I know it's foolish but I wish I had held on to him tighter. I fought so hard for him when he was little. If you only knew! And now, he could be throwing it all away, just like when he went away to the war. I know he got through by some miracle, even survived that awful wound. Why can't he just stay at home safely, and be grateful?'

Betty looked at her.

'You wouldn't have wanted him to stay as he was . . . a poor little thing wasting away in that bath chair. That was no kind of life.'

Alice nodded slowly.

'It's so hard. I want to gather him up and protect him and nurse him, the way I did when he was a child. But I have to stand back and watch. It's a dreadful thing to have to do.'

'He's a grown lad, Alice. You can't do anything but sit by. But wouldn't it be better to do it with a smile, however afraid you are? Why don't you suggest he goes to see the specialist? There's folk about that knows about these things, even if we don't. It's ignorance that makes us afraid. He'll be able to find out for himself, make up his own mind. But if I know that lad of yours, he'll not stop till he's done everything he's dreamed about. He'll find that blasted Blue Poppy of his, one day. He'll climb those great mountains. Nothing will stop him. You'll see! Remember, you can't keep a bird in a cage. Let him go free and he'll come flying back one day. He's got to spread his wings. It will make him stronger in the end.'

Alice was quiet for a moment, then she nodded slowly.

'You always did see things so clearly.'

Betty stood up and smiled down at her. 'It's hard. I don't have bairns, but if I did, I would feel the same if one of them was weakly. You always feel you want to go about with a feather bed held under them in case they fall down. . . .' She hesitated. 'It's hard for me too. In my own way, I'm that fond of Charlie. As though he were my own kin, I suppose, odd though it is. . . .'

Alice looked up at her.

'I felt it,' she said at last, with difficulty. 'It was something between you. It used to make me very jealous. I often think I drove you away because of it.'

Betty shook her head.

'Nay, you never drove me away. I made up me own mind. I had my own life. It was past the time for staying. And speaking of that, I must go. I don't want to see Charlie just now. Later maybe, but not just yet. Just send him my best.' She put her cup down on the table.

Alice put a restraining hand on her arm once again.

'When I said, I . . . I . . . felt there was something between you, there's something you should know. I have to tell you. It's praying on my mind. I should have written, but it was such a delicate subject. . . . please, let me finish.'

But before Alice could say any more, there was a sound of carriage wheels on the gravel outside.

CHAPTER 28

The same old carriage had been waiting for him, smelling of must and age, with mould spots on the cushions, even the same pair of aged greys who seemed to have been around forever. Alice had refused to countenance a car, considering such things dangerously newfangled. Although in some ways she had changed a lot, grown softer and more tolerant, in other ways, she was just as intransigent as ever.

At last the carriage swung ponderously into the drive. It looked a sad place, the walled garden dark with rain. Already, in the softer South, the spring flowers were well-advanced in the beds around his rooms in Cambridge. Still, Charles peered out at the gardens of Bambeck Hall with a sense of excitement. From here, he could just see his new glasshouses. Round the corner, in the lower garden, more beds had just been restored. It was part of his plan to feed the house, as they had once fed it before the war. He had ordered new plants for the terrace. At least his mother would have a blaze of colour to look out at on dull days.

The house came into view, and, perversely, considering how many unhappy memories it held for him, he felt a sudden rush of affection for it. There was a shiny new Riley outside, perhaps one of Alice's friends – more ready to move with the times. Connie was waiting at the door. As they passed through the black and white squared hall, she was taciturn. Once, she would have burst out with all sorts of gossip, but those days were over now. He was becoming a stranger.

The thought of Betty came into his mind. Betty, who in this very hall, had fallen and knocked herself out, while reciting *The Lady of Shalott*. His idea! He had kissed her when she was lying in her sickbed, and then she had run away. Then, because of his clumsy insensitivity on that evening up at High Greenrigg among the daffodils, he would probably never see her again.

'Excuse me, Mr Charles,' Connie burst out as they approached the drawing-room door. 'Your mother has a visitor.'

He remembered the car. As Connie opened the door, he saw his mother lying on the long sofa under the window. Since Christmas she had lost flesh, and her pale sandy hair was almost white. How long had she looked like that, and yet he hadn't noticed? A wave of guilt overcame him.

There was another woman there, standing in the shadows, very tall, brilliant hair shining out from the blackness of her dress. Alice turned towards the door.

'Charles! How lovely! You remember Betty!'

He must have looked a complete fool, standing there in the doorway, with his mouth hanging open. Behind him, he heard Connie's gasp of surprise, before she clattered off down the stairs to pass on this startling piece of news to the kitchen.

Charles took a deep breath and strode across the room, clasping Betty's unwilling hand in his. She was forced to look at him.

'Betty! How wonderful to see you. How are you?'

'I'm in good fettle, Charles, thank you.'

It was seven years since they had seen each other. In that time she had grown into a stunning, assured young woman, severely dressed, but with a certain spare elegance. She had such presence, but then, she always had. And, he thought ruefully, the same ability to unnerve him and throw him into a spin with that sharp blue gaze.

Alice, lying on the sofa, looked from one to the other. She leaned forward and spoke across the room.

'Charles! We've been talking about this wretched expedition of yours. I never did hear of such a thing!'

He bent down and kissed her cheek.

'Mother! I'm sorry. I know the idea must worry you. But I am so fit nowadays. I seem to have outgrown all those childhood troubles. And I really will take care. I give you my word.'

Alice thought then how well he looked – not her white-faced invalid boy any longer, but full of suppressed excitement, like a child let out on a treat. How changed he is, she thought, half-resentfully. How he patronises me, as though I am an old woman.

'Betty has been trying to convince me that I must let you go. She always was on your side! But I am not convinced!'

He glanced over at Betty, noting that patches of red had come up on her neck and throat, vivid against her white skin.

'Good old Betty! I knew I could rely on you!'

Betty gave him a withering look.

'You would do a sight better to concentrate on your work and stop worrying your mother when she's in bad fettle! I'm not here to defend you!' She turned and walked towards the door. 'If you will forgive me, Alice, I have an evening's work ahead of me!'

Charles was not to be put off. He moved quickly across the room placing himself in front of her, and smiled half-teasingly.

'You haven't changed, Betty.'

'I daresay, but I must be going.'

'Come on now, I haven't seen you for so long. Won't you stay . . . just for a little while, stay for dinner, even?'

'No, I've jobs to do of my own, Charles. You don't own me now.'

Alice was watching the exchange from the sofa.

'Betty! Please do stay. It's rare nowadays for me to have company. I could ask Connie to arrange something special. It would be such fun. Do say yes!'

Betty hesitated by the door.

'Thank you, Alice, you're very kind, but I have Mary, my assistant, to tell about the evening milking. It won't do itself, and she's always in a dream.'

Charles grabbed her hand again, refusing to let go. Rather than have an unseemly struggle, like a pair of quarrelling brats, Betty let it lie there. He looked at her.

'We have a telephone now. You could telephone High Greenrigg. I'm sure you have a telephone, Betty. Don't deny it. Mind you, here at Bambeck Hall, Mother makes us keep the wretched thing in the scullery! She doesn't trust any of these gadgets.'

The shadow of a smile passed across Betty's face. They were all so charming; it was seductive. The uncomfortable feelings she had been experiencing since Charles had walked through the door were beginning to subside. Perhaps she owed it to Alice. In any case, it would be nice, just for once, to put her feet up and be pampered, to stay for a while and listen to his plans. She couldn't deny she cared enough to know.

She stood against the door, still uncommitted. 'I have a milk round to consider. My customers won't wait for their milk in the morning. And the shop to provision. I have a shop now – Jackson's in Penrith. Perhaps you know it?'

She had seen Ollie in the shop several times buying butter, but she had stayed 'in back' and not made herself known to him. It was awkward, Betty reflected, how separate the world of 'trade' and the old upper classes still were, with people like her caught in the middle, neither fish now fowl.

'I have the orders to do. It's a busy shop now. . . .'

It wouldn't do for them to think she belonged to them. These upper classes, they picked you up and put you down like a plaything. No, she would never belong to anyone again.

Charles was looking at her in that uncomfortable way, as though he was reading her mind.

'Stay a little while, please.'

She hesitated. It was on the tip of her tongue to make a sharp comment about having to earn a living, unlike some folks. What would Alice know, after all, or even Charles, lecturing at that fancy college? But it would do no good to be unfriendly, She could afford to be a little gracious.

'Very well, thank you. I'd be glad to.'

She saw the expression in Charles's eyes, and turned away. 'Could you show me the telephone?'

'Of course! And while mother has her rest, we could walk around the gardens. Would you like that? You might have a few tips on growing flowers you could share with me. And I so much want to hear about your business.'

Was he laughing at her? She shot him a glance.

'I shall have to see how Mary is placed,' she said guardedly. 'But, yes, I would like to see the glasshouses and the garden, if you have time.'

Charles opened the door for her and almost fell over Connie, who had obviously been listening at the keyhole. She and Betty stared at one another for a moment.

'Well!' said Connie at last, quite unabashed. 'Aren't you the one?'

Betty extended her hand.

'How are you, Connie?'

'And why didn't you make yourself known?' Connie asked, seemingly without rancour. 'Too high and mighty, I suppose. Well, you've grown into a very smart young lady, very bonny indeed! I told them in the kitchen.'

They stood in an awkward little group by the open door, Betty wishing the ground could swallow her up. Connie too had grown into a bonny lass. Black curls framed a pale face, now alive with curiosity. She was not at all the sad, scruffy little creature Betty had once shared a bed with.

'Connie, I'm that sorry. It was rather difficult. I never thought I'd get so above myself to not say, "Hello".' What a traitor she had been! It was all her own fault for trying to be something she wasn't. Too concerned to hang onto her own dignity to give other folks the time of day!

'We've heard all the crack about you from Ollie,' said Connie. 'He says you have a fancy shop in Penrith now and a smart motor car, and a milk round and three horses to pull carts. Is that true?'

Betty nodded, embarrassed.

'We'll all be that glad you've done well for yourself. I'm to marry a farmer's son next back end, did you know?' Connie went on. 'You'll have to come down to the kitchen after and I can tell you all about him.'

'I'm that glad for you, Connie!' Betty said impetuously. 'Is Mrs Callerthwaite still here? She might give me an earwigging if I come down. She was never that fond of me.'

Connie giggled.

'Nay, that old Sour Face is long gone and good riddance, begging your pardon, Mrs Fergusson. Aye, she's gone, and I'm cook and chief house-maid and maid of all work, with only a tweenie to do the grates now!'

Alice tinkled her bell imperiously from her seat on the sofa. Connie raised her eyes.

'Some things never change, ay Betty? Nay, I'm right glad you've done so well for yourself. It does my heart good to see you. But don't go getting so high class you forgets your friends. Ollie and me and Nellie, we'll be having our tea soon. Just you come by if you can before dinner and we'll give you all the gossip.'

Betty felt tears sting her eyes, for something lost. She was acutely conscious of Charles looking at her, understanding. He took her arm with a gentle pressure, and guided her through the hall, out towards the back kitchen, where the telephone was kept.

'I shouldn't have come back,' Betty said at last, having telephoned Mary and left a list of instructions. Practical things always made her feel better, and she was quite composed now. They were walking in and out of the paths in the garden, looking at the early spring flowers.

'Don't say that! I can't tell you how glad we are to see you!' He pressed her arm impulsively.

'No' she shook her head. 'I will always be caught between these two worlds. I can't find a spot where I belong. I'm that ashamed I didn't say anything to Connie. She and I never got on, but I cared for her in my own way.'

'Don't always be so hard on yourself, Betty.'

She shook her head.

'No, I've sorted it in my own mind now, Charles. I'm telling you, it's been a sharp lesson for me, one I'll never forget!'

'Connie doesn't bear you any grudge.'

'Aye, and that's what makes me feel a gay sight worse about it. She didn't really expect me to say, "Hello"! I'm supposed to be a fine lady now with all the airs and graces, just because I've made a pile of brass. Too good for the likes of Connie and all my friends.'

Charles stopped on the path and turned her to face him.

'Betty, you know as well as I do, it's a difficult world nowadays. Everything is changing, and thank goodness for that. We don't want to go back to the old ways. You and I, in our own way, we are both breaking out. Fifty years ago, I would have been running the Bambeck estate, (if I were still alive) and breeding little fourth generation aristocrats. Though, perhaps not, come to think of it, with this condition of mine. Mother doesn't think I should ever marry, in case I have a heart attack on my wedding night! And Ashington, the specialist, has an idea about this illness being inherited! That's the fashionable theory at the moment. And you've taken your own path. That will never be easy, whatever generation we live in.'

Betty bent down and examined one of the daffodils which were strug-gling to stay upright in the sharp evening wind.

'I want to know how you are nowadays, lad. You look a sight better than the sickly creature who tipped himself out of his bath chair on that rainy day. Though I'm sure you're as stubborn as you ever were!'

Charles laughed.

'I'll tell you everything, and you can tell me about what you have been up to! Come on now. I want to show you my garden.'

She had admired his glasshouses and the newly restored peach house. She had a mind to put in some glasshouses of her own one day, for her flower business. She told herself this was all useful to her; time well spent. Charles told her about his plans to create a blue and white garden, and to build a rock garden in the manner of Reginald Farrar, even to create a wild garden for native species. She wasn't so impressed to hear he would be cultivating weeds. Fancy and impractical, she called it. But then he always had his head in the clouds. Then they climbed the terraces to the top of the garden, where they could look out across to the blue Scottish hills beyond the Solway. The wind had quite died away. Betty sat down on a boulder and looked over to the east, where the Pennines were now almost invisible in the dusk. Charles squatted down on the grass beside her. She could hear him breathing hard.

'Are we friends now, Betty?' He said at last, when he had caught his breath.

'Ay, lad, we are.'

'I'm sorry about what happened that night, up at the farm, but I haven't forgotten and I often reproach myself for it.'

'Ay, well. I was grieving then.'

He walked a few yards up the path, and then came back down again to stand beside her, restless and nervous.

'Could you care for me, Betty?'

'Ay I do, lad. You know that well enough.'

'No, I don't mean. . . . You know how I feel. I haven't changed. I still remember that day . . . up here, on this very fell. I will never forget it.'

She shifted uncomfortably on the hard stone.

'You do feel something for me, Betty, don't you?' He persisted. 'We were part of each other that day. No one can ever take that from us.'

He sat down behind her, looking over towards the darkening hills.

'Aye, I can't deny that, but it doesn't make any difference. No differ-ence at all. You've got your own life to lead, that Blue Poppy out there still to find. I've a practical turn of mind. I like to get things done and to make some money at it. You're a dreamer and good luck to you. If there were no folks like you about the spot, we'd never have new flowers in our gardens.'

He smiled down at her.

'You always did have a comical way of putting things, Betty.'

She shook her head. 'No, I mean it. Some folk, I reckon are there to explore and dream and make new things, and other folk are there to make new out of what they've got. I'll always be up to my armpits in suds or something practical. I don't have dreams the way you do. I'd just be a tie to you, and you'd be a tie to me.'

They were quiet for a few minutes. A thin wind had sprung up, blow-ing across from the Pennines, sharp with a scent of late snow. New Herdwick lambs, in the fields below, blared for their mothers, seeking their flanks before the dark came down. Something infinitely sad touched her for a brief moment. Then she shook herself free.

'Do you remember the day you helped me climb the stairs, and I asked you to marry me?'

'Ay, but that were a long time ago.'

'Well, would you consider it still, after all this time?'

She stood up and dusted the dried moss from her skirt.

'And what about all those fashionable theories about your heart. Heredity, and all that?'

He came back to her and took her hand.

'Oh, Betty! You were the one who taught me not to take any notice of doctors! And even the doctors say that as long as I don't marry a close relative, there really isn't any chance at all of passing it on. No one even knows if it is really a congenital condition. No one in my family as far as I know has ever had it. This narrowing of the heart valve is quite rare, I believe.'

'You can't tell what folks have died from in the past, lad.'

'It's all about heredity, Betty. Just like those old stud books of father's, and the genes in plants. . . .Mendel's work, that sort of thing. You see it in plants all the time. It's a fascinating branch of science.'

'Ay, very fascinating, I'm sure, playing around with other folks' lives. We're not illustrations in some blasted plant book, Charlie. We're flesh and blood and bone. I'd sooner make my own fate!'

'But why?'

She could hardly bear the pain in his voice. Turning away, she started to walk away between the bare beds. He pursued her. 'I know you care for me! We've always been meant for each other, right from the beginning. You know it too!'

She walked on, as fast as she could in her cumbersome skirt.

'Nay, we're too close, Charles. I can't explain it to you. There are some things you're best not knowing. They aren't even my secrets to tell. Nay, don't ask me. But even if those things weren't there, getting in the way, I don't want to depend on any other folk, not ever again. I've got my plans now and a bit of freedom. I don't want anything else.'

She picked up her long skirts and started to walk faster.

'Here I am, clarting about when I should be seeing to the milking, and in me best black too. I always did get into a scrow when I was with you. I'll not stay for dinner, if you torment me one more time!'

He stopped in his tracks. She was forced to turn and face him. His face was very white. The sight of him distressed and irritated her even more.

'And you can stop looking like a banty hen that has lost her bairns. Get yourself off on that expedition, and stop worrying about me. I've fine plans of my own.'

He reached out a hand.

'And I can manage very well myself, thank you! While we're on the subject, you're going to have to work yourself to get up those mountains. I heard you breathing like a dying cat when you were walking up the terraces. It's not so long before you go. You'll have some gay hard work to do getting yourself in good order. You've spent too long at your books.'

She wished she had never come, opening up old wounds. They hurt as though they had never begun to heal, the pain as bad as ever.

She had gone down by herself to the kitchen to see Connie again, and had sat, trying to get her composure back, catching up on all the news, just as though she had never been away. Ollie was a white-haired old man now, and rather grumpy with her, not liking change in any form, but Nellie, hugely fat and breathless, had given her a great hug as though she was a lass again. She had felt quite at home, at last. . . .

CHAPTER 29

In the dining-room, it had all been different. Connie in a starched apron, behaving distantly, as she served up the food; not betraying by word or gesture that they had just been laughing fit to split together in the kitchen. Betty had to concentrate hard on the shining forks and spoons and getting the right knife for the fish, even though she had good silver of her own at her table on occasions, and she had been to some fine dinners as the Secretary of the Chamber of Commerce in the town. She had nothing to be ashamed of. So why was it, in the stiff atmosphere of the dining-room, with the ticking grandfather clock, the stiff, silk flowers in the tall stand, the life seemed to have ebbed out of them all, and they all become like cut-out pictures in one of those cardboard penny theatres?

Despite that, in the smoky buttery light of the oil lamp, that treacherous softness had stolen over her again. She toyed with her food, watching his foolish white face, the way he tossed back his black hair when he talked. He was her lad, both ways, kin and heart, whatever she told herself. But she would never have him.

He had begun to grow away already. This summer he was going back to the Alps, to get strong, he said to her, laughing at her fierceness now, no longer with that hurt expression she had seen in the garden. She should have been glad. And yes, he would go and see Ashington (this in response to Alice's entreaty), but they didn't understand, he was so well nowadays, hardly ever out of breath. It was the chance of a lifetime. He was looking forward to it.

How she loved his enthusiasm, his brave, idiotic dreams. She would give everything she had to protect him.

Alice seemed preoccupied. Once, when Charles had left the room for a few moments, she drew Betty down beside her, seeming to want to say something. Then he had come back, laughing, laden down with books to show them both all about the region he would be visiting on his expedition. The moment passed. When Betty left, Alice had kissed her affectionately, and pressed her arm, making her promise to come back and see her soon.

Charles helped her into her car. In the darkness, he had kissed her very gently on the cheek, holding her hand. This time she had not stopped him. They were old, old friends, after all, though at his touch she had felt her bones turn to jelly, like some dreadful Victorian heroine out of the penny papers. And there was no denying some deep tenderness and understanding between them in that moment.

Getting a firm grip on her feelings, she had wished him luck heartily and told him to write, but no, not to try and see her again. She would be busy with her own life, after all.

Later, driving home in the spring darkness, the headlights picking out the first primroses and cowslips on the banks, it was harder to think that they had said goodbye.

She got out of the little car outside the farm, and stood for a moment, alone in the dusk. Now, in May time, it hardly grew dark at night, though it had been such a bitter cold winter there was hardly a leaf as yet on the trees. It was a harsh country. She stood, gathering her strength for half a night's work, getting orders ready for the morning and then an early start to help Mary with the milking. The sad, bubbling call of a curlew fell through the dusky night, the bird swooped from the fellside above her, seeking its nest on the bare ground.

Charles and Alice sat for a while by the dying fire, Alice with her habitual glass of whisky. It was a companionable silence, both of them thinking about the events of the day.

'I don't know why you don't get married and settle down, Charles,' Alice said at last.

'Don't start that again, Mother. We've been through it all before.'

'If only you would get rid of these silly ideas of yours, and just find a nice wife . . . come back to Bambeck. It would be so lovely. You don't really need to be so restless all the time, pursuing these idiotic dreams of yours.'

'If I did marry, there is only one woman I would want. . . .' He gazed into the fire. 'And she has made it clear that she doesn't want me. And no one else will do.'

Alice sat up and put her glass down with a bang.

'Betty?'

'Of course, Mother. Who else would it be?'

'But that's impossible! You must know that!'

'Why on earth should it be? I love her, after all. I have done for years. Surely you knew. But she's too busy with her own life for me. She has made that very clear.'

'But marriage would be quite out of the question.'

'But mother. . . .' he was laughing at her now. 'You are quite impossible. Without wishing to be indelicate, or to offend your sensibilities, I do have enough experience to assure you that I will not have a heart attack on my wedding night! And even if my heart condition might be inherited, any children I might have would be absolutely all right, as long as I don't marry a close relative. Let's face it, mother, you're a frightful snob, and it does you no justice!'

'No!' Alice said vehemently, as she got to her feet with difficulty. 'You have to understand. You have to see. I tried to tell Betty this afternoon. Somehow there just wasn't a right moment. It is such a difficult matter. But you must read this letter, Charles. You will see there could never be any chance of marrying Betty, ever. Go, on read it! I found it when I was clearing out the papers in the library last week. It wasn't until I had made a few enquiries, discreetly of course, that I finally found out the truth.'

She pulled an envelope from the desk drawer and brought it over to him, dropping it on his lap. Mystified, he turned it over and over, seeing that it was addressed on the outside, in a fine copperplate, to Hannah Bowman of Stainton, a name which seemed half-familiar. He pulled a piece of paper out of the envelope, saw the crest at the head of the page, and turning it over, read the signature.

'This is from Grandmother!'

'Yes.'

'But who is Hannah Bowman? That name rings a bell.'

'Betty's grandmother.' Alice stood beside him, looking down, holding on to the back of the chair for support.

'But that's ridiculous. They didn't even know each other.'

'I think you may find that you are wrong.' Alice's voice was tight, controlled. 'There most certainly was a previous connection, if that letter is to be believed. I have made some enquiries, though it was all so hushed up it hasn't been easy. The letter should be believed, shocking though it may be. Read it!'

He smoothed the paper out on his lap, squinting over the faded writing. A letter from his grandmother, Maud Fergusson of Bambeck Hall, written in some distress, sending money for Hannah Bowman's child.

CHAPTER 30

In the last few weeks, the hall had filled up with boxes, tea chests, leather holdalls, all the essentials of an expedition. Now they had been sent ahead to Victoria Station, and it was time to say goodbye.

Charles walked for the last time through the walled garden. The stone steps were slippery after overnight rain. He remembered how once he had climbed those steps, secretly, day after day, to make himself strong, believing that one day, he could climb to the top of his own mountain, right to the top. Looking back it seemed foolish, stubborn even. Yet he was glad he had listened to that voice within him, and to Betty's voice spurring him on. Those dreams were still with him. He had never let them go.

Strangely, Betty was still with him too, all the time, in his head, urging him on. He had been twice to High Greenrigg to say goodbye, but Mary, now Betty's farm manager, had told him that Betty was in London, over-seeing a new shop. She wasn't expected back for some months. It seemed she had forgotten him. Perhaps it was as well. After the revelation of the letter, he had been in a turmoil. They were cousins. Everything was different. How could he ever face her, knowing that a member of his own family – her family too by that twist of fate – had committed such a dreadful crime. Charles was a gentle man, even a little unworldly, and the revelation of what his grandfather had done to Hannah Bowman had shocked him profoundly.

He wandered down the terraces, noting the summer flowers making a blaze of colour against a sharp blue sky, and the two new gardeners busy in the glasshouses. The estate was becoming more profitable since Charles's innovations. Some of Alice's friends were rather inclined to sneer at a country estate setting itself up as a business venture, selling vegetables and flowers to people like some common shopkeeper. But he

179

had never had much time for such stuffiness, and Alice, whatever her
views, seemed happy for him to have his way. He had reflected, ruefully,
that with the expense of an expedition, he was going to need a steady
income from somewhere, to supplement the miserable salary from his
Cambridge Fellowship.

Then, from another direction, had come more encouraging news. He
had been asked to undertake some plant hunting for Bees, the seed firm.
If he was successful in his first expedition, this too might be a source of
income in the future. The great gardens of the North were crying out
for new plants, particularly from the Sino-Himalaya. There was a huge
demand waiting to be fulfilled, and the seed companies were prepared
to pay well for new specimens that could be grown in British gardens.

Alice was in her own little garden in a corner of the bottom terrace,
planting out a rockery. He squatted down beside her and took her hand,
gently removing the gardening glove.

'Mother, it's time I was leaving.'

She straightened up and smiled up at him.

'I shall think of you everyday, Charles. Just come back safely to us all.
That is all I ask.'

He saw tears in her eyes, and was mortified by his selfishness. It was
costing her so much that he was going away.

'I did keep my promise. I went to see Ashington. He's just about to
retire. He must be eighty and he's as pompous as ever! He told me that I
was as fit as a flea, and that the exercise would be good for my heart. I'm
quite better. I really am!'

It was a lie, and they both knew it. Although Ashington had not actually been able to find anything wrong with Charles, he had given him a
dressing down and told him he was a fool.

'Betty has written to me,' Alice said, bending down and making a hole
in the earth with her fork. 'She is doing so well. She is setting up a London
shop now, in Covent Garden.'

There was a little pause. Alice carefully removed a gentian from its pot
and placed it in the hole.

'There! That will be a picture! You know, Charles, I really am enjoying
working on this little bit of garden. That was Betty's idea. She came to see
me a few weeks back, when you were away in Cambridge. I didn't say
anything about the letter, as we agreed. I'm leaving that for my solicitors
to do when I die. At least she will have the chance to know the truth some
time in the future. I think we have to do that for her at least, don't you?'

He bowed his head.

'To think we are both related to that monster! I'm ashamed.' He bent down, picking up a handful of soil from the newly-dug plot beside him, and crushing it in his hands.

'I keep going back to something Betty said to me, that day she came to dinner, when we went for a walk in the garden. Do you know, I have this strange feeling she may know already about grandfather . . . may even have known for a long time. She is such a proud woman, it's hard to tell. Whatever the truth, we have to make it up to her somehow. I owe her so much.'

Alice nodded.

'I have arranged that Arnisons should look after the letter, and some other documents I found. If anything should happen to me, the letter will pass to Betty. And that little cottage on the estate, where she was born, is to be given to her in my will. I hear from Ollie that she has a new house being built on the hillside outside Bambeck, with the electricity and an acre of heated glasshouses! And she has that shop now in Penrith selling dairy produce. Very successful, I believe, with a stable of horses for her milk rounds and a fleet of vans. Now she will have this shop in London. What a girl! I don't suppose we can offer her much she hasn't got by her own efforts. But it might mean something to her to have her mother's cottage. It was the least I could do.'

Alice bent down again and dug her fork in the earth.

'I don't know. Thank goodness Betty has only inherited your grandfather's determination, and his hair, of course! Not his incontinent nature. Your grandmother, now, she was quite hopeless. All she could ever think about were those blessed mountains of hers, and of going back out East. She was such a dreamer. You really do take after her. She always used to say you were born with mountains in your eyes. It used to irritate me. But she would have been so pleased with you, Charles.'

'We were very close, and I still miss her.' He shook his head. 'Poor grandmamma! What a life she must have had. So little happiness. But at least I am going back, as she wanted me to. We will even be staying in the dak bungalow she left me. It's maintained by the British Raj, so I understand, for their political staff, but travellers can stay in it. Actually we do still own it, though they rent it through our estates. I'm surprised it's still standing. But I shall think of dear grandmamma when I am there. I hope she will be proud of me. Maybe I will even fulfil my ambition and find her Blue Poppy!'

He hesitated. 'You know, I feel if I could do that, find that Blue Poppy of hers, not only will she rest in peace at last, but somehow, I will feel more at peace. Above all, I will have proved something to myself that is rather important. Terribly fanciful, I'm afraid.'

Alice shook her head, half-smiling.

'I don't know, head in the clouds, just like your grandmother. Oh, she was right about you! Go on now, before I cry! Ollie's waiting. Find your Blue Poppy, if you can. Make a success of it all. Just come back home to us, safely.'

She began to dig another hole fiercely with her fork. 'Go now,' she said, smiling up at him. 'And hurry up or you'll miss your train.'

As they got to the bottom of the hill, he turned back and saw Bambeck Hall outlined against the trees. On this early summer morning, rooks were flying up in the great elms. It was a really beautiful place in the sunshine. He was mad to be going away. If he came back in one piece, he would never go away again. . . .

CHAPTER 31

It was a long journey up to the North in the hot season. Charles was plagued by a stomach bug he had picked up in Calcutta, and Thompson, the expedition leader, was weak from an attack of malaria. As they finally arrived high in the foothills on the little hill railway, he breathed the cool, dust-free air with relief.

Charles's family bungalow provided them with a few days to rest up while the sirdar organised the mule train. There was a strange familiarity about the lawns, the verandah, that view over the forest, like some distant memory. He supposed that, in a way, through his grandmother's stories, he had known it all his life.

The world of the European bungalow in the foothills was oddly reminiscent of an English country house. Roses bloomed extravagantly, while white-coated servants flitted obsequiously in and out of the shaded rooms. Yet in some ways it was still utterly different; spicy food, the scent of incense burning before the statue of Shiva, marigold petals strewn on the veranda in the morning. Strange and yet comfortingly like a memory of something he had once known, to be woken by the sounds of chanting at dawn, and the liquid note of the bulbul bird running like water through the landscape. But he looked in vain for that one magic element in the garden, the Blue Poppy, which he had seen in that old photograph of his grandmother's. He knew that plants of some blue *Meconopsis* were reputed to grow to a great age, but, however hard he looked, he could not find a single rosette.

There above him in the early morning, before the dust and heat hid them in haze, were occasional glimpses of the Himalayas. It was as though they had been there all his life, on the horizon, beckoning him on, but it was frustrating, tantalizing to have no more than a glimmer of a distant peak, before the clouds covered them once more.

On the second night, Thompson roused himself from his sick bed enough to play a game of croquet on the lawn with Charles and Dawson. They had sat out on the verandah watching the moon come up over the forest, listening to the night owls. Eventually the others went to bed, but Charles sat out a little longer.

It was very quiet. He looked out over the trees, their tops silvered in the moonlight, thinking about Betty. He missed her so much.

He became aware that Kadji, one of the 'boys', was standing silently by his side, holding out a small wicker box.

'What is it, Kadji?'

'Mr Charles, a man comes to the gate, sir. He gives me this. He says he worked for your father. In this place, many years ago.'

Charles got to his feet, peering into the darkness beyond the compound.

'No. I'm sorry, Kadji. There must be some mistake.'

Kadji stood looking at him.

'Yes, sir. The man says, Colonel Fergusson was here, with his lady. Very beautiful. Long time ago. He is very old. But I said to him, Mr Charles is not very old. It cannot be his son.'

Charles started down the veranda steps.

'Where is this man, Kadji? I will speak to him.'

Kadji looked agitated, and ran down ahead of him.

'Please sir, man is gone. Very old. Would not talk. Please take box. I promised.'

Suddenly standing there in the velvety dark, Charles had a vivid vision of the old photograph his grandmother had shown him all those years ago, and which had inspired so many of his dreams. That faded sepia likeness, with his grandfather and grandmother standing on a green, hand-tinted lawn, that enigmatic third figure smiling beside them.

'It wasn't my father, Kadji! It would have been my grandfather. My father's first name was Charles too, but everyone knew him as Thomas. He was born out here, but I am *his* son, Colonel Fergusson's grandson.'

Kadji shook his head stubbornly.

'Old man says the box must come to Mr Charles. Yes, sir. Everybody in village knows you are Mr Charles. He says, beautiful Mrs Fergusson had a son. Very much happiness in house. He calls him Charles. The old man says, you are son. He promises beautiful Mrs Fergusson he will keep box for son.'

'No, no, my father, the other Mr Charles, Charles Thomas Fergusson, died in the War. He never came out East. I know my grandmother would have liked him to, but he was never interested. I suppose she started working on me instead, and here I am!'

Kadji smiled and nodded his head, not understanding. He held the box out pleadingly to Charles, and he took it. He wondered what could possibly be so special about any family treasure that his grandmother had wanted to leave it here. He looked out over the darkened garden. So many memories must have been left behind in this place.

'Thank you, Kadji. Are you sure the old man is not waiting? I would like to speak with him.'

'Old man has gone now. It was his father who served your father. Mrs Fergusson was very fine lady with big soul. Everyone loves her. This man does not forget. She asks him as sacred duty to take care of box until she returned. Maybe she will come back. She was very sad lady when she went. Cry, cry. If she doesn't come back, we must give box to her son, Charles when he comes. She will make him love the East, so he will come back. These things have been a burden on his soul, and on his father's soul. But now you have come, his father's spirit can rest.'

As quickly as he had come, Kadji faded into the shadows. Charles was left wondering, had there ever been a man at the gate? Kadji had spoken with such passion. He would probably never know. . . .

He looked again at the small wicker box. The old man, Kadji's own father, perhaps, must have kept that box for years in his hut in the hills, waiting for Mrs Fergusson to return . . . or her son. Squinting in the soft light of the paraffin lamp, he examined the lock. It was almost rusted through, green with damp and age. A twist would do it. They had been so close, he and his grandmother. Her stories of mysterious Tibet and the diplomat who had come down from the 'Roof of the World' to stay with them in this very bungalow, had fired his imagination from the beginning. It was because of her, and Betty, that he was here at all.

Was anything in life really random? For a moment, standing in the dark garden, a great precipice seemed to open up in his view of the world. The Eastern mind, with its mysterious ways, would have understood such things perfectly. He had a lot to learn.

He turned up the lamp so that it flared and hissed in the darkness, casting shadows along the verandah. Standing the box on the table, he twisted the lock, gently. It came away in his hand. Slowly, his heart beating fast, he prised the box open.

Inside was a small, leatherbound book. Beside it, a coral and turquoise amulet, beautifully wrought in silver. He lifted it gently. The beautiful thing shone and winked at him in the glow of the lamp. A letter lay underneath. He squinted at the writing. Even though he had been expecting it, seeing his name, 'To my son, Charles' on the front of the letter, gave him a strange thrill. Some extraordinary emotion ran through him like an electric shock. It was as though everything had come together in this moment, and was waiting to be revealed to him here. He started to read.

My dearest Charles,
If you have kept faith with the spirit of the great mountains, you will come back one day. And it is against this day that I have kept this diary. When you have read all that I have written, you may understand. I have just now learned that we must return to England, and that I may never see my beloved again. There is nothing for me any more. My life will be over. I can take nothing away but my memories, and you, my baby son. Please, read so that you will understand. I will try to implant in you a dream of the East. If you return, it will be because you have already understood. I leave this box for you. This diary, and this amulet, which your true father gave to me, and which is the match of his own, I have placed in this box. One day you will wear it in his memory.
    You will read in this diary how all these things came to be so. Please forgive me, and draw strength from your understanding.
                          Your loving mother,
                          Maud Fergusson

He sat for a long time on the verandah, the letter in his hand, listening to the sounds of the night. If his father had made this journey, would it have changed him? Would he still be alive somewhere, instead of lying in a military cemetery on the battlefields of France? Instead, somehow, his son had been mysteriously led here in his place, by his dreams of the Blue Poppy and of those mountains which now lay beyond the horizon, beckoning him on.
    At last, hesitantly, he opened the leatherbound book which lay on the table. He caught his breath. There on the first page, perfectly pressed, was a specimen of a blue *Meconopsis*, echoing his thoughts. Even in the dim light, he could see that it was the same, vivid, heart-stopping colour as that Blue Poppy he had stumbled across in the Library at Cambridge. Underneath, a few words had been scrawled, as though in great haste.

The servants come for us. All our luggage has gone. I have taken one flower of his Blue Poppy, to keep safe for ever. His gift still blooms in the garden, but I cannot bear to remove the flower buds as he has instructed me to do. This is the first year. My Blue Poppy will bloom for this season, alone in this garden full of memories, and then it will be lost to the world. It will never bloom again, but just now I cannot bear to destroy something so beautiful. It is all I have left. This garden will return to the jungle again, and all will be lost. My heart is empty.

Charles knew that, for most of the Blue Poppies, if the flower buds were not removed in the first season to prevent the plant from setting seed, it would never make a rosette – that coronet of leaves from which the plant would make growth year after year. It would not bloom again, and would be lost for ever. He would look in vain for it in the garden. Yet who was this mysterious person who had given his grandmother the Blue Poppy. Why was it so precious to her that she could not bear to destroy it?

Hours later, he was still reading the leatherbound book by the dim light of the paraffin lamp, poring over the faint copperplate writing.

Kensin Lo has taught me many things, but I cannot accept and love my husband again. At first when I learned that he had betrayed me with a servant girl, I was so angry. That it should have been poor innocent Hannah, whose family were good Quakers, was doubly terrible. The poor child was in my care. Her baby has been christened Violet. Matthew Bowman had taken Hannah to wife, out of pity for her condition. I could not share a bed with a man who had done such a thing. I tried to send money for the child but Matthew would have none of it.

It seemed that no good could ever come of such a tragedy. But Kensin Lo has taught me the way of the Buddha, and I have learned some acceptance. He has great powers of wisdom, and the power to love and transform others. Since he came to stay with us, so much of my hidden spirit has been revealed. I have found a deep and lasting joy in life.

I am with child, and there is an even greater joy in me. My husband forced himself again upon me during this time, but I know this is not his child. I would cry 'Rape!' but who would heed my call?

There is no such thing between a husband and wife.

I wait for Kensin Lo to return. He predicted that we would have a child together. He wishes to take me back with him. I must live a lie with this creature who tries to come to my bed. I wait. But where is Kensin Lo? I look over the mountains where he is now, and I remember his promise, but he does not come.

The child is born, with much difficulty, and it is a boy. I have named him Charles Thomas, and I am saddened only that he does not bear the mark of his true father, hardly resembling him at all, except in his eyes and his dark hair. Yet these are impractical sentiments. If things go badly, and Kensin Lo does not return, it is better that the child favours me. He is the flower of a great love, and, despite all, I am filled with joy.

Kensin Lo has not returned. It is time for us to leave. I am helpless. Day after day I think I will speak but I do not. The creature thinks the child will be his own. I would not tell him otherwise, although he so revolts me. The child must grow up in England. I would not have it suffer. It is fitting that I must bear the burden instead, deprived for ever of my love. There will be no other children. I wake every morning after a night of crying, and raise my eyes to the mountains 'whence cometh my help.' But it does not come. I know he loves me as I love him. If he has not come, some terrible thing must have befallen him. That is worse for me than death . . .

I play the wife. This week before our departure, we have visitors from the political service, up from the plains, to pay their respects before we leave. I do my part. The child cries a great deal. I would have given him the breast myself but it is not considered fitting. He has a nurse from the village, Kadji's wife. She sees my grief but only smiles and says nothing. I am in a prison and cannot speak.

I must go back to England and all will be lost. Perhaps my baby, when he grows, will come back. I must try, if I can, to give him such a love of the East, and the great mountains, that he will return. I will leave this box with Kadji's family for safekeeping. Perhaps one day my little son may learn the truth. It is all I can do. It may not be too late for him to find his rightful father. . . .

It was nearly dawn before he finished reading. Laying down the book in its box, he walked out softly onto the verandah, and looked out over the lawn. The sun had not yet risen, and the grass was drenched in grey dew.

Sweet peas, twisting up the verandah support, gave out a faint scent. A mynah bird was tapping on the mosquito mesh at the window. As Charles came out in his bare feet, it stopped for a moment, regarded him with its head on one side, then resumed its probing for trapped insects in the wire.

Charles took a deep breath. He felt as though he had, in that night, lived through a hundred years of grief. Strangely, it was not the revelations about his own ancestry which, at that moment, so affected him. The helpless sadness which so drenched the end of the diary, those last words scrawled before departure, these were the things which moved him most. It was as though the tears, which smudged the copperplate, were still fresh and new on the page. No wonder at the end of her life, his grandmother had seemed so sad, wandering a little in her wits, only seeming to come alive when she talked about the East.

He thought of his father, stiff and awkward, a military man down to his shining boots, a perfect English gentleman. He had never shown the slightest interest in the East, nor in the high places, which had drawn Charles like a magnet from his earliest years, so colouring his dreams. He and his father had had nothing in common. In everything his father had been the English squire, quiet and kind, considerate of his tenants, a proper gentleman (not like his grandfather) but always remote. Only in the darkness of his colouring and a faintly Oriental look, did he betray his ancestry at all. These things would have only become significant to anyone who knew the secret of his parenthood. But for Maud, it must have only been with the birth of her beloved grandchild, this dreamy Tibetan child with mountains in his eyes, that she could be sure that Kensin Lo had left her something of himself. It was Charles, not his father, who was the living embodiment of his true grandfather. He was here, today, because of Kensin Lo. He had inherited the spirit of the mountains. Strangely, the letter, skipping one generation, had, in some mysterious way, really been meant for him.

The sun was coming up above the trees. He slipped the amulet around his neck, and putting on his shoes, crossed the dewy lawn, to the rough, steep track beside the house. As he did so, the bulbul bird began its soft liquid song somewhere in the undergrowth, heralding the day. He climbed and climbed, until he stood on a promontory, looking back over the valley. The world below was filled with mist, like a great river, and there, above, flushed to rose and gold with the morning sun, were the Himalayas, revealed to him in all their glory for the first time, as they reached, snow-covered to the infinite sky; those impossible shining mountains which had called to him since before his birth. The silver amulet, catching the first rays of the sun, glowed with a rosy, crystal light, as though it too had been released from darkness.

CHAPTER 32

Coming through the door of her brand new fellside house, she saw the unfamiliar letter lying on top of the pile. Despite herself, she felt that familiar lurch in her stomach. She had filled up her life so full that there was hardly a crack for any feelings to squeeze through. Her business was very successful. She had seen how popular those first daffodils had been, and how the lure of fresh spring flowers had encouraged customers. First they came to patronise her milk round in the town and, later, to visit the shop. It had seemed sensible to open a shop in London, where she had access to the very first spring flowers from the Cornish coast, rushed up in protective boxes on the overnight train. And alongside the flowers, she was selling the freshest Cumberland butter and the cheeses, which she and Mary Haskett, now her business partner, had made together.

She had coined a slogan for her chain of shops – *Flower Fresh*. The painting of a wild daffodil, by an artist from Cumberland, decorated her labels. The idea of farm fresh produce had proved very successful among the newly affluent city dwellers, nostalgic for country life. Her shop in Covent Garden sold all her dairy products – curds, little pots of Cumberland Rum Butter in stone jars, and earthenware dishes of fresh farm butter. Some of the dairy products were from her own farm at High Greenrigg, and some were produced by women outworkers from the outlying farms. She made sure that all her outworkers were given a percentage of the sale price, not the usual miserable pittance. With her usual hard-headed business sense mixed with reforming zeal, she saw that they worked better for having a share in the business from the beginning.

The flowers were a lure, and once in the shop, the feel of the place caused a sensation among customers. Reminiscent of a dairy, with its cool, slabbed floors and earthenware jars placed on the wooden shelves, it had become very popular. So much so that there were sometimes queues stretching out into the cobbled square.

She found she was spending less and less time up in Cumberland, staying part of the week in her new rooms in London. But it was still good to come home, to get off the train after the smoke of the city, to the flower-filled station with the familiar station master greeting her as an old friend, and a blackbird singing in the evening. That was really when she felt she was home at last, and could put her feet up after a long week, before the telephone started ringing again!

Where was he? Could something terrible have happened to him. She didn't think that could be possible. Surely something inside her would have known. But why hadn't she heard anything for so long? Now, at last, there was a letter, lying on the hall table, beside a bowl of late purple lilacs, mocking her.

Absentmindedly, she made herself a cup of tea and cut a slice of cake, putting off the moment when she would open the letter. She had a meeting in the town that evening. The District Council was to make a decision on her plans to develop a bakery in an outlying village. It would mean more employment for the women who were stuck out in those outlying farms, with no life of their own.

Suddenly, she could bear it no longer and, setting down her tray, she reached for the letter. It was a year since she had heard from him. She had been down to see Alice twice, now that she had moved into the Dower House. Alice had showed Betty the new garden. The sight of Charles's flowers, just now coming into their full glory, had affected her powerfully. Neither of them had heard a word for so long, only a brief letter posted in Bombay, more than a year since. He had written to say that the long voyage was over, and they were setting off into the interior. Now, here was news of him at last.

My Dear Betty,

I have by some miracle received two letters from mother at once, brought by runners from the valley, before the rains made everything impassible.

I am writing this without much hope of its getting through. We have had a late monsoon on these slopes and the trail is quite washed away lower down. I am sitting in my tent, very late at night now, rather cold and wet, after a beastly day, thinking of you. Perhaps that does not sound too flattering, but thinking of you is actually very comforting. We have had a very frustrating time up here. Rain on the lower slopes, then as we came higher up, heavy snow, which at this time of the year is a disaster. How does one identify a bush rhododendron when it is covered in snow and looks like all the others? Thompson has been rather depressed. Only Dawson keeps our spirits up.

Anyway, I can't sleep. Water is dripping down my neck. For the thousandth time on this trip, I resolve to inspect the tent inch by inch in the morning to find out where the weak spot is, but then I forget. I will paint the scene for you! Above me are wooden racks where our specimens are drying and seeds hanging in little canvas bags. We have a very clever arrangement with a small paraffin stove, not to keep us warm, but for our precious plants! The whole thing is rather reminiscent of a wet washing day in England. The air is drenched with moisture lower down, and even the snow up here is not the nice crisp Christmas card variety, but wet and soggy. It gets into everything. However, one enormous advantage of being this high up is the total absence of leeches! Anything else is bearable if there are no leeches.

Despite all this grumbling, I am, I confess, very happy. It is wonderful to be at this altitude. In the few minutes a day when the weather clears – enough to give us false hopes of a fine day – the sight of rank on rank of snow-covered peaks, seemingly below us (and in some cases really so), the roar of the river far down in the gorge, and the odd scarlet rhododendron fighting its way through the snow cover, is enough to give any man a feeling of almost pure contentment. I am in my beloved mountains, and who could wish for more?

But it is the nature of humankind to crave the impossible and I do find myself wishing that you could be here to share it with me. I read in mother's letter that you have succeeded in your own summit attempt and now we must address you as Cllr Mrs Jackson. I do congratulate you. Mother writes that you are fighting hard for Agricultural Workers' Rights through the Labour Party; she expresses some grudging admiration – not easy for a lifetime Tory sympathizer! Thank you so much for going to see her. She writes with great warmth about your visits, and is obviously rather fonder of you than of her only son, who has turned out to be such an eccentric, no-hoper. I hope she will forgive me. Her life sounds very happy at the Dower House. A very respectable family are renting the Hall. The rent comes in useful in these hard times. Strange that we should all have found contentment once we moved away from the Hall. It was such a dark and dreary place, wasn't it? But, perversely, I do rather miss it all, despite the feeling of wonder I have for my perfect mountains.

I will give this letter, and one for Mother, to Pesang, who is returning to the valley tomorrow, on the way to visit his home village. It is written more in hope than certainty of your ever receiving it. But I did want to tell you that I have made a decision. We are coming to the end of the collection period. The plans are to make our way back down in a few days. Yesterday evening, when we were sitting round the fire (no one very keen on leaving its comforting warmth to seek out a cold, wet tent!), the porters spoke to me of a 'sacred lake where the Blue Poppy grows'. They told me there are 'many, many flowers', of a strange kind which they have not seen before. Of course they are not botanists and this may be a wild goose chase, but I remembered the words I saw written some years ago, in a field note in the library in Cambridge.

Dawson and I have questioned the porters. They seem quite clear about where the sacred lake can be found. We have decided that Dawson will be left in charge of finishing off the collections here, and packing up the specimens, which he is very willing to do. He has a wife and family waiting for him at home, while I do not have so many commitments. With Professor Thompson's permission, I intend to go off on my own with two porters, and Tsering and Numbu, to try to find the lake.

It is too good a chance to miss and if they are right, it is no more than three days' trek from here. With luck I may even be able to join the others before they sail.

Anyway, that's the plan, and I did want to write one letter to you just before I left. You must know how much I think of you and how much I regret. You have your own life, and your own causes; you have made that clear. I do want to tell you, however, just once, that I care for you very deeply. In fact, you are everything to me.

The snows are going to make things a bit tricky, but I am sure we will get through.

> With love, always,
> Charles

CHAPTER 33

Feeling the need for quiet he had walked ahead. He wanted to be alone in this place, without the shouts of the porters, their laughter, their constantly intoned prayers. As he climbed towards the pass the vegetation changed from the carpets of anemone and potentilla, which had filled the grass with colour under the trees. The rutted mountain path, where the mules slipped again and again, was edged with bare yellow grass. Stunted firs and dwarf rhododendra clung to the steep slopes.

The two porters with their mules were making one of their frequent stops for tea and tsampa. They would not catch up with him for a while. He was fighting a battle with himself. The chest pains were very real and he was frightened. They must already be at 16,000 feet but he didn't think he was suffering from altitude sickness. Tsering had given him some strange greasy mixture one day on the Napso-La, and since then he had had none of the unpleasant side effects of going too high.

He walked on up the track, taking it slowly. The narrow V of the pass at almost 19,000 feet, hung far above him on the skyline. Beyond that pass, if the porters were to be believed, lay the sacred lake.

The pain in his chest seemed to have lessened a little. He laboured slowly up the path, climbing above the roar of the little river, onto the high, bleached grass.

Then it came again, a crushing weight. Fine flakes of snow stung his cheeks, carried from the glacier above him. The wind had been muzzled in its ferocity by the curve of the mountain. Now it hit him with its full force. There was no shelter. The weight on his chest grew and grew, until he found himself stopping for seconds at a time, lost in a fog of pain. He knew then that he was very ill. Somehow he must get out of the wind and rest. He would find shelter and wait for the porters, drink from his flask, have a little sleep. Then he might be well enough to carry on.

Below him was a small circular cliff and a hollow beside a waterfall. It would be out of the wind and near enough to the path to wait in safety until the porters caught up. With difficulty, staggering a little under his pack, he clamboured down. He half-fell on to the rocks at the bottom of the ravine. It was a different world. The absence of wind sang in his ears. It was hot in the intense Tibetan sun, but deep frost lay in the shadows. Minute flakes of sparkling snow drifted down from above, the sun shone on the boulders and there were tiny patches of grass and ferns. A few tiny flowers bloomed here, taking advantage of this haven from the arctic wind.

He unstrapped his pack, frightened by how unsteady he was, and lay down, close to the waterfall. A shining mist soaked the air with a crystal vapour, iridescent in the intense sunlight. The sound of the water was thunderous, yet it was also the quietest place he had ever been in his life. The quiet entered into him. Lying by the clear torrent on that bright sharp day, cut off from all but dark blue sky, the burning sun, the crystal water rushing by him, he felt a hesitant, reverential joy which filled him utterly. The scent of juniper, the grey rock, tiny lichens and mosses hiding under the stones, which glowed like minute forests of red and green and gold, all was irradiated mysteriously with this same light-filled joy. He was entirely at peace.

'If I should die now,' he thought, 'I would have had this happiness. This moment. There could be nothing more.'

The pain came again, brutally. He would never now find his Blue Poppy. This was it. The deepest, the purest, the best . . . it was enough. Yes, this was the answer. Better, infinitely better, to rest quietly in this perfect place, while the porters passed by. Even if he were never found. . . .

When he opened his eyes again, the shadows had moved. His eye was caught by a splash of blue to the right. Behind the nearest group of rocks which had previously been in frosted shadow, in a spot protected from the wind, a single Blue Poppy had opened its petals shyly to the sun. Golden stamens erect, it danced before his eyes against the grey rock, a vision of heaven. He struggled to his feet and scrambled up the last few yards of wet, slippery rock towards it, the roar of the fall and his own blood growing ever louder, his eyes fixed on the unearthly blue. It was so perfect, so delicate, so utterly frail. And yet here it was, just as he had dreamed it, springing up through the dry shale at the base of the rock, sheltered from the scouring wind. A butterfly of a flower in this harsh country; its glowing petals spread out with the sun shining through them as through stained glass, the stamens heavy with gold. It was here. He had seen it. They existed for each other and nothing, no one, could ever take that away.

In the next second the pain sprang on him as he had never known it before, a leopard of a pain springing from the hard rock. With the roaring of blood and water in his head, the darkness came.

CHAPTER 34

He had no sense of where he was, or how long he had been there. It was a cold place, with the sound of the wind sighing about him. There was a distant sound of chanting and, as he slipped in and out of consciousness, the chanting was played over and over again in his head – curiously peaceful.

Waking again, he felt a great sense of peace once more. The chanting began, and some flickering, reflected light, like candlelight, washed and moved over the walls like water over stone. In the chanting, which seemed like a prayer, he heard the same sounds over and over again, *Om Mani Padme Hum, Om Mani Padme Hum*. Part of him remembered those words from a past life. *The Jewel in the Heart of the Lotus*. He fell into a deep, quiet sleep.

It was full daylight. He was in a small, white room, like a cell, with one arched window high up, unglazed. An incredible light was pouring through the window, staining the walls a burnished gold. This is what heaven must be like, he thought, and then he remembered the strange dreams and the terrible pain in his chest which had come before oblivion. A Blue Poppy, alone on the mountainside, beckoning him on. Then there had been blood-red robes, butter lamps, the deep roar of the great radongs and the sound of cymbals clashing. Tibetan faces were smiling down at him.

They were such vivid dreams. He wondered if they could be true. Had he lived these things? And what of the other dreams? A woman, red-haired, standing on a hillside, crying. Were these dreams also true?

This time he was almost sure he was awake. A bubbly feeling like champagne tingled right through his body. Apart from a strange sensation in his chest, he felt amazingly well. He lay on the low, wooden platform, quite warm with his covering of woollen rugs, looking at the rough-plastered, shining walls, the sunlight streaming in in a great beam through the high window. He felt no curiosity about why he was there, no sense of wanting to get up and explore this world. It was as though his body were light and free, as though something had been released from him, a burden that had been weighing him down for most of his life.

The door opened quietly. A monk in maroon robes, with a dark Tibetan face, his head shaved, came into the room with a wooden tray. There was a bowl of some green liquid, the herbal scent of it filling the cell, a leather tsampa pouch, and a little silver bowl of tea.

The monk smiled down at him, not speaking, but laid the tray down on the floor beside him, squatting beside it. He passed a bowl to Charles, encouraging him to drink the strange greenish liquid. Then, taking a little of the tsampa flour in the palm of his hand, he rolled it into balls with a little of the tea, offering it to him. Charles was amazed to see his own hand go out and take the tsampa. It was so thin and there were long nails on the ends of the fingers. He must have been ill for a long time.

For days he lay suspended as if in some golden time in the little cell. The monk, Jingme, came and ministered to his needs. He was too weak to stand, but Jingme took care of him, washing him and cleaning him in a matter-of-fact, quiet way. There was a deep sense of perfect peace and acceptance, and the knowledge that he was safe. In some mysterious way he knew he had been healed. That heaviness, which had been in his chest since he could remember, had been lifted. Not only did his heart feel lighter, but likewise his entire body.

Days and nights passed. The days were distinguished by that same brilliant snow light. The nights were never dark. Visions walked across the walls, lit by a single butter lamp which fluttered in the wind. In those visions, he seemed to see his life mapped out. Gradually he pieced it all together, this little life of his. He remembered clearly then, how he'd seen that perfect Blue Poppy growing on the scree, just for him. It had not been a dream. He could remember every detail of it, the corolla, the calyx, the rosette of spiny green leaves, the soft golden hairs on the straight stem like the hairs on a woman's arm. Above, two flowers opened shyly to the sun, a perfect blue, with gold stamens. It bloomed just for him. Somehow, he knew it was his grandmother's Blue Poppy. He might never find it again, yet, in his newly enlightened state, the thought gave him no pain. He had seen a perfect vision of beauty, and the fragile, transient nature of it made it even more precious. It seemed to him that he had found a perfection which he didn't need to possess. His dream was fulfilled. He had been filled with joy, and that was enough. He didn't need to search any more.

How long he lay there in that dreamlike, joyful state, he couldn't have said. His whole life seemed to have been interwoven with the distant chanting, the sun slanting through the window, bells tinkling, the quiet monks shuffling about their duties.

One morning, the monks helped him from his bed, and he was able to look out of the high window for the first time. What he saw took his breath away. He had been able to feel the zinging light of the mountains, smell the snow wind. But seeing the vista was perfection. The monastery was poised in some high eyrie, looking across at an endless panorama of frozen, white mountains under a deep violet sky. Looking down he saw that in some mysterious way the monastery was part of the mountain, seeming to grow out of the very rock.

Days passed in that airy place, looking out over the high Himalayas. He ate and drank little, just the amber Tibetan tea from his own silver bowl, tsampa, a little clear soup, occasionally those strange green concoctions that the monks brought him. Despite his frugal diet, he grew stronger. So it was that he lived in this light, strange state, learning and changing. His mind began to touch on those things that he had hardly begun to understand before. And always in his mind the image of the Blue Poppy, set against the white background of his little cell, seemed to draw him back into himself. It was as though that Poppy had been there especially for him to find, in that moment of truth and almost death. And now he was reborn, he had been given something back, something infinitely precious.

When he was able to walk about, he began to come down and join in the prayers in the huge dark temple. Here, ancient hangings, thankas of the Buddha, created timeless corridors. The red-robed monks chanted endlessly. Butter lamps flickered, and there was a thick smell of ghee and the smoke of incense. It was then that he seemed to dip down into some time that he hardly understood.

Time passed and yet did not. The weather grew colder. The snow peaks were darkened with cloud. More snow appeared on the peaks. Thunder crashed around the mountains, and hail fell in through the open window of the cell. Gratefully, Charles accepted one of the thick wool robes which the monks wore. Then, suddenly, it was spring. The tiny monastery garden, hollowed out of the high rock, was full of tiny flowers; primulas, saxifrages, strange bush roses he had never seen before at this height, all sheltered and tended lovingly by the inhabitants of the monastery.

One morning, he woke with a strong feeling that it was time for a new beginning. Here, in this place, he had completed one journey. Now it was time for another. Until then, he had felt no desire to leave. Yet now, between one night and the next, it was time to go. As he lifted himself from his bed, he saw that there, laid out before him on the floor, was his old sleeping bag and his tent, his personal effects, even the shaving kit which he had not used for so long. Like every other strange thing that had happened to him in this strange place, it seemed perfectly understandable and natural. And there before him too, under the narrow windowsill, back-lit by the dawn light, was Jingme, the monk who had become his friend. He sat cross-legged on the floor of the cell, waiting for Charles to wake, a steaming copper bowl of water before him. A maroon cloth was laid out on the floor. On it was a silver bell and a bowl of burning incense.

Jingme smiled his brilliant, peaceful smile, holding out his hands with the tea bowl.

'Please, drink first. You must wash, and make an offering. It is time to meet our Abbot, the Rinpoche, Precious Jewel. You must prepare. I will lead you to him.'

Charles unpeeled the layers of robes which he had worn for so long. There was no odour to them in that dry, germless air. He looked down at his own body, still thin but growing stronger. He saw with surprise that there were two scars on his left side. One, the mark of the bullet which had almost killed him in the trenches, the other a strange crescent-shaped scar, like a thumbnail mark, just below the fifth rib.

He washed himself, shivering a little in the mountain air from the window. Jingme had placed in one pile the clothes in which he had been found, strangely alien to him now in that simple cell: his old battered tweed hat, khaki trousers, gaiters and boots, even a tie, the whole pile like a shed snakeskin, holding the shape of his old life. In a second pile was a worn sheepskin chuba, a coarse cloth shirt, some baggy woollen trousers, a pair of brightly decorated felt boots, and a Tibetan fur hat. He picked those up and began to dress.

He made an offering as he had been taught to do. Then, looking up, he saw Jingme waiting gravely by the door, holding out on a cushion the amulet which his grandmother had left for him, which the monks must have kept safe for him all this time. He placed it around his neck. It was time to go.

He entered a tiny cell, even smaller than his own. There was a simple floor covering, some butter lamps burning, an incense holder where aromatic twigs smouldered, occasionally glowing red in the draught from the window. A frail old man stood, his face in shadow, looking out of the window at the snow-covered mountains. For a moment he was framed there, a stooped figure in a dark red robe, the only sign of rank a yellow sash over his shoulders. Jingme had given Charles a white silk katag – a silk scarf – to present to the Abbot. He stood there now, holding it out in his hands in the approved manner, waiting. For some reason, his heart was beating fast.

The silence in the cell grew deeper. Charles was aware of the little sounds, the spluttering of the butter lamps, the hiss of the twigs. The sun had gone in and occasional grains of hail fell through the stone window onto the floor with a pattering like dry rice. And there was a kind of underhum, like a chant in the room.

Without turning towards Charles, the Abbot stood still by the window. Charles saw that he was spinning a simple copper prayer wheel, and was indeed chanting a prayer under his breath. He waited.

The alpine storm passed. Sunlight flooded into the cell. The ancient lama turned to Charles and gave him a joyous smile which lit up his whole face. Charles, with a profound sense of shock, saw, looking back at him, a reflection of his own face, ancient, but indisputably his own. The Abbot was wearing a coral and turquoise amulet which flashed in the crystal light. Looking down, he saw that it was identical to his.

'Your grandmother waited for me for many years. I had been ambushed by Khampas on the road back to Lhasa. They left me for dead, and indeed I lay in that time between life and death. But I did not die. I was cared for by nomads. In the end, I recovered. By then it was too late to find your grandmother again. So for many years, I devoted myself to seeking the True Path. . . .

'Our family were nobles at the courts of the Dalai Lamas. My father before me was a great plant-hunter. He had travelled to the Americas in search of seed for the Norbu Linka, the Dalai Lama's summer palace in Lhasa. Our family had helped design the Palace gardens. It was so beautiful there. If you could have seen it . . . the willow trees, the flowers. We used to have picnics by the river.

'I was sent south on a political mission to India. I stopped here, in this monastery, where my uncle was Abbot at the time. One day, walking on the mountain, I found the Blue Poppy which you too found. I collected seed from the one seed pod which was ripe. I was very lucky. Later, I planted that blue poppy in her garden . . . the garden of my beloved. Little seedlings I had raised on my journey. It brought her much pleasure, but sadly it was too delicate. The country was too lush, too rich; it would not have thrived for long. Yet for a little time it gave her happiness. I like to think so. But I believe there is another, somewhere in this land. Finer. More robust. I glimpsed it once, by the sacred lake. It is such a colour as you cannot imagine. The blue of Lake Manasarovar at dawn. It is my gift to you.'

'Did you know of me, Grandfather?'

'So many years, I have waited for you. Now you are here, I can at last leave this earth in peace. You are my true son.'

'But my father is dead. I am your grandson.'

'I knew of your father's death. How could I not? The son of my earthly body, dying in pain and fear. No man should die so. I thought I too should die. But now you have returned to me. You are my true heir. Let me embrace you, so that my earthly body can leave in peace. I have waited so long.'

How many days he spent in the Abbot's cell he could not have told. Afterwards he could not remember having either eaten or drunk, but he must have done so, for he felt neither weary nor cold. He began to understand much that he could not put into words.

'I have always known of you. When you were sick, I said prayers for you. Now you have come back, and I am twice blessed. . . .'

'What should I do?'

'Keep your prayers, spin the wheel, seek wisdom, remember the mantra I will teach you. Find your Blue Poppy. Do not forget us while you are on this earth. I will be reborn in another body when it is time. We will find each other again.'

The Rinpoche moved forward and lifted a silver bowl from the corner of the low altar.

'Drink this. Now you are healed, you must find your way back to the valley where you found the Blue Poppy. Above that valley will be a sacred lake. There you will find, at last, what you truly seek. Then it will be time for you to go home. But do not forget what you have learned. And first we will sit together in the sun and meditate for a little while.'

His grandfather placed the incense in a silver holder; aromatic smoke drifted up into the little cell. He rang a bell and a monk came in with a tray. Three butter lamps flickered in the dark. There was a small offering of rice. Side by side they sat down together, cross-legged beneath the window.

CHAPTER 35

Betty sat in the upstairs room on the window-seat, looking out over the front garden, so overgrown now that it was hard to see there had ever been a path and a gate. It was a beautiful day. She had been here all afternoon, just sitting or wandering about, touching memories in her mind. She had never been over the threshold of the cottage since she had left it as a tiny baby. Yet she had known from the first moment she had pushed in through the broken door, stepping gingerly over the debris in the little hall, that here was a sense of home.

Betty had arrived back that lunchtime from a tiring week in London. She had spent too many nights alone in that soulless sitting-room in her flat, looking out over the endless brick skyline. Mary had left her a message that there was nothing to be done until the following morning, when she had arranged to oversee the milking on the three farms. For a little while, no one needed her. She had no meetings and nobody to organise. The Cumberland house had suddenly oppressed her, with its expensive oil paintings on the walls, its modern fitments and all the conveniences that money could buy. She had unpinned her hat and left it on the kitchen table. Ignoring the car, she walked out into the afternoon sunlight, away down the road, still in her smart London clothes, not even knowing where she was going. It was quite foolish, not at all the sort of thing she should be doing, but there it was. She had found herself wandering between hedges and stone walls down the lane towards Bambeck, pulled by some deep instinct, as a swallow, winging its way home, seeks its old nesting place.

Strange and touching that there should have been such accord between Alice and herself at the end. She welcomed that hard-headed respect they had had between them and Betty knew how much the old lady had cared for her. All that time Alice must have known they were kinfolk, she and

Charles, but she had never said a word. It wasn't until Betty had opened the letter from the solicitors, telling her that she had been left the cottage, that she had known for sure. Alice had enclosed the letter from Maud Fergusson to Hannah Bowman with the papers. It was enough.

She had left going upstairs till last. There had been tragedy here, her family's tragedy. If only her mother had not died giving birth to her on that April night, they might all have been together for a while, secure in this little house. There might have been all sorts of happiness she could only guess at. Yet her father would still have gone off to the war. You couldn't bring it back, any of it. It was no good being angry with the past.

She had opened the door onto the staircase, gingerly climbing the rickety stairs. Her father had never come back to live in the house. There had been other tenants in for a while after her mother had died. But neither the tenants nor, it seemed, the Fergussons themselves, had looked after the place. It had just been left to decay when the last tenants had finally departed.

At the very top of the stairs, her foot had gone through the step, and she almost fell. The floor boards were rotten. She must go carefully. There were only two rooms, opening off the landing at the top. Which one had been her parents' room, the room where she had been born? The bigger one, she supposed. She ducked her head, and went in. There was faded wallpaper on the wall, roses and forget-me-nots, some sort of cheap Victorian stuff. Had her mother chosen it, all those years before? It was marked with mould now, half off the wall. It gave her a little stab of sadness to see it. That sense of her mother was suddenly very real, a memory which had been planted there by others, but which had grown and been embellished by the growing child over the years. All at once, she felt vulnerable and scared, as though her life had all been a pretence, that inside she was no more than that small motherless child, lonely and afraid.

Had her mother died in this very room? There was a bedstead in the middle of the floor. It would have to go. She couldn't bear to think about it. This Victorian preoccupation with Death gave her the shivers. Always harking back. But wasn't that what she was doing now? What was the matter with her?

Would her mother have been pleased with how she had turned out? Suddenly it mattered a great deal that she would. But of course she would never know. Her mind was running on, finding a refuge in practical things. The damp would need fixing. There was no bathroom. There, in the corner, the rain had been coming in. That might mean a new roof. Well, that wasn't the end of the world. She would have to put in the electric light. No tenant would want the cottage unless she made some improvements. And she could charge a better rent.

There was a faint slapping noise on the window, making her jump. A yellow rose was lying against the pane. Each time the breeze moved the stem, the blooms dashed themselves against the window with a soft plashing of petals. With some difficulty, she pushed open the window. You could see over the fields from here, beyond the tiny garden and the road. Pale fronds of barley rippled in a green-gold sea. There was a scattering of scarlet poppies and the brilliant blue of cornflowers. And beyond all that, the ridge of Bambeck Fell, outlined against the sky, dark even on this summer's day.

Her eye was caught again by the cornflowers in the barley field. How much she had always loved blue flowers! Or had she just absorbed Charles's love for them since he had become so much of her life, woven into everything? It was hard to remember a time when that hadn't been so.

He was so far away now. In Tibet, maybe. Was he still alive? She hadn't heard from him for so long. She had sent a telegram to his last-known stopping-place just before Alice had died, telling him of her illness. That was many months ago. Charles had once written to Alice that there was an 'excellent Englishman' manning the telegraph in Lhasa. It sounded very modern and unlikely. Alice had been reassured and she had made Betty promise that if anything should happen, Betty would send a telegram to let him know.

Would he be there now? And would he ever choose to come home? It was so long since they had heard anything. After all, there was nothing now for him here. Now she was his only kin, his only friend in England. Had Alice ever shown him that letter? Did he even know that they were kin? How she missed him! The ache in her heart had never left her, in all those years. She supposed it was because they were cousins, and she had given him so much. And in return he had helped to shape her into the person she had become, given her a confidence in her own ability which she had so desperately needed. They had shaped each other.

There was a crash downstairs, followed by a man's voice, angry. But this was her house! How dare someone break in, disturbing the fragile sense of the past she had felt around her. She was too angry to be afraid. Stomping out of the little room, she reached the top of the landing to see a figure blocking the stairway at the bottom. In the dimness she could only see his shape hunched up.

'What the devil are you doing, lad?' she shouted, lapsing as always into her own speech when she was angry. 'You're trespassing! Get yourself out before I give you a skelping you'll not forget.'

The shape, which had been bending over massaging its shin, looked up at her. The stairs were dark and she felt a sensation of fear. She was all alone and he looked a great tall thing, wearing some kind of headdress. Who knew she was here, to think of it, excepting Ollie Plaskett who had given her the key?

'Go on with you! This is my house, so just keep yourself out!'

She advanced down the steep steps. The figure stood still, looking up at her. She saw behind him that the door had finally given way and was lying in sections in the hall. A strong smell of dust and rats came up from below.

'Well, Betty! This is a fine welcome after all these years!'

Charles! Here, before her on the stairs, as real as could be! Wearing some kind of exotic furry hat and the oddest britches she had ever seen.

She longed to touch him, but something, a different kind of fear this time, held her back. He was that tall nowadays, as thin as a string bean, burned a deep bronze by the fierce mountain sun. He was hardly her Charlie at all. And there was something else different about him, not just the Tibetan clothes. Some vitality, as though he had been, in some odd way, newly-made. She felt it at once. It made his presence there, so close to her, even more unnerving.

They sat either side of the tiny windowsill, just touching. It was as if he had never been away. Just to begin with, there had been such joy inside her she could hardly speak, but she soon got over that. Now they were talking and teasing and fighting almost as they always had.

He had just come from the train. Old Ollie, faithful as ever, had met him with the cart. It was Ollie who had told Charles where he could find her. He had wanted to see her first.

'You would have given them a fright on the train dressed like that, with some kind of queer bonnet on your head.'

'I've grown so used to these clothes, Betty. I never gave it a thought. No wonder people were staring at me!'

He took off his strange-looking furry hat, and laid it beside him.

'There! Is that better? I didn't mean to give you a fright. I just wanted to find you. That's all I could think about, all the way up on the train. Seeing you again.'

There was a little silence.

'It's good to see you, Charles.'

She was surprised by how dry her throat was. Her voice sounded strange. Powerful feelings were running about inside her in an odd way, making her feel queer.

The afternoon had gone now and the slanting light lay along the fronded ears of barley, painting them red-gold. It was getting chillier in the room. How long had they been there? He moved closer to her and put his arm round her shoulders. Entirely naturally. An odd pain ran down her arms, right to her fingers, as though her heart were constricted. It was an intense pain, a feeling which left her almost unable to breathe. It frightened her. Maybe she was having a heart attack. How ironic that would be, if she popped her clogs first, before him, after all.

'Are you cold, Betty? I've got my knapsack at the bottom of the stairs. Ollie's taking the rest of my stuff up to the Hall. There's a sheepskin jacket in there, and you only have this thin dress on.'

With this other hand he touched the collar of her dress, feeling it with his fingers. 'It is pretty stuff. You always look so good. You always did.'

'You don't see me when I'm dressed up on the farm. In my overalls covered in cow muck!' She spoke briskly, trying to shake off that feeling which threatened to overwhelm her. She stood up, lifting his arm away. 'The lads give me hell, but I have to show them I'm as good as them. If I won't get my hands covered in clart, I wouldn't be much of a farmer.'

She stood in front of the window, looking out. It was no good feeling like this. She would never have him. They were kin after all.

He came to stand behind her. She could smell that indefinable scent of his: bookish; the pipe smoke smell she loved, overlaid with other more exotic scents of some place far away.

'I thought you would come home smelling of yak butter.'

'These are my best clothes. The rest of my stuff's pretty aromatic!'

She turned and smiled at him. They were suddenly easier with one another, secure in that light-hearted teasing they knew so well. Now they weren't touching any more.

'God forgive me', she thought, 'I am thirty-eight years old. I have been through all this. I just have to get a grip on myself.'

'We have a lot to talk about.' He said at last. 'You see, I suppose I thought . . . I don't know. . . . We know each other so well, and you are so special to me. I always loved you, in my way. Of course I did. To begin with we were like family to each other, weren't we? But then . . . it was different.'

He sighed and looked out over the darkening fields beyond the window, the fells silhouetted against the reddening sky. The silence in the room had a quality all of its own. She struggled to break its power, walking over to the window, turning her back. The silence remained.

'Did you know, all this time, like, that we were cousins?' She asked.

It was hard to speak about. She had never talked about it to anyone, not since Old Jinny had put her right all those years ago.

'I saw the letter just before I left England. Mother showed me. It was an awful shock. In the end, she couldn't bring herself to tell you herself. She promised to leave you the letter in her will, with this cottage. We both loved you, you know. I suppose we were afraid it would ruin your life, somehow.'

He paused and sighed deeply. Her heart constricted in that queer way again, but she wouldn't move towards him.

'I've known for a long time. Since I were a lass.' Betty spoke, still looking out over the darkening fields. 'There's no need to worry yourself about me. I've always been all right.'

He nodded, seemingly lost in thought.

'Tsering, Numbu and the monks, taught me so much about life,' he went on at last. 'I don't need anything much in the way of material things now, and I don't want them. But I have always, always, wanted you.'

She shook her head vehemently.

'No. You're forgetting. We're family. The only family each of us has got now. It wouldn't be right. And in any case, we're that different, Charlie.'

He didn't seem to be listening to her.

'I've had a long time to think about it – all on the way back, on the voyage. To plan for the future. You see, it seems to me that I don't want to go on without you any longer. It just isn't sensible.'

The pain in her was such that she thought she must cry out. It was all there, clinical, set out as a scientist might see it, the ordered dissection of their lives. Only his voice was shaking, which wasn't quite as it should be. She could hardly bear it any longer, but he wouldn't stop.

'I'm really making an awful hash of this. It's just that I really want us to be together, make our lives together. . . . Could you see it like that?'

His head was bent down, and he wouldn't look at her. It was dreadful. She spoke firmly, her back to him so he couldn't see her face.

'Me and William, we never had any bairns. It wouldn't have worked out too well for me, what with him dying. But I wouldn't want anyone else to care for, not ever. I have my independence and I've fought for it. Even if we weren't family, I wouldn't want it! You don't have to worry yourself about us. We're friends, and more than friends, but we're too long in the tooth to go laiking about with all that sort of nonsense.'

She had forced herself to speak stoutly, but inside she was empty, cruelly sad, so grief-stricken that she hardly knew what she was saying.

He got up from the bedstead, and came over to stand behind her. The physical presence of him after all these years, the warm breath of him, that scent she remembered, his black unruly hair which he never could get to lie flat. It was too much. Ridiculously, she felt tears spring in her eyes. He was talking to her again, but she didn't dare to turn and face him.

'There is so much to talk about, so much to tell you. Things I've learned. I've come to see that our lives have been intertwined since long before we were born. Everything we have become. . . . The last few years I haven't thought of anyone else but you. I just wish you had been there, in the Himalayas, seeing them for the first time. They were your mountains too. You gave them to me.'

It had grown cold in the room. The shadows had crept in beside them without their noticing, but still in the sky was the lingering light of the long Cumberland evening. It would not grow really dark for a long time.

'I can't go back tonight, Betty. Not to that place. It's too full of memories. Would you mind if I just made a bivvy here? Like I used to do in the fells? I've got my sleeping bag and a flask of cold tea and some stale sandwiches. I shall be in the lap of luxury. It's warmer than the Chang Tang plain, I can tell you.'

She said nothing. At last he spoke again, quietly.

'I had thought we might . . . go back together, to Tibet.' He paused uncertainly. 'Only I suppose that would be rather an unfair thing to ask. I see that now. . . .'

She shook her head vehemently.

'I've had a struggle, Charles. I'm just getting where I want to be in the world. I've got the farms, and the shops, and the constituency. I've got my own life. I don't deny I feel for you. Maybe more than I should. But don't talk to me about loving. I never knew what that felt like, except to give good folk trouble they could do without.'

He was looking at her in that odd way of his, which always made her cross. When she was angry, she inevitably felt better. It was as though he was always peaceful, and her natural state was forever to be in a temper.

Not that anything was ever that simple.

'You're welcome to be here, Charles,' she went on, trying to sound practical and cool, swallowing her irritation. It was necessary to put the things they had said and felt, in those last hours, as far from her as possible. 'I've Jed in to do the stock tonight over at Greystoke, and Mary's running the spot, like, so I can be a bit late and it won't harm. I'll stay a while and talk to you and you can tell me about all those places you've seen. We can have a right good crack.'

'Just like old friends?' He was still looking at her that way and smiling gently. Only this time it made her so uncomfortable with that queer feeling in her chest again, she had to take a deep breath to make it go away.

A sort of awkwardness had come down between them again. It was as though they had broken some taboo, as though something had been stripped from them both and they stood before each other with nothing. There were some mats in the corner of the room, not very clean, but one had been wrapped inside the others for safe keeping and was cleaner than the rest. She was glad of some activity to keep her from feeling too much. Between them they laid the cleaner rug on the bedstead, so they could sit more comfortably. Then Charles went down for his rucksack, and he laid his sleeping bag on top of the mat, and they wrapped themselves in it. It was cold in the room now, but they warmed each other's hands.

Betty put on Charles's spare sheepskin, which did indeed stink of rancid butter, so all the farm cats would be after her when she got back. It was just like when they were young. If it hadn't been for that feeling between them, it would have been the same as in those days when she had dragged him up the stairs at Bambeck Hall. But now it wasn't, it wasn't like that at all.

'I'm afraid I won't be able to stay long.' His voice was quiet. 'Just a few hours. I've got to get back to London tomorrow afternoon. To visit some Army department. They're looking for people on the North-West frontier. I thought it might do for me. It's rather unstable out there, and I do speak some of the dialects. And if there's another war, perhaps I might be of some use. I can speak up for the tribesmen, that sort of thing.'

'You, in the Army again! What sort of dummlehead are you!' A familiar exasperation overcame her. 'When are you *ever* going to settle down and rest? Take it easy! I have never heard such rubbish!'

He smiled his slow smile, shaking his head.

'I want everything to be held in trust for you, to do whatever you want with it. It's yours by right anyway. All I want is a piece of the walled garden where I might build a house one day. A little white house, maybe, like Tsering's home in Tibet. And I would like you to plant these for me, if you will.'

He felt in his pocket and took out a tiny canvas bag, undoing the string which held the neck and scattering the fine black dust in his hand.

'I found them at last, by the sacred lake. A new variety. Growing in the same valley as my grandmother's poppy. I found that too, Betty. Just as I had always dreamed. Do you remember? Then I climbed even higher, under the glacier, and there was this other beautiful *Meconopsis* growing on the plateau, just below the snow line. Fields of blue, wherever you looked. I wish you could have seen it. Those snow peaks. That fabulous blue. A new variety, more robust. Double petals and a blue you can't imagine. I knew at once how special it was. I named it after you. After all, it is yours. I would never have got there without you. It was so beautiful, Betty. You can't imagine. It would have taken your breath away. Would you plant this for me, in the walled garden, so that it will be there for ever? For me to come back to?'

Carefully, gently, he emptied the seed back into the bag, and tied the string around the neck. Then he reached out for her hand, and taking it, he turned it palm upwards, placing the small canvas bag in the hollow of her hand.

'This is all I am, Betty. All I have become.'

Some time later, when it was really dark, they lay down in each other's arms and, although a grown woman and having put all such things aside, to do this seemed as natural as if they were children. There was so much hurt to be healed, so much to be shared. So much to tell, and the world was very far away.

She supposed everyone would know by the morning and there would be a scandal, and the lads on the farm would never take her tongue-lashing again without sniggering behind her back, but for this night she hardly cared. And as for him, he had lived close to his feelings for so long he had nothing to hide from himself. So they loved one another naturally, finding, tentatively and shyly, that all they had learned before was nothing compared to this.

Was this then what all the fuss was about? This feeling like the beck bursting its banks? She supposed it must be, but she couldn't let it overwhelm her like this. She had fought too hard to let it all go. . . .

CHAPTER 36

When she woke in the little room it was long after dawn. Cool air was blowing in at her from the field beyond. Usually, by now, she would be well on the way with the milking, summer or winter. Mary would have woken her at 5 a.m. with a cup of tea. Mary! What would she think? What would they all think? She must get back.

It was only then that she turned over, conscious suddenly that the warmth beside her had gone. He wasn't there! He had left her without saying a word, leaving her sleeping. How could he? Foolish though it was, she swallowed back tears. She was going soft! No doubt about it.

There was a ragged curtain half-shading the window. The moon had risen some time in the still hours of the night. They had lain together and she had watched his face, looking out at the moon. He had been stroking her skin, that passion, that thrill rising up in her. It was all new. Frightening. Exhilarating. The moon was so bright that he had pulled the curtain across, so that they could sleep at last, entwined in each other's arms. . . .

Now, violently, she pulled the ragged curtain back from the window. The ancient rings parted company with the scraps of cloth and the whole lot fell in a cloud of dust at her naked feet. She stared down at it, helplessly.

Where was he?

Inside her there was a terrible sense of loss. Unbearable. Twice she had lost in this room. Her mother, and now him.

She turned back the makeshift bed, not caring that she was weeping. Her clothes lay forgotten on the floor. That good frock she had bought in London only last week. Fine linen from a French fashion house. Fitting for her station in life. Crumpled now on the floor, with her silk stockings, her shoes. Her silk underwear bought in Paris on a business trip that Spring –

everything tangled together.

She smoothed back the old sleeping bag. What was she doing here? Naked, weeping, in a derelict house? Was what she had fought for, so easily lost?

All for love?

There, she had thought it. That was it, wasn't it? She loved him. She would always love him. He was the other half of her.

After last night, they were one body, joined by fire and love. It would always be like that. Wherever he went in the world, they would always be one person. He had told her about his grandfather. How he had found Kensin Lo in the remote monastery deep inside Tibet. How the monks had healed him. The whole story. They were not kin, after all. How strange life was, the way it fell into place. Now there was nothing to hold them back. She had meant to tell him that, but somehow the words had never come. But surely her body had told him, after all, that she would be his forever.

But now he had gone. He had made love to her, and now he had gone, and left her alone. Not a word. No kiss. Nothing.

How pathetic that she was weeping. She laid her head down on the rough lining of the sleeping bag and cried. Shaking with uncontrollable tears. For all that she had lost. Independence. Serenity. Peace of mind. Pride. It was all gone. She was lying naked on a makeshift bed, weeping, like some gypsy woman.

Something in the folds of the sleeping bag pricked at her cheek. She sat up and fumbled in the folds. Yellow petals fell to the floor. A rose! He must have placed it beside her while she slept. When she had turned over in her sleep, she had covered it up. There was a page of paper beside it. Some rough handmade stuff, torn from a notebook.

His awful writing, so familiar from the schoolroom long ago. It had never got any better. She took the sleeping bag and wrapped it round her, crouching by the window. She squinted at the page, her heart doing somersaults in her breast. To care so much. It was terrible to be so vulnerable.

'I will love you for ever. There will never be anyone else.' That spidery writing. 'You know that. I came to find you. To ask you to marry me. To go back with me. . . .'

He must have written that, in the half light, perhaps sitting on the windowsill, watching her sleep. . . .

'In my mind I saw you riding across the plains with me, on mule-back in the Himalayas. It seemed so real. But it was only a dream. As soon as I heard what you had to say, I understood the truth. I could never take you away from all you have, all you have achieved. I am so proud of you, my darling. But I would never ask you to share the life I have now, with all its hardships.

I am leaving now. I couldn't bear to say goodbye. Unlike you, my dear brave girl, I have always been a coward. . . .

I will love you forever.

Your Charles.'

No getting away from it. She had sent him away. She had told him, straight out, that all she had built up, all she had achieved was more important than him. She had said it, and then in the whole of the sweet, beloved night, she had never thought to unsay it. She thought he would have known. . . .

Ollie, grumbling to himself, had opened the door of the house for her. He was getting creakier in his joints every year, and it hadn't improved his temper. He stood, staring open-mouthed at Betty's dishevelled appearance.

'Tha looks like summat cat's dragged in,' he said bluntly.

Betty ran her hands abstractedly through her hair.

'I didn't have a brush in my handbag. Ollie, is he here? I have to find him.'

'He's been gone a while since.' Ollie could barely conceal his curiosity. 'Been and gone back to London. Got me out of my bed at the crack of dawn when all decent folk are asleep. Made me open up the house. Ferreting about, muttering, he was. Looked right upset, if you ask me.'

He looked at her closely.

'Here! He was looking for you, lass, last night. Did he catch up with you? Have you two had a row or summat? He looked like he'd lost a florin and found tuppence, I would say!'

Betty stared at Ollie, trying to gather her wits. It would be all around Bambeck by lunchtime, no doubt.

'I have to find him, Ollie. Please help me.'

So that was how she ended up in the estate cart, with the old horse, straw round her ankles. Sitting on the scratchy planks in her best linen frock and good shoes, being driven down the fell at top speed, with Ollie on the reins making a great performance of it all. And why was it when you didn't want to be seen, that everyone was out on the road? The vicar at the church gate, raising his hat. One of her tenants loading eggs in his yard, wanting to pay his rent, running after them down the road. Old Mrs Prendersby from the top corner, the worst gossip in the village, coming up the main street with her basket. And there was she, Councillor Betty Jackson, a business woman of some station in life, looking as though she had spent a night on the tiles. Face it! She had. All dignity gone. Sitting in a wretched farm cart, knee-deep in straw, hatless, with her dress rumpled and no doubt her hair all askew, clutching her bag. For all the world to see.

All of a sudden, she didn't care. Whatever it took, she would find him. She would go to him wherever he was. Barefoot and hatless on an elephant if needs be. Mary had a good head on her. She could run the farms and the businesses. But none of that mattered. She loved, and was loved. She would find him, and they would be together, at last. Whatever it took. . . .

Charles cut a sorrowful, solitary figure on the platform, a battered suit-case at his feet. He had been back to Bambeck Hall briefly. Taken another change of clothes and a few of his books. Said goodbye for the last time. He should have felt light, free. After all, wasn't this what he wanted? He had given it all away. It would be Betty's now – as it should be. He was free to roam the world, wherever the fancy took him, searching for those rare, beautiful plants which were his passion. He had a contract with a seed firm. The prospect of a job to go to on the North-West frontier. Dangerous territory with its warring tribes. But a job he would love, in a place close to his heart. The only trouble was, he was leaving behind all he cared most for in the world.

He felt inside as though he had died. There was a place in his heart so wounded he couldn't even think about it. A terrible emptiness.

Betty. He had done it for her. For her sake. He steeled his mind to remember that. She had suffered enough for his dreams. Now the very best thing was to go away forever – to let her get on with her life. She had made it clear that she would never leave her own very successful life behind. And who could blame her?

He looked down the valley. There in the distance was the plume of smoke from the approaching train. Five minutes and it would be there, drawing up alongside the little platform. His life in Bambeck would be over for ever.

There was a sudden commotion outside in the station yard. A clatter of hooves on the cobbles, and the squeal of a cart brake being applied with unnecessary force. Someone cutting it fine for the train. They were lucky the train itself was, unusually, late. . . .

Then she was standing in front of him, her hair falling half-pinned around her shoulders. That wonderful colour. Her eyes that intense blue. He felt himself drowning again, in that familiar way. How he loved her.

'Where do you think you're going, lad? Without me?'

There were violet shadows under her eyes. The signs of tears. She had never looked more beautiful.

'Making me come after you like a right fool and everyone watching, when you should have known I loved you, without the words being said. You should have known.'

He opened and shut his mouth. Behind him, the slow train puffed up the side of the fell towards him.

'I messed up your life enough, Betty. My family and I. I thought it was for the best.'

'For the best!' Her eyes were blazing.

Charles was conscious that Ollie was leaning on the station gate, watching in fascination.

'So you go sneaking away like a la'al weasel after the hen's eggs – away in the dark and never saying goodbye?'

With a thunder on the rails, and a screech of brakes, the old train pulled in to the platform. Doors opened. The morning arrivals in Bambeck – two old farmers and a young girl with a basket of cheeses – opened the carriage doors and alighted on the platform.

Betty and Charles stood glaring at one another, wreathed in the steam from the engine. The girl with the cheeses, recognizing her employer, hovered beside Betty for instructions. But Betty was oblivious to everyone except Charles. Ollie, with rare tact, shepherded the lass away. For a few moments he was occupied with telling her where she needed to go with her cheeses – to Betty's new warehouse in the village. To his eternal regret, he missed the moment when Betty, taking a step forward as though she could no longer help herself, was suddenly in Charles's arms. For when he turned back, they were wrapped in a passionate embrace, oblivious to the disapproving glances of alighting passengers.

Ollie, hardened though he was to all of life's dramas, felt a sudden lump in his throat. The lass came back to his side to beg for a lift back into the village, and when he looked again, a great gout of steam was blowing along the platform, enveloping the figures in an impenetrable fog. The whistle blew. With a shudder and a slamming of doors, the train began to move away.

When the steam had cleared, the platform was deserted. The train receded down the track, before disappearing round the bend. The empty rails stretched away, forever parallel, to a far horizon between the distant fells.

EPILOGUE

I drove through the old grey town, half-recognizing old photographs. Evidence of her was everywhere. In the smart grocer's emporium, 'Jackson and Haskett', on the corner of the market square. Charles and Betty had been married in a simple ceremony in Sikkim, but she had never taken his name. There on the corner of the square was evidence of her philanthrophy – the smart façade of the agricultural co-operative, endowed by her for the benefit of wives and daughters of the fellside farmers. Somewhere nearby, I knew there was an Agricultural College, specialising in dairy practice for the women of the villages – founded by her and still funded by her charitable trust. My grandmother's considerable fortune, managed from the UK by her business partner, Mary Haskett, had mostly derived from her successful chain of grocer's shops linked with florists. She had used it wisely, never forgetting where she had begun.

I drove out of the town and up the motorway, looking for the village sign. It would all have changed so much since my grandparents' day.

I saw the sign for Bambeck Hall, and turned left off the narrow fellside road. I drove in through the entrance, past the sandstone bulls rearing up, open-mouthed and silent. The drive was full of potholes. An unattended JCB and a concrete mixer were parked to one side, alongside piles of shingle. I noticed the local builder had put a sign up at the gateway. . . . *Conversion into family units. Six ready now.* There was a developer's address in Penrith.

I parked the car in front of the concrete mixer and walked up the drive, shivering a little in the unaccustomed cool of the evening. This was my first visit to England. I was more used to balmy evenings in the little hill town in Northern India where I had been brought up. My grandmother had made the journey in the hot season, pregnant already with my

221

mother, to join Charles in the old family bungalow in Sikkim. My mother had often joked that she learned to ride a mule before she could walk.

Bambeck Hall was suddenly there, framed by rhododendrons and beech trees. A few of the units were occupied already. I could hear children calling somewhere. Towering above the distant fells, the house seemed weighed down with its own importance. I felt it, standing there in the June dusk. My grandfather would have been glad to see children playing in its gardens, sliding down the banisters and clattering over the marble floors. He had never been able to do that, after all, when he was a child.

I walked on through the stone archway. There were more units round the back, with little courtyards. One or two had hanging baskets. A child's scooter lay abandoned across the path.

Beyond the back of the house, the vegetation had been allowed to grow rank and untamed. Overhanging branches of trees crowded across the way. A tree blocked the lane. I had to step over it in my tight skirt. No one, I guessed, had been this way for a while. After my grandparents had travelled into Tibet for the last time, they had never returned. It had been their last great adventure.

Then I saw the sign. 'Visitors for the White House only. Strictly Private.'

I fought my way on down, regretting my smart suit and unsuitable shoes. There was a long red wall, half-obscured by a Filipus Skifsgate rose, smothered with white blossom, which was clinging to the sandstone. I barked my shin on a half-hidden lawnmower. Then I saw the house.

It was built into the side of the wall, in an odd way, so that it seemed to grow out of the stone itself. Tall, oblong and whitewashed, somehow it managed to look entirely Cumbrian and entirely Tibetan at the same time.

I felt in my bag for the key. The door was still in good order. I pushed tentatively and stepped inside. A pigeon flew up and out with a clatter of wings, giving me a fright. It was an illusion that the roof was complete. After all it had never been finished. But Charles would have liked it like that, open to the wind. It was dusk now, and bats, like tiny stones, hurled themselves in and out of the spaces where the sky was. The back wall had a gap where the door had fallen in. I could see now where the garden had been laid out.

I picked my way through. It was much lighter outside, and easier to see. Strange how in the North it hardly ever seemed to get dark in June. It must almost be Midsummer's Day. The terraces were still visible; a sundial covered in bindweed.

Quite suddenly, standing there, looking down over the blue transparent folds of the distant fell, I felt the ghosts. My grandfather, who had dreamed this house and this garden in Lhasa, and my grandmother, who must have given those builders hell! I put my hand into my bag and felt again the smooth old leather of my grandmother's diaries, the bundles of letters. It was all here. The ghosts would be here too, in the garden and in the shell of the house, with all its dreams. I felt it strongly. They would not be found in that vast Victorian pile whose turrets I could still see beyond the beech trees. This house, this garden, was where they came alive to me again. I could almost hear their voices. They seem to be woven in with the cry of the Herdwick ewes calling for their lambs, and more distantly, the sounds of yak bells. Somewhere, too, I could almost catch the scent of the juniper fires on the Chang Tang Plain.

I remembered the last time I had seen my grandparents. I had been standing with my mother on the steps of the verandah in their old house in Sikkim. Charles had just finished strapping on the last of the panniers and grandmother was fussing as usual, about whether he had taken enough clean underwear. He had just smiled up at her, mischievously, like a little boy, and she had melted. Right there he had taken her in his arms and kissed her until she started laughing, pushing him away. My mother had sighed loudly. She was always embarrassed by her parents. But I had thought it was wonderful. They were so old and yet they could still fight and kiss like young people. I was determined to be like them when I grew up.

They had come inside into the cool of the house, to say goodbye. The servant, Kadji's great-grandson, had brought mint tea. My grandfather had taken me on his knee and given me the amulet I am wearing today. He told me to keep it safe. Then my grandmother had kissed me and handed me her diaries, to keep safe for her too. I knew instinctively I would never see them again. My mother was trying not to cry. She had always found it hard to express her emotions. My grandmother had embraced me once more, enveloping me in that exotic, wonderful perfume she always wore. Then she had hitched up her skirts and mounted sidesaddle (my grandfather insisted on it, although she always rode astride when he wasn't around) pinning on her hat and they had left, the mules swaying up the dusty track. I had stared and stared until I could see them no more. My mother told me they were going into Tibet to help the people there. It would be very dangerous. She wished they wouldn't go.

But what I remembered more than anything, was how they had kissed each other in the yard, and how happy they had seemed on that last day, with the prospect of adventure before them, and how my grandmother always took a smart hat with her on her travels. In case she met a king, she said. She never had, and my grandfather never stopped teasing her about it, but it made no difference. It was part of that character I had loved so much. I would have liked to have gone with them on their journey. . . .

An owl cried in the dusk, making me jump. All that had happened to them both, all the struggles, all the battles they had fought, would it all come to nothing in the end? When this house had finally tumbled down, and the Hall had been 'sympathetically converted' and all trace of the terraces and the stone walls had been smothered for ever, would anything remain? Was that what it was all about in the end? Two people who, in a few years, would be remembered by no one still alive.

My eye caught a brief flash of colour. There, in a broken corner of the sandstone, protected by the wall, a flare of blue, sudden, startling, even in the dusk. A blue *Meconopsis*, shy, sleepy, its petals almost closed, but, indisputably there. I bent down, squinting at the copper plate whose letters had been blurred by years of weathering. Yes, this was it. My grandmother's Blue Poppy, the famous *Meconopsis*, *Meconopsis bettiana*, now grown throughout the world, its rare blue colour and double petals celebrated by gardeners everywhere.

The dream of an invalid boy, and of his grandmother, my great-great grandmother. As alive, as true, as real as the first day Maud had seen her own Blue Poppy in that garden in Sikkim, more than a hundred years ago. As blue as the Tibetan sky, it flowered here in the dusk.

Among the ghosts.